ROBOT FRENZY

By Erik Craddock

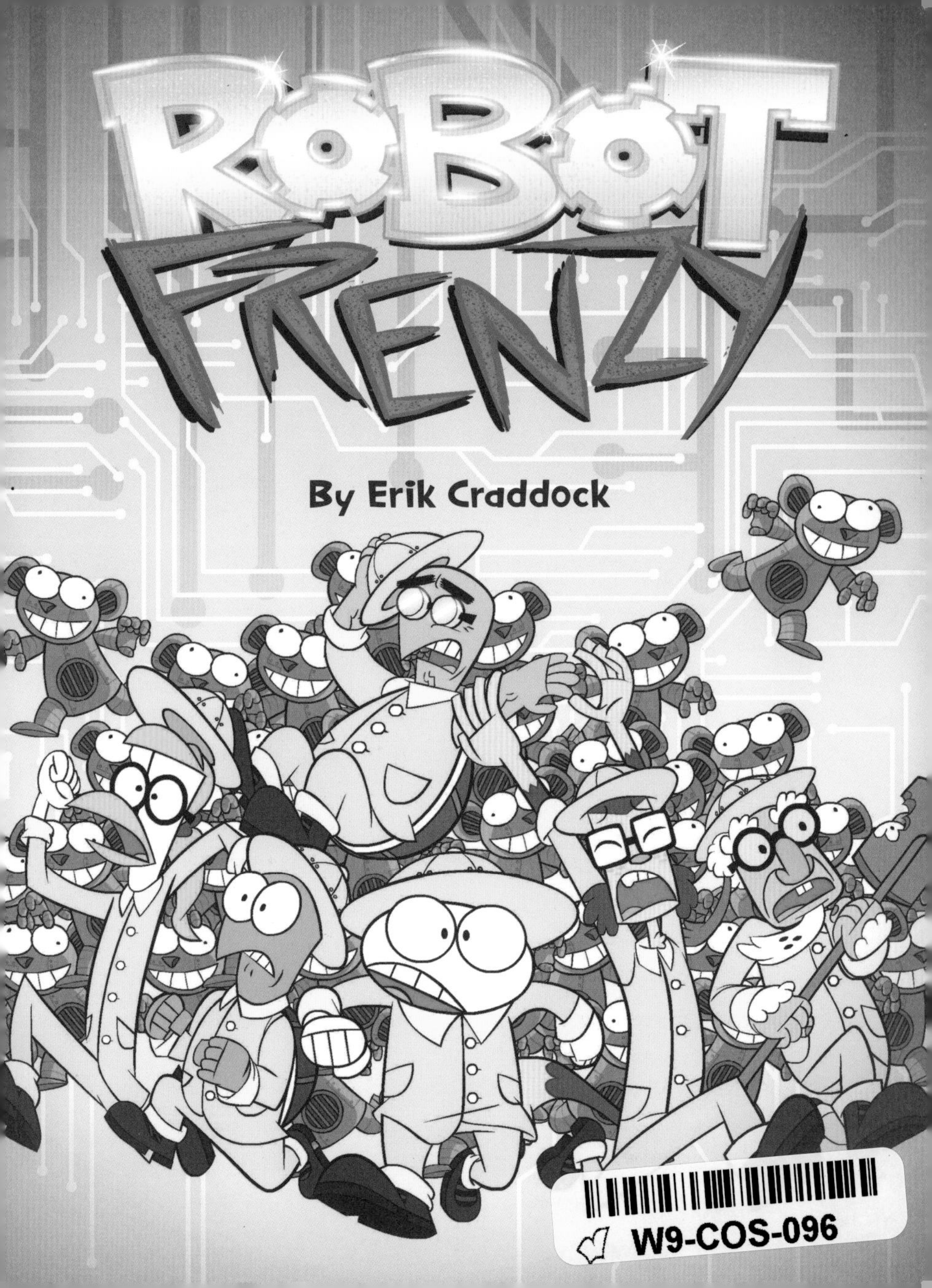

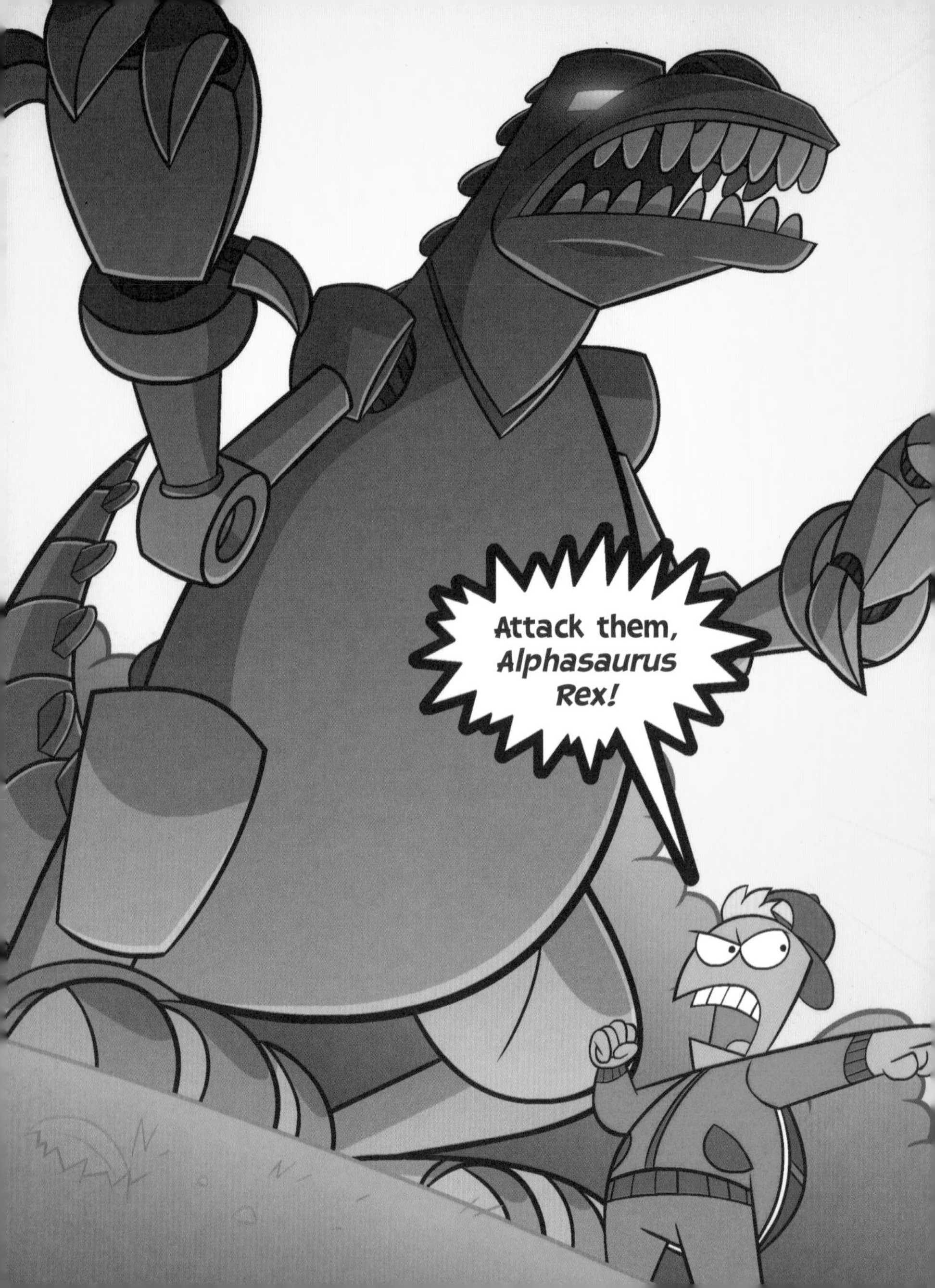
Attack them, Alphasaurus Rex!

Visit us on the Web! randomhouse.com/kids
Educators and librarians, for a variety of teaching tools, visit us at RHTeachersLibrarians.com
stonerabbit.com

Library of Congress Cataloging-in-Publication Data
Craddock, Erik.
Robot frenzy / Erik Craddock. — First edition.
p. cm. — (Stone rabbit ; #8)
Summary: "When Stone Rabbit and his friends create robots to help out with chores, a glitch in the programming sends the 'bots into a malfunctioning frenzy that threatens to destroy Happy Glades!" —Provided by publisher
ISBN 978-0-375-86913-6 (pbk.) — ISBN 978-0-375-96913-3 (lib. bdg.) — ISBN 978-0-307-98145-5 (ebook)
1. Graphic novels. [1. Graphic novels. 2. Robots—Fiction. 3.Chores—Fiction. 4. Rabbits—Fiction. 5. Animals—Fiction. 6. Humorous stories.] I. Title.
PZ7.7.C73Rob 2013 741.5'973—dc23 2012049524

MANUFACTURED IN MALAYSIA 10 9 8 7 6 5 4 3 First Edition

Random House Children's Books supports the First Amendment and celebrates the right to read.

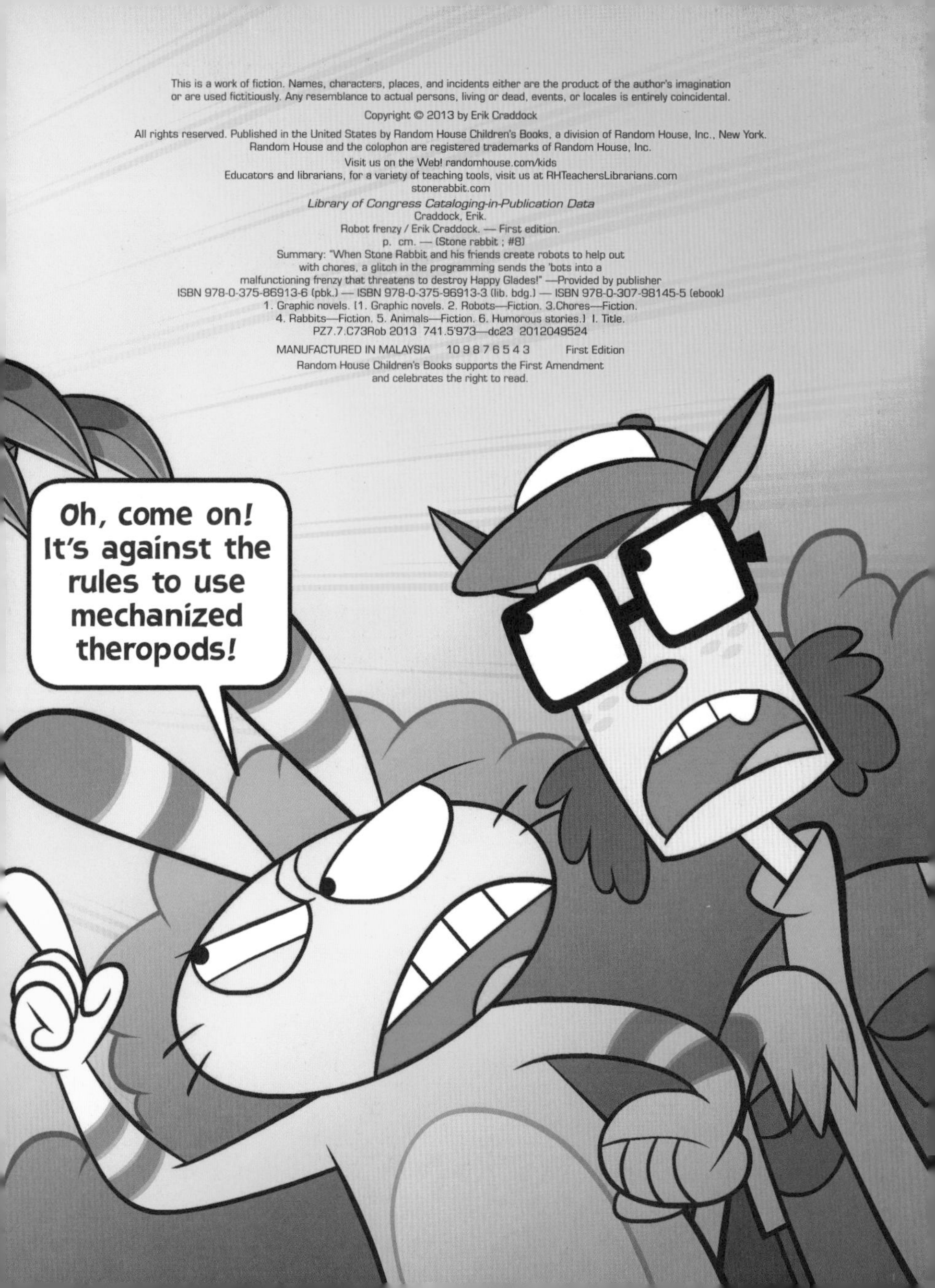
Oh, come on! It's against the rules to use mechanized theropods!

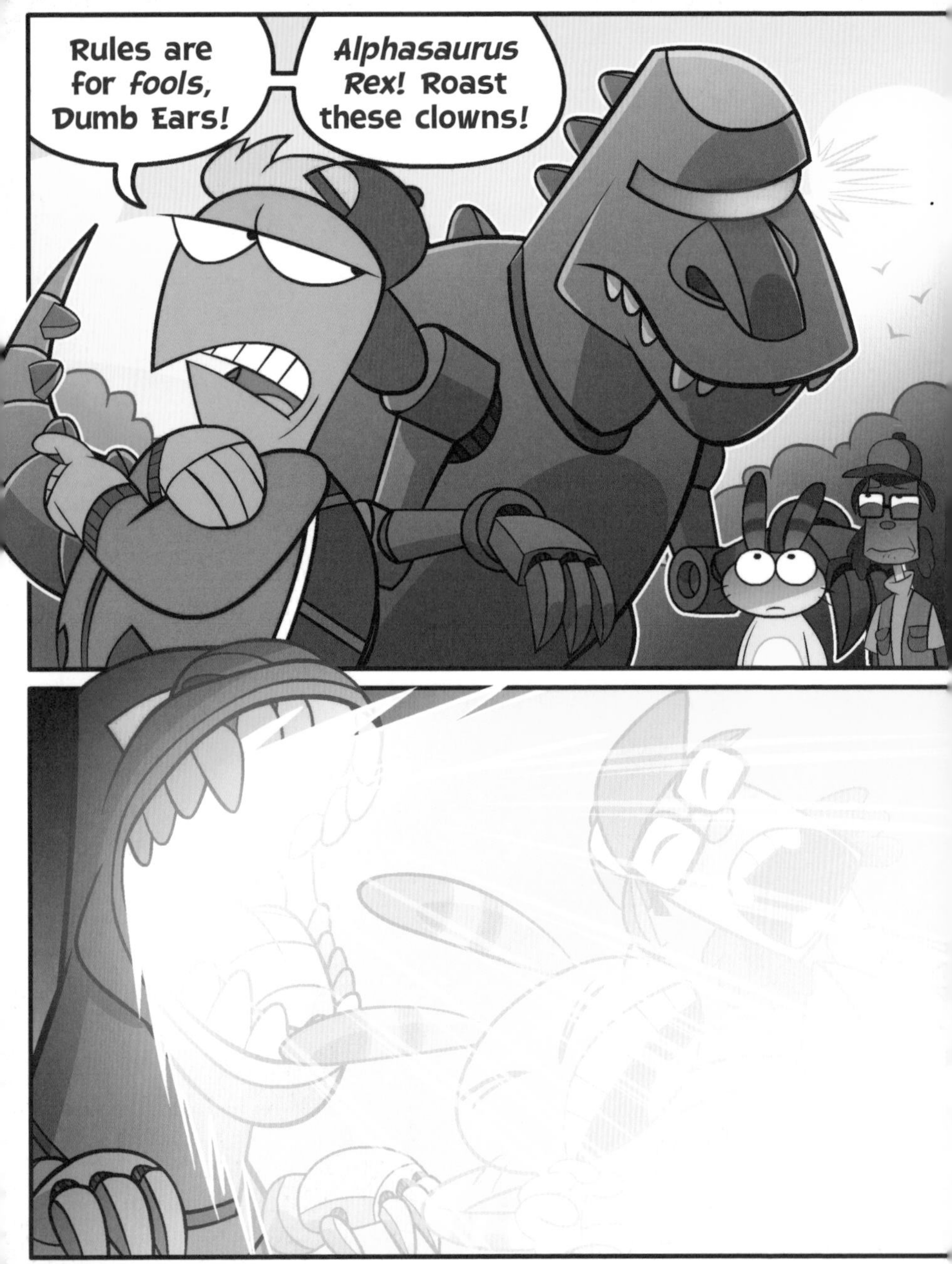
Rules are for *fools*, Dumb Ears!
Alphasaurus Rex! Roast these clowns!

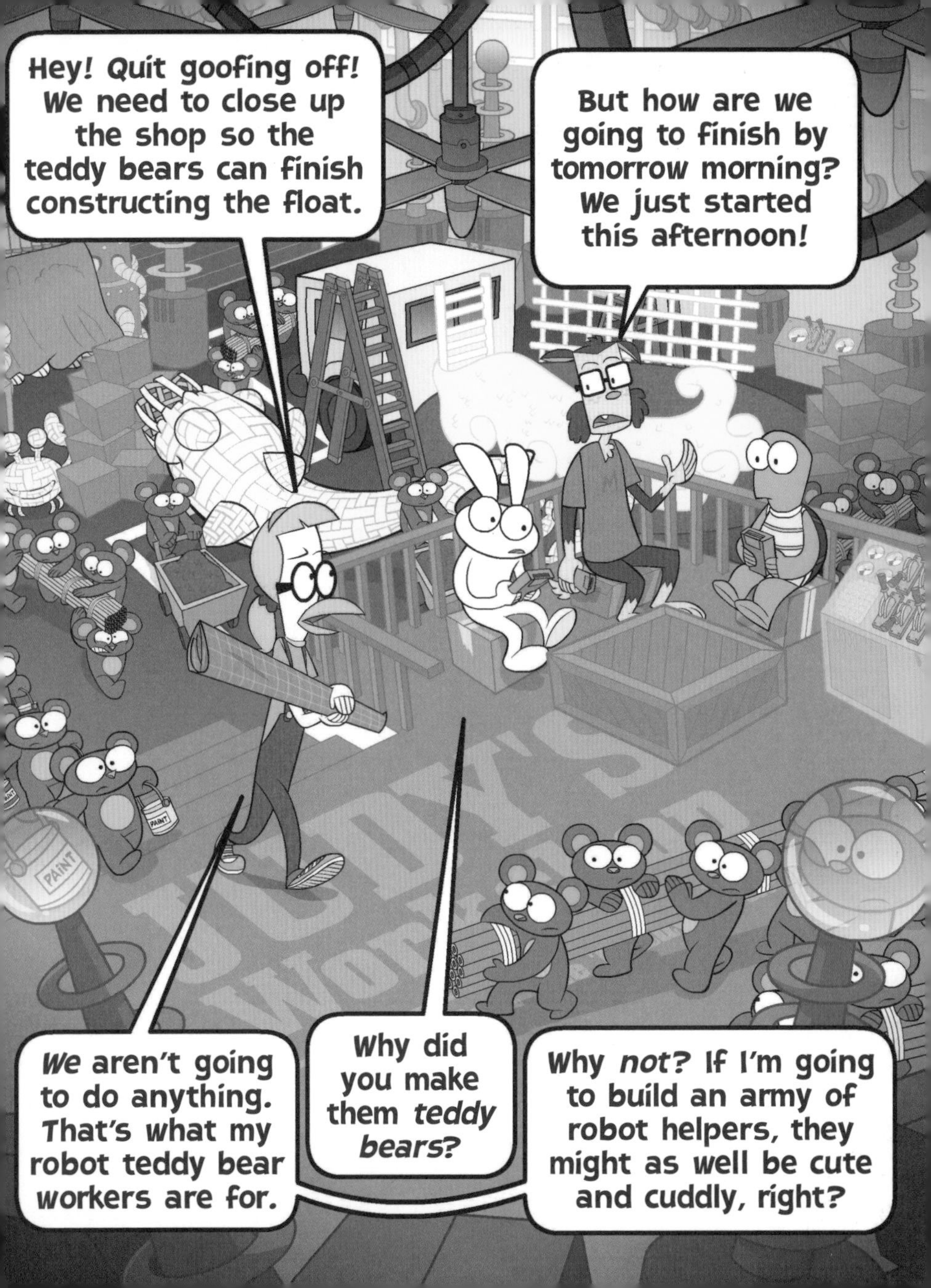
Hey! Quit goofing off! We need to close up the shop so the teddy bears can finish constructing the float.
But how are we going to finish by tomorrow morning? We just started this afternoon!
We aren't going to do anything. That's what my robot teddy bear workers are for.
Why did you make them *teddy bears*?
Why *not*? If I'm going to build an army of robot helpers, they might as well be cute and cuddly, right?
PAINT
PAINT
PAINT

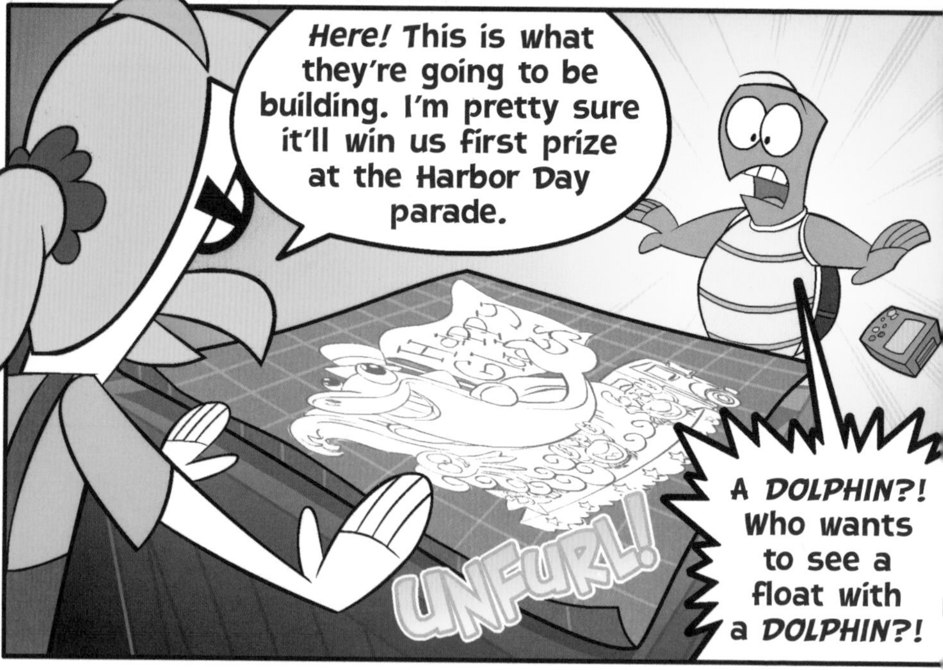
Here! This is what they're going to be building. I'm pretty sure it'll win us first prize at the Harbor Day parade.
UNFURL!
A *DOLPHIN?!* Who wants to see a float with a *DOLPHIN?!*

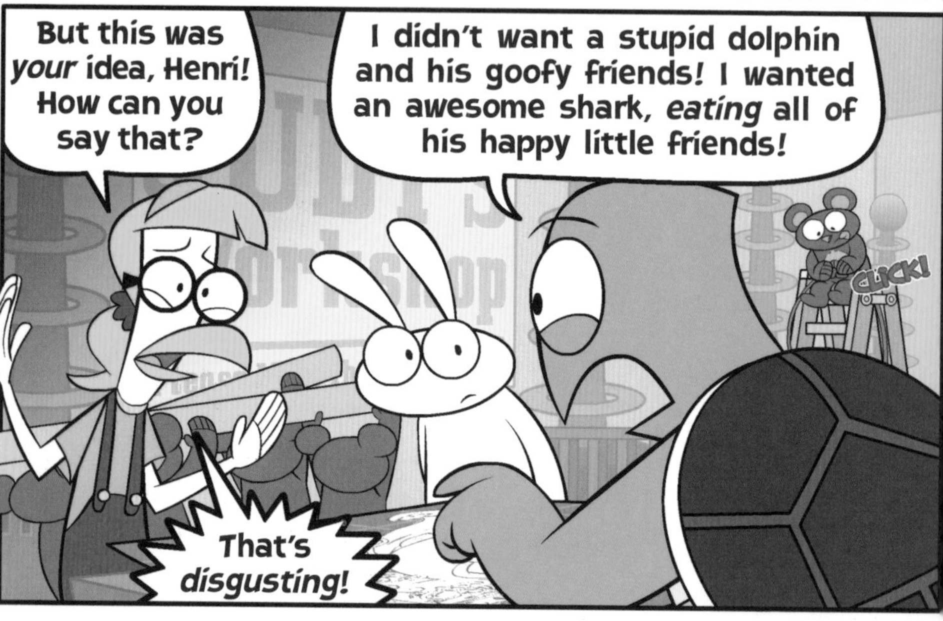
But this was *your* idea, Henri! How can you say that?
I didn't want a stupid dolphin and his goofy friends! I wanted an awesome shark, *eating* all of his happy little friends!
CLICK!
That's *disgusting!*

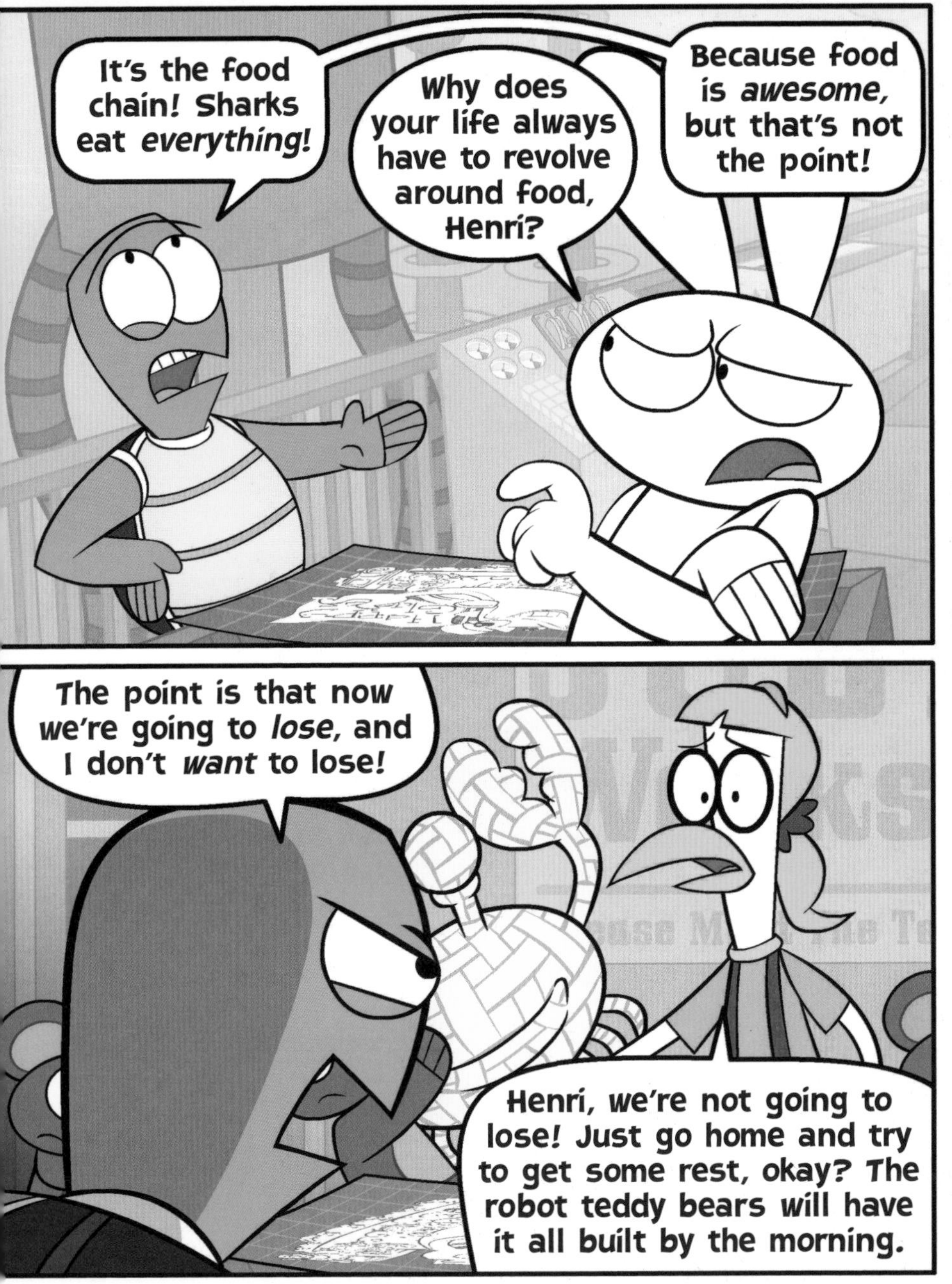
It's the food chain! Sharks eat *everything*!
Why does your life always have to revolve around food, Henri?
Because food is *awesome*, but that's not the point!
The point is that now we're going to *lose*, and I don't *want* to lose!
Henri, we're not going to lose! Just go home and try to get some rest, okay? The robot teddy bears will have it all built by the morning.

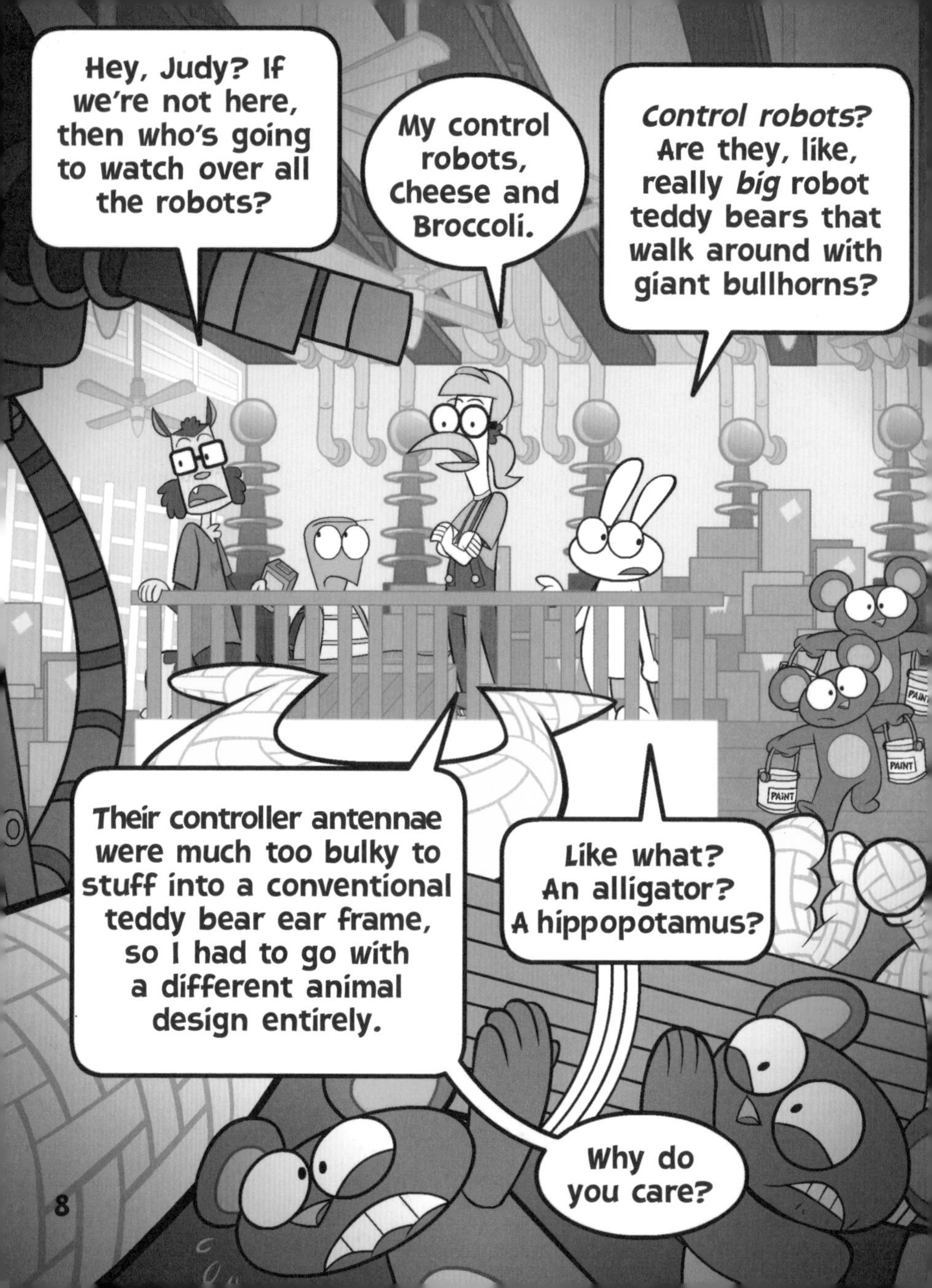
Hey, Judy? If we're not here, then who's going to watch over all the robots?
My control robots, Cheese and Broccoli.
Control robots? Are they, like, really *big* robot teddy bears that walk around with giant bullhorns?
PAINT
PAINT
PAINT
Their controller antennae were much too bulky to stuff into a conventional teddy bear ear frame, so I had to go with a different animal design entirely.
Like what? An alligator? A hippopotamus?
Why do you care?

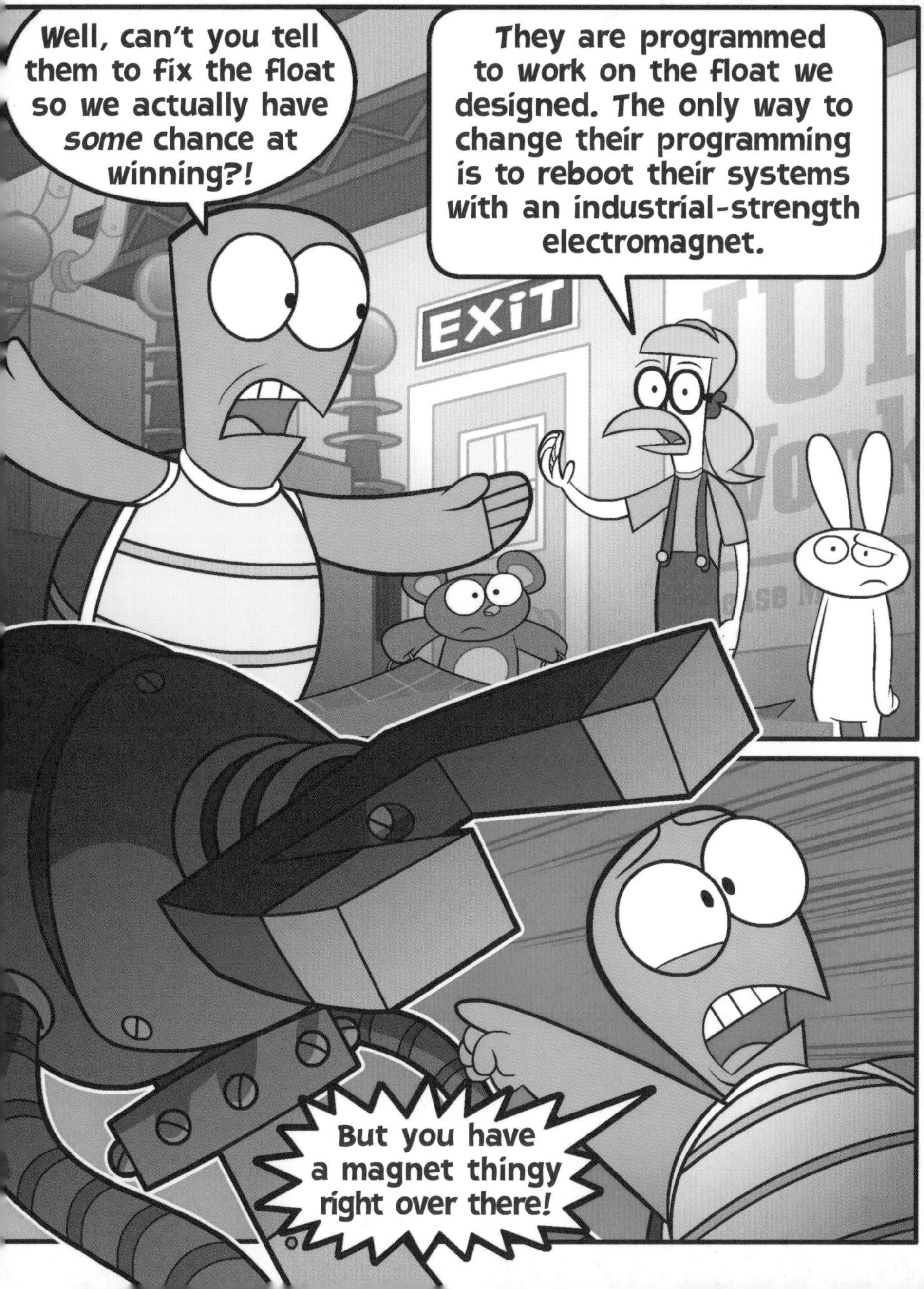
Well, can't you tell them to fix the float so we actually have *some* chance at winning?!
They are programmed to work on the float we designed. The only way to change their programming is to reboot their systems with an industrial-strength electromagnet.
EXIT
But you have a magnet thingy right over there!

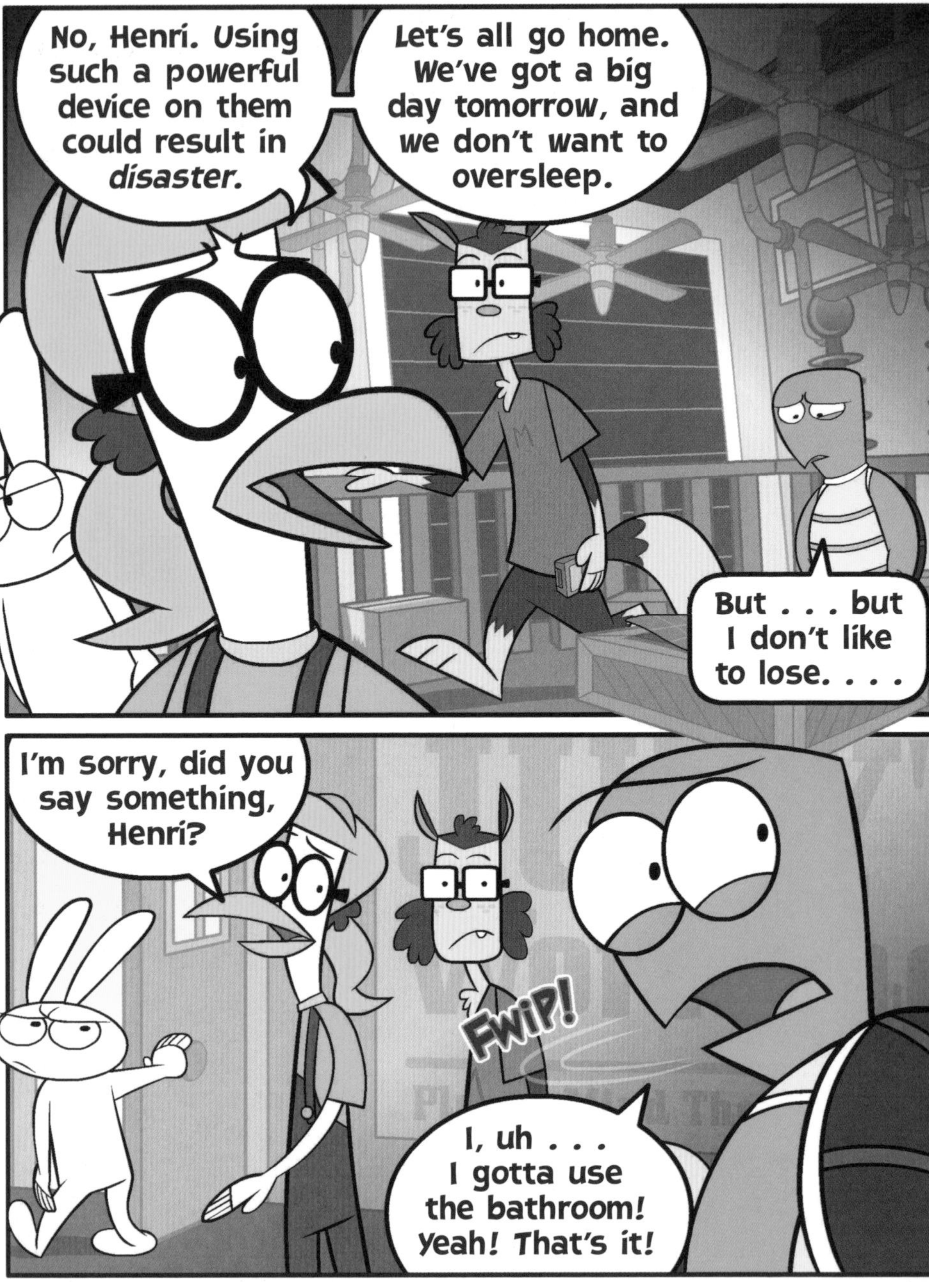
No, Henri. Using such a powerful device on them could result in *disaster.*
Let's all go home. We've got a big day tomorrow, and we don't want to oversleep.
But . . . but I don't like to lose. . . .
I'm sorry, did you say something, Henri?
FWIP!
I, uh . . . I gotta use the bathroom! Yeah! That's it!

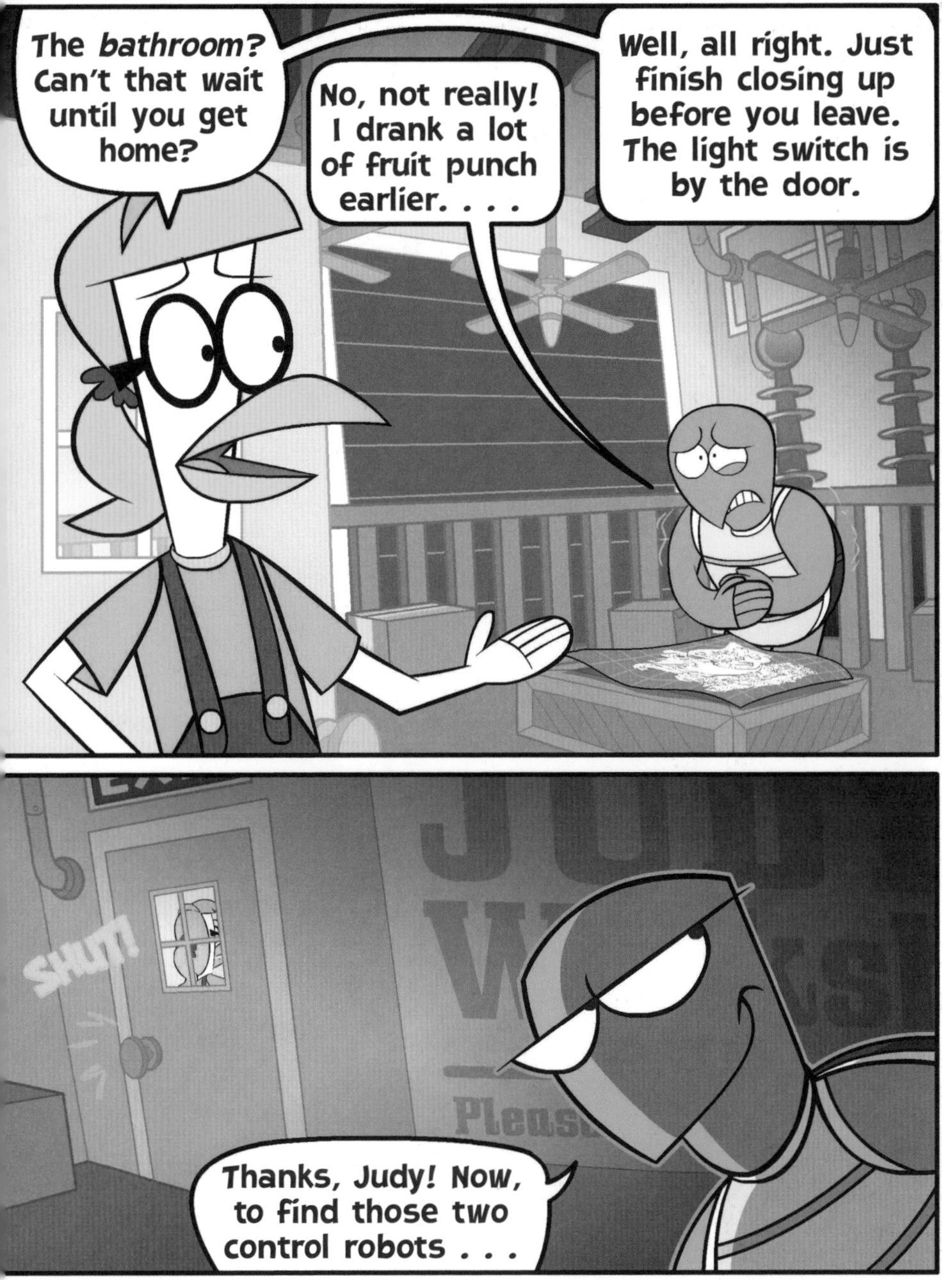
The *bathroom?* Can't that wait until you get home?
No, not really! I drank a lot of fruit punch earlier. . . .
Well, all right. Just finish closing up before you leave. The light switch is by the door.
SHUT!
Thanks, Judy! Now, to find those two control robots . . .

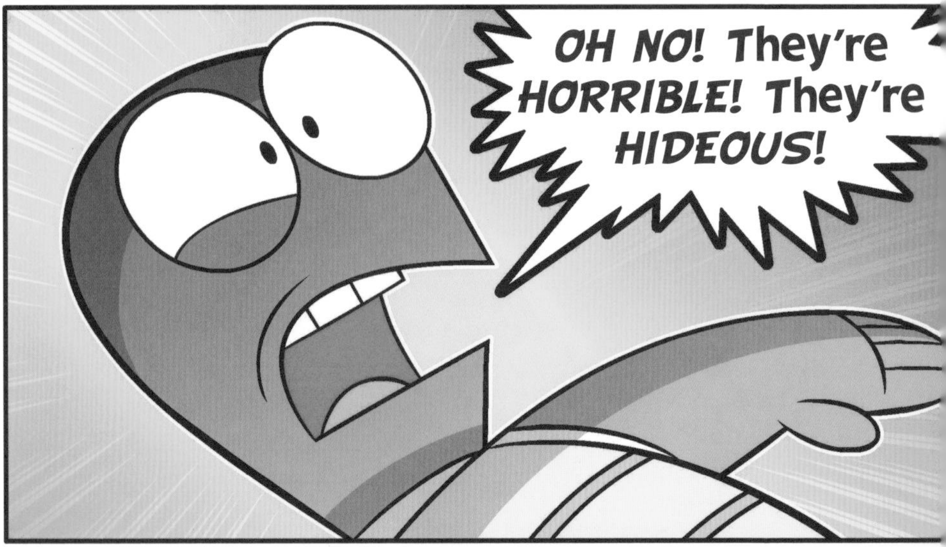
OH NO! They're HORRIBLE! They're HIDEOUS!

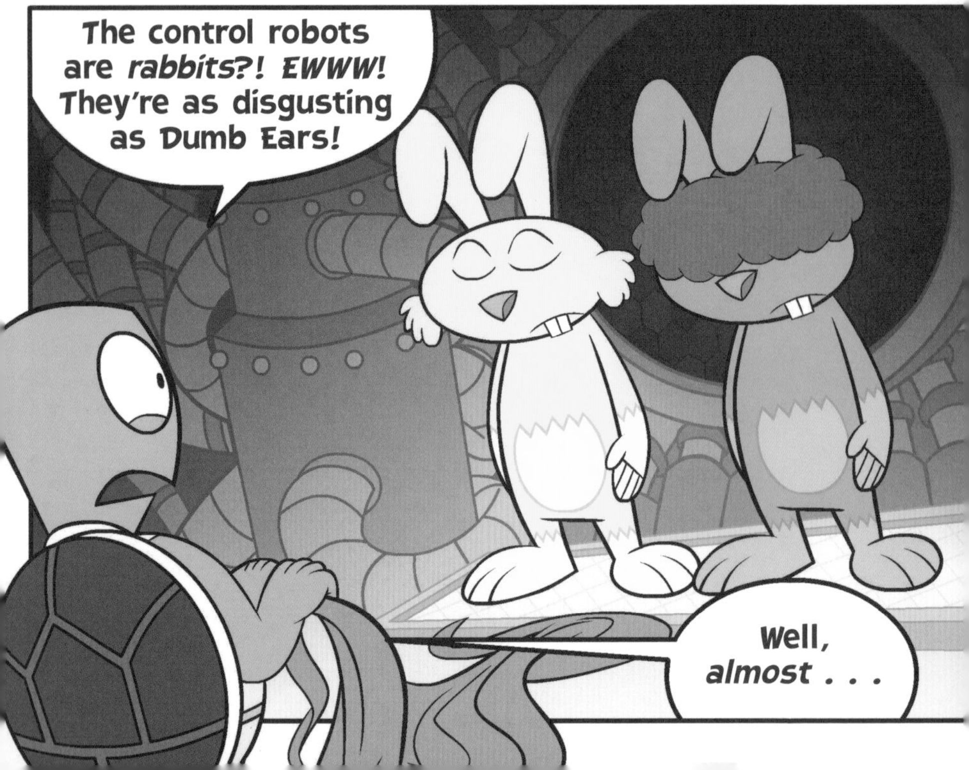
The control robots are *rabbits*?! *EWWW!* They're as disgusting as Dumb Ears!
Well, *almost . . .*

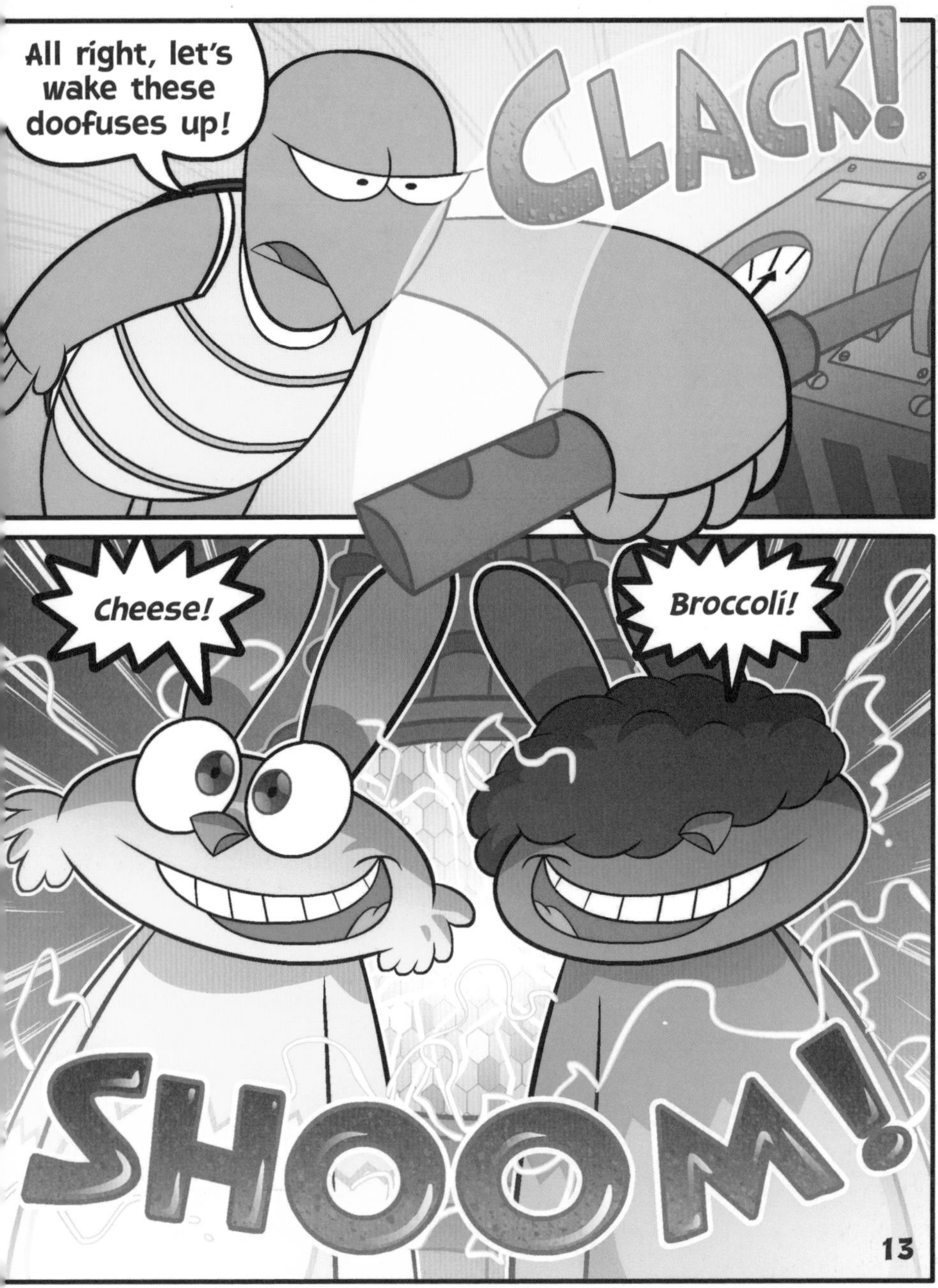
All right, let's wake these doofuses up!
CLACK!
Cheese!
Broccoli!
SHOOM!

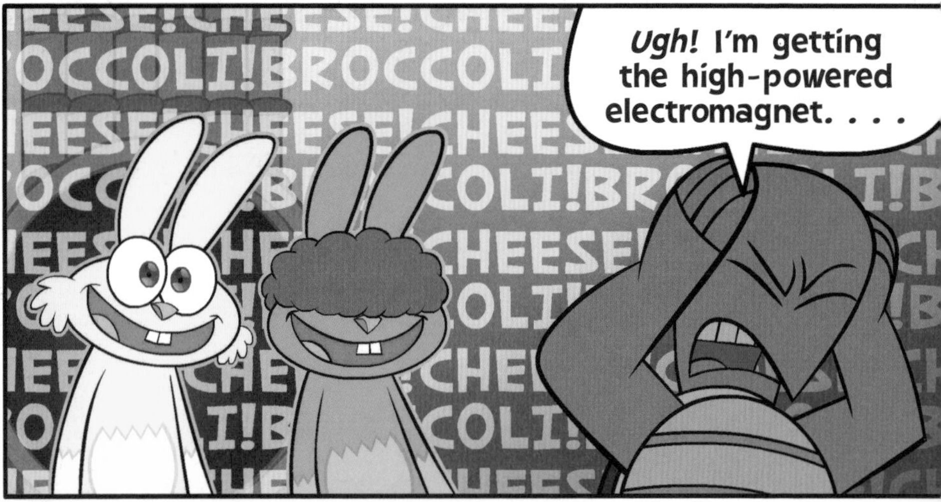
Ugh! I'm getting the high-powered electromagnet. . . .

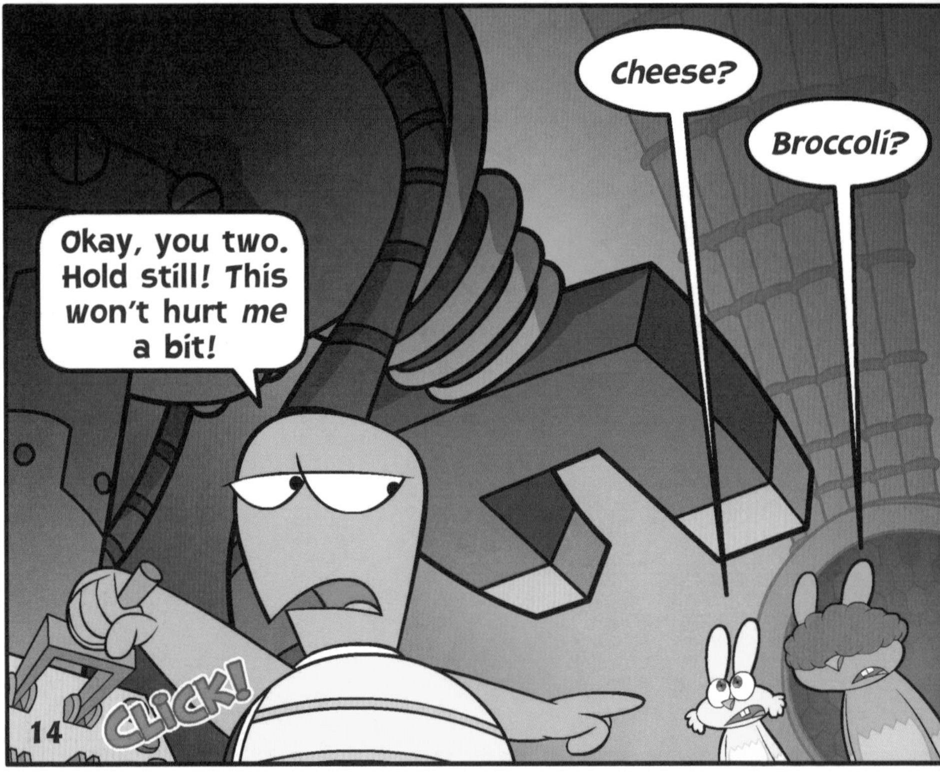
Cheese?
Broccoli?
Okay, you two. Hold still! This won't hurt *me* a bit!
CLICK!

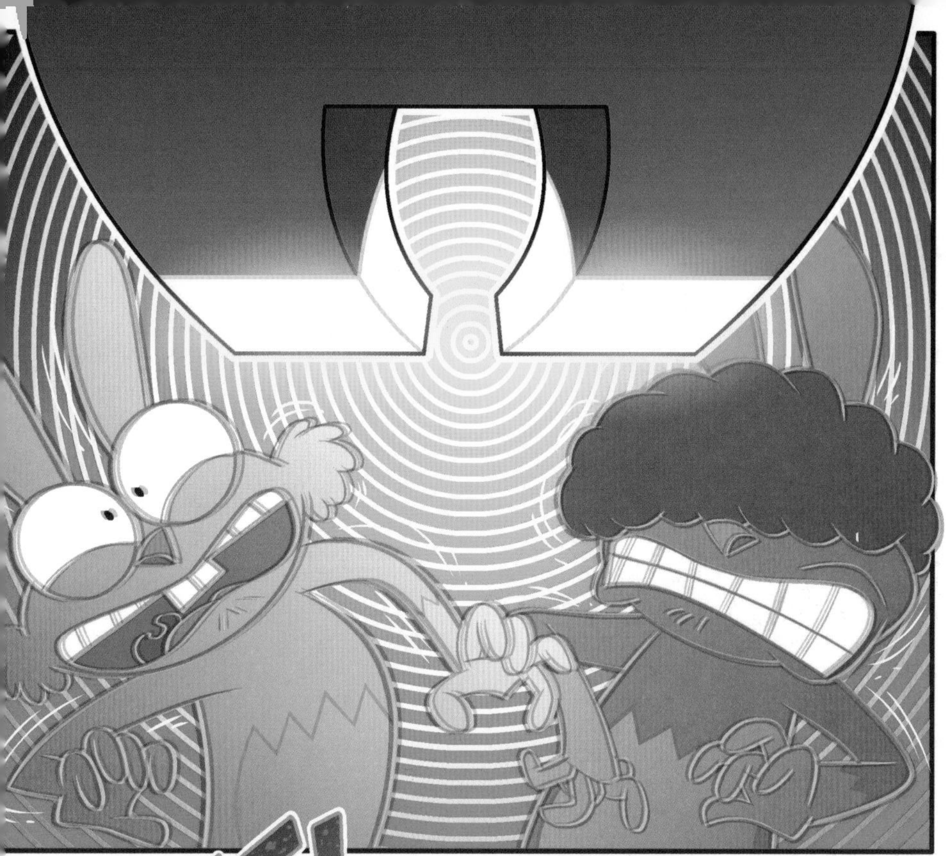

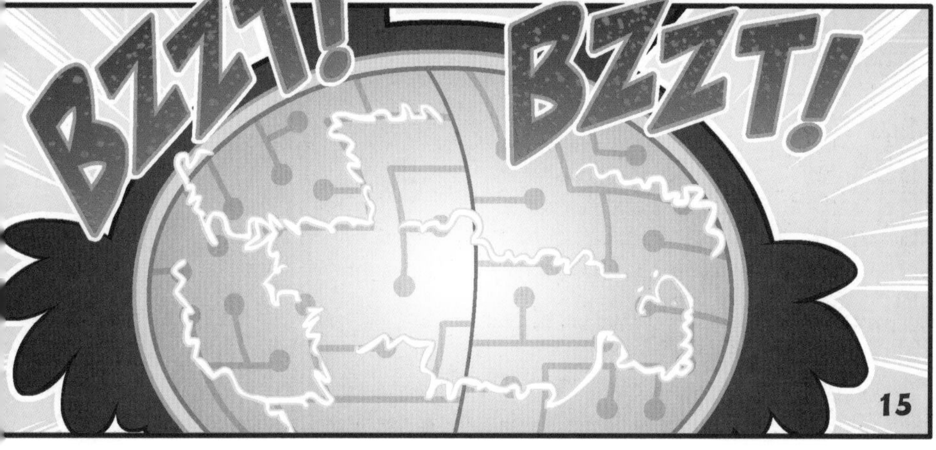
BZZT! BZZT!

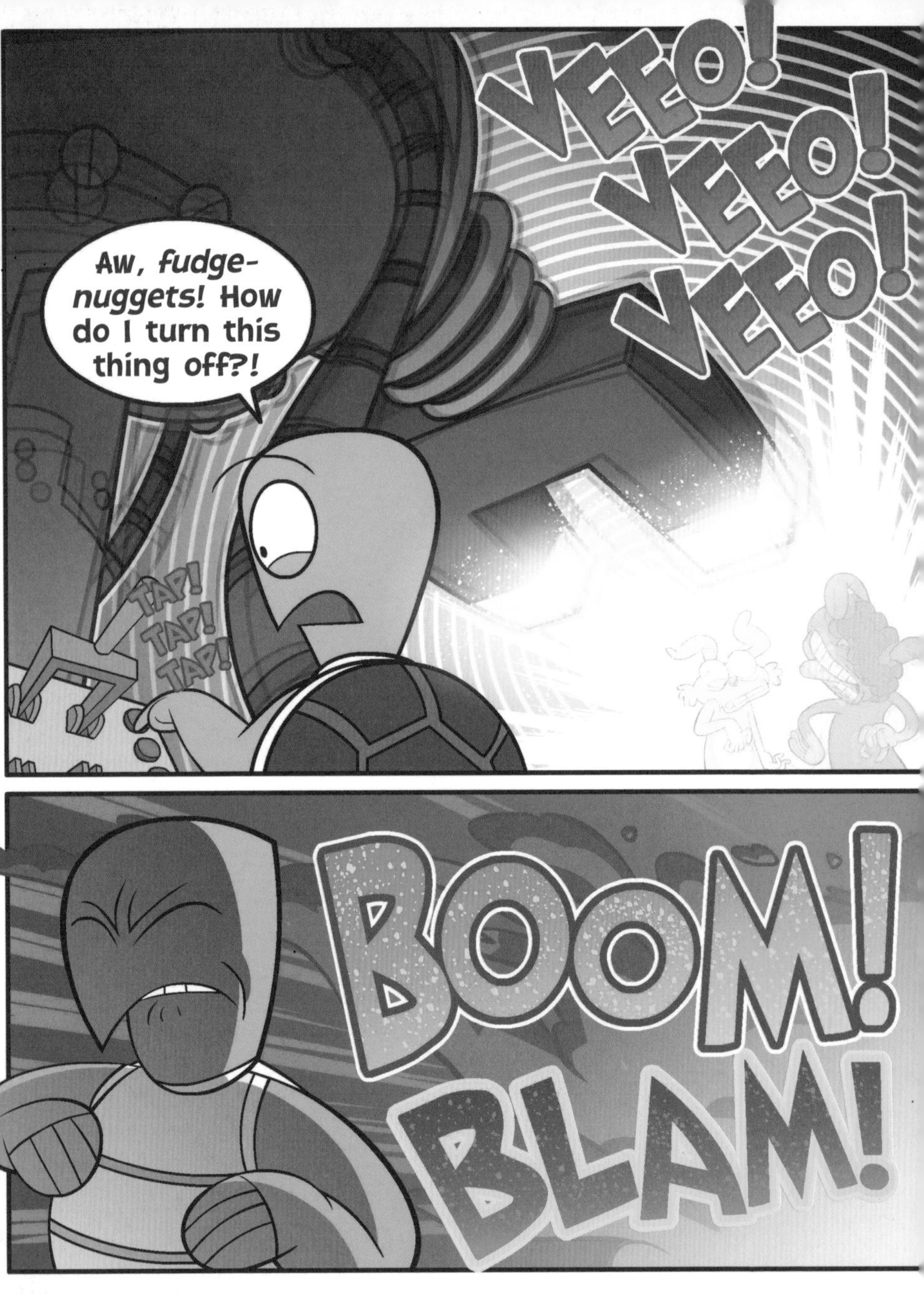
VEEO! VEEO! VEEO!
Aw, fudge-nuggets! How do I turn this thing off?!
TAP! TAP! TAP!
BOOM! BLAM!

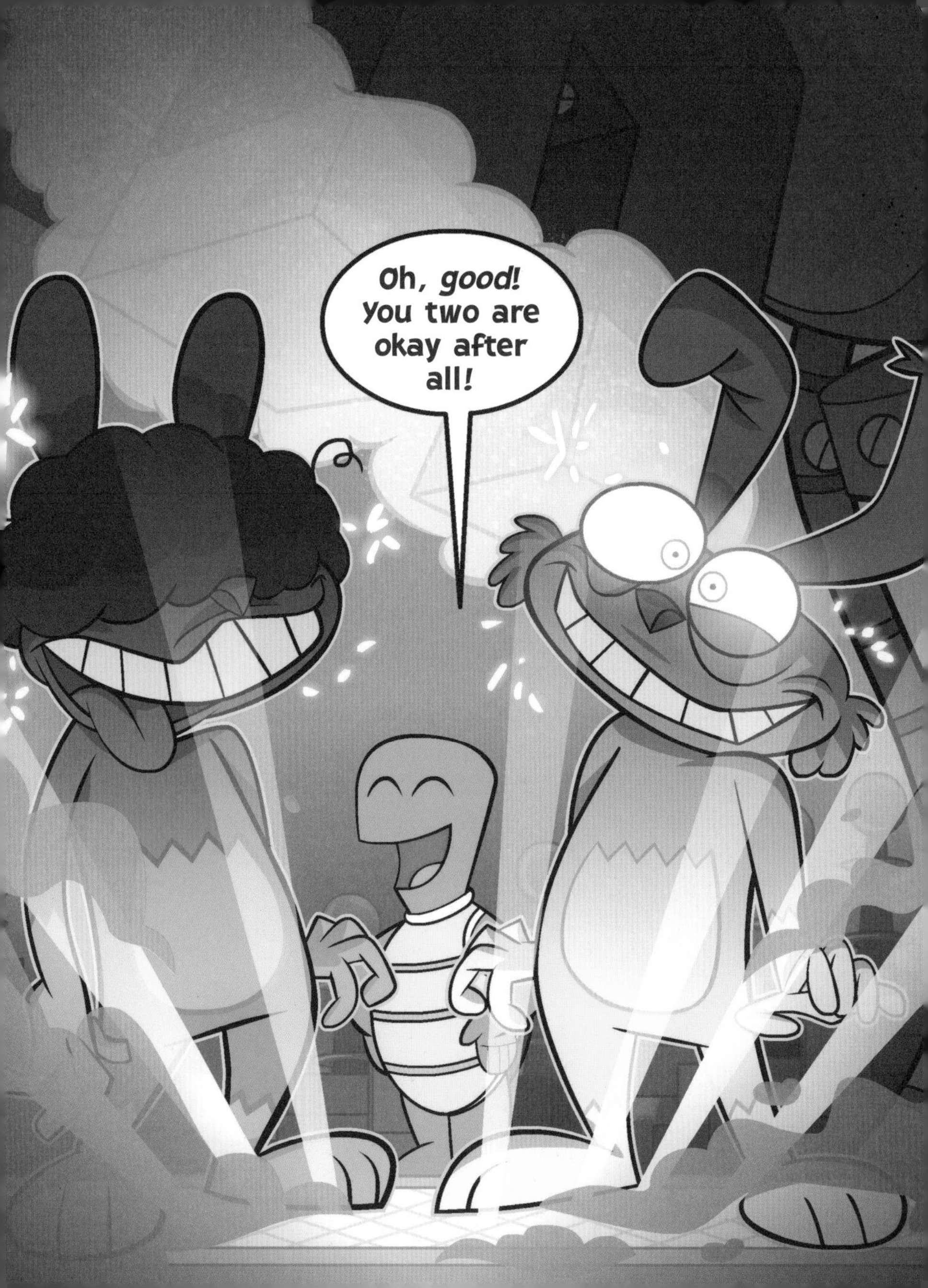
Oh, *good!* You two are okay after all!

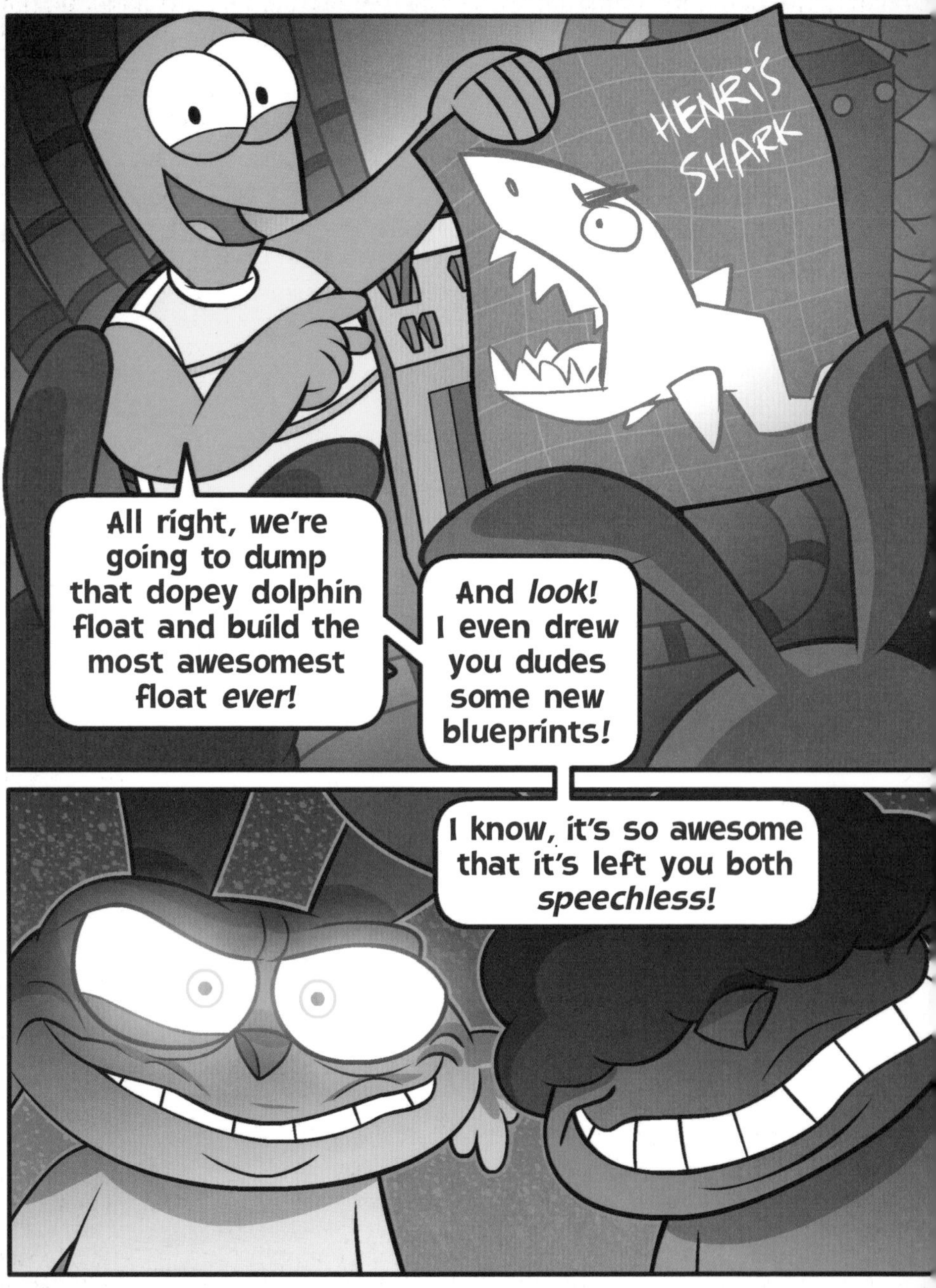
HENRI'S SHARK
All right, we're going to dump that dopey dolphin float and build the most awesomest float *ever*!
And *look*! I even drew you dudes some new blueprints!
I know, it's so awesome that it's left you both *speechless*!

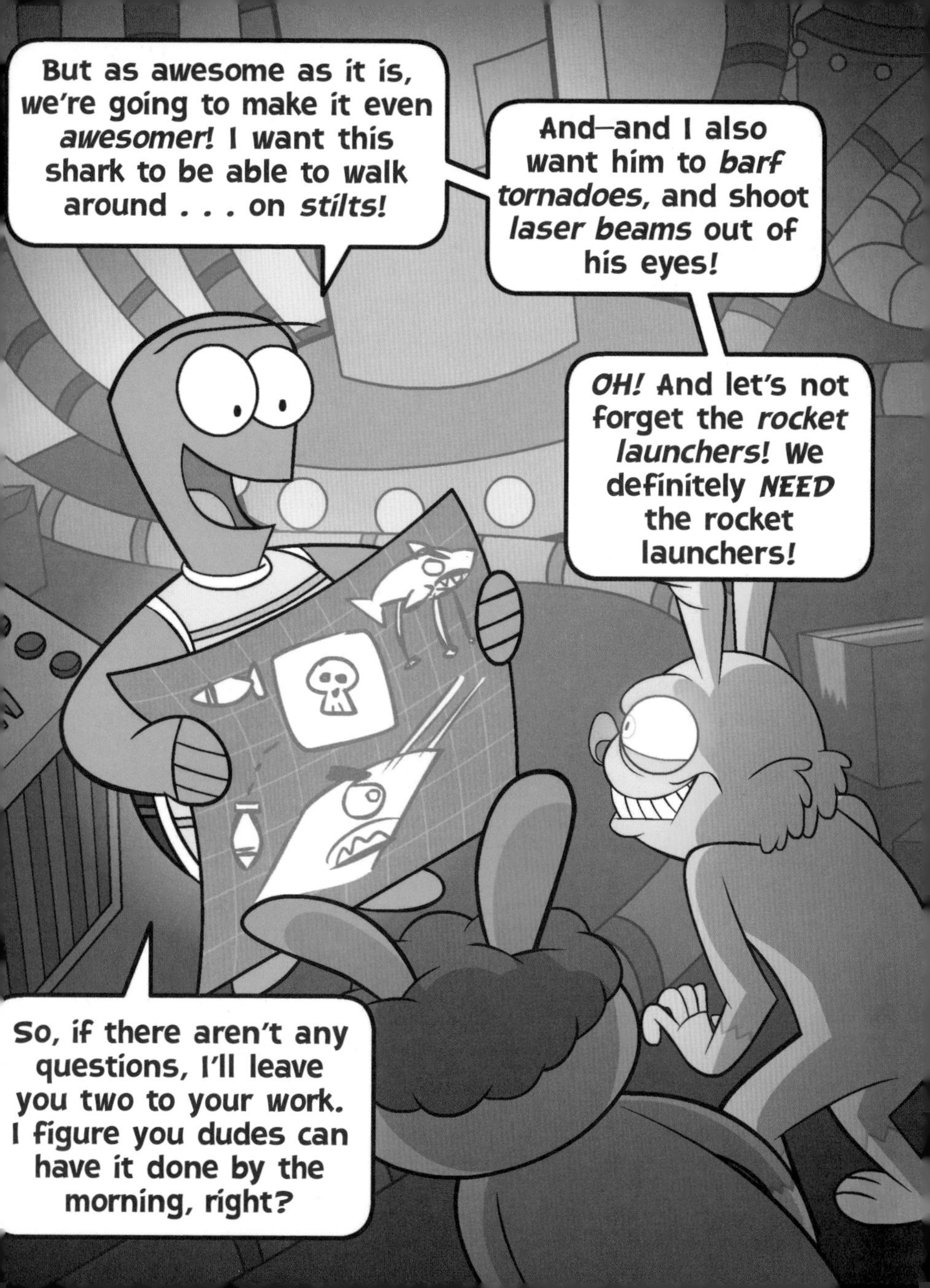
But as awesome as it is, we're going to make it even *awesomer!* I want this shark to be able to walk around . . . on *stilts!*
And—and I also want him to *barf tornadoes,* and shoot *laser beams* out of his eyes!
OH! And let's not forget the *rocket launchers!* We definitely *NEED* the rocket launchers!
So, if there aren't any questions, I'll leave you two to your work. I figure you dudes can have it done by the morning, right?

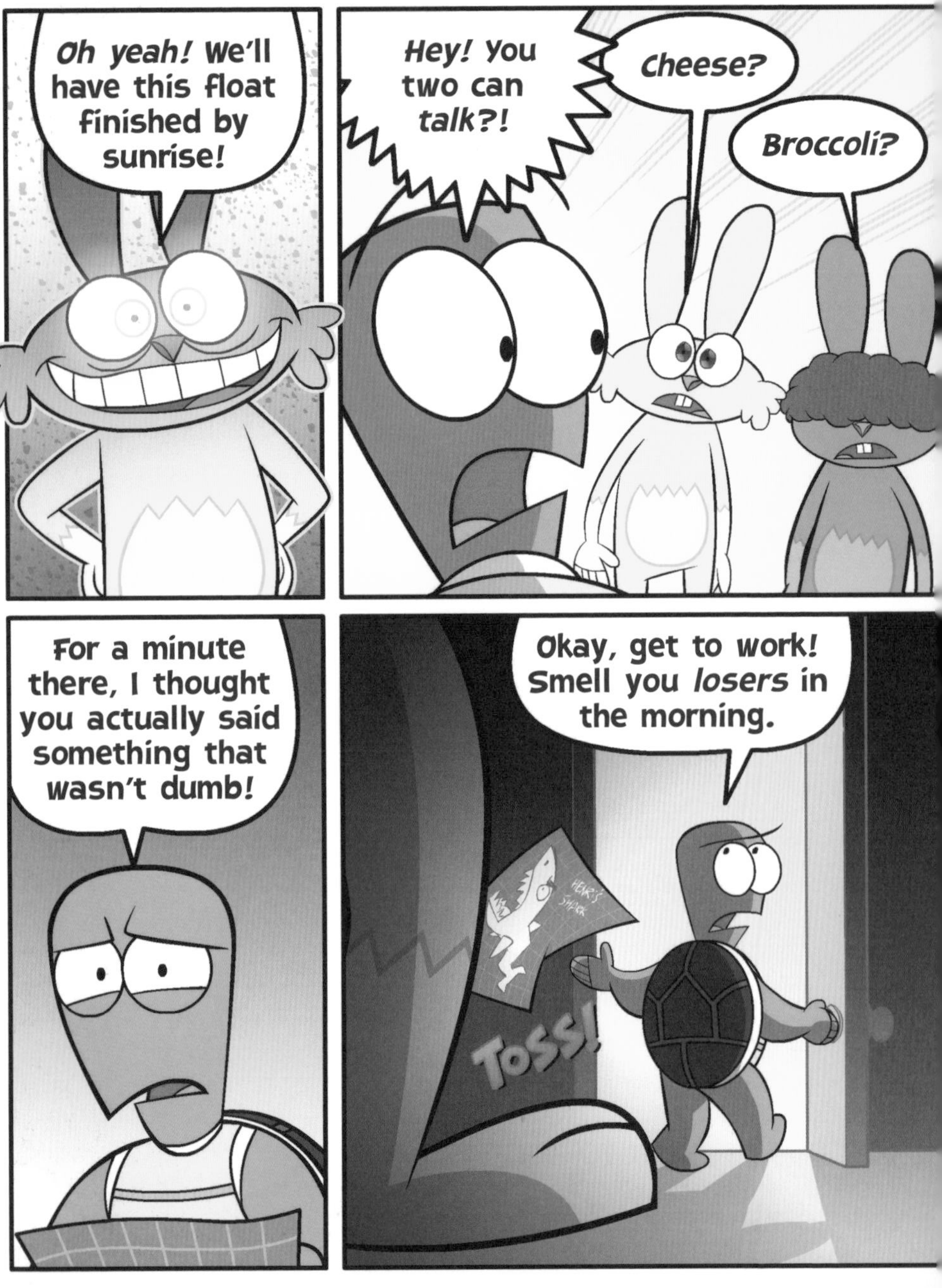
Oh yeah! We'll have this float finished by sunrise!
Hey! You two can talk?!
Cheese?
Broccoli?
For a minute there, I thought you actually said something that wasn't dumb!
Okay, get to work! Smell you losers in the morning.
TOSS!

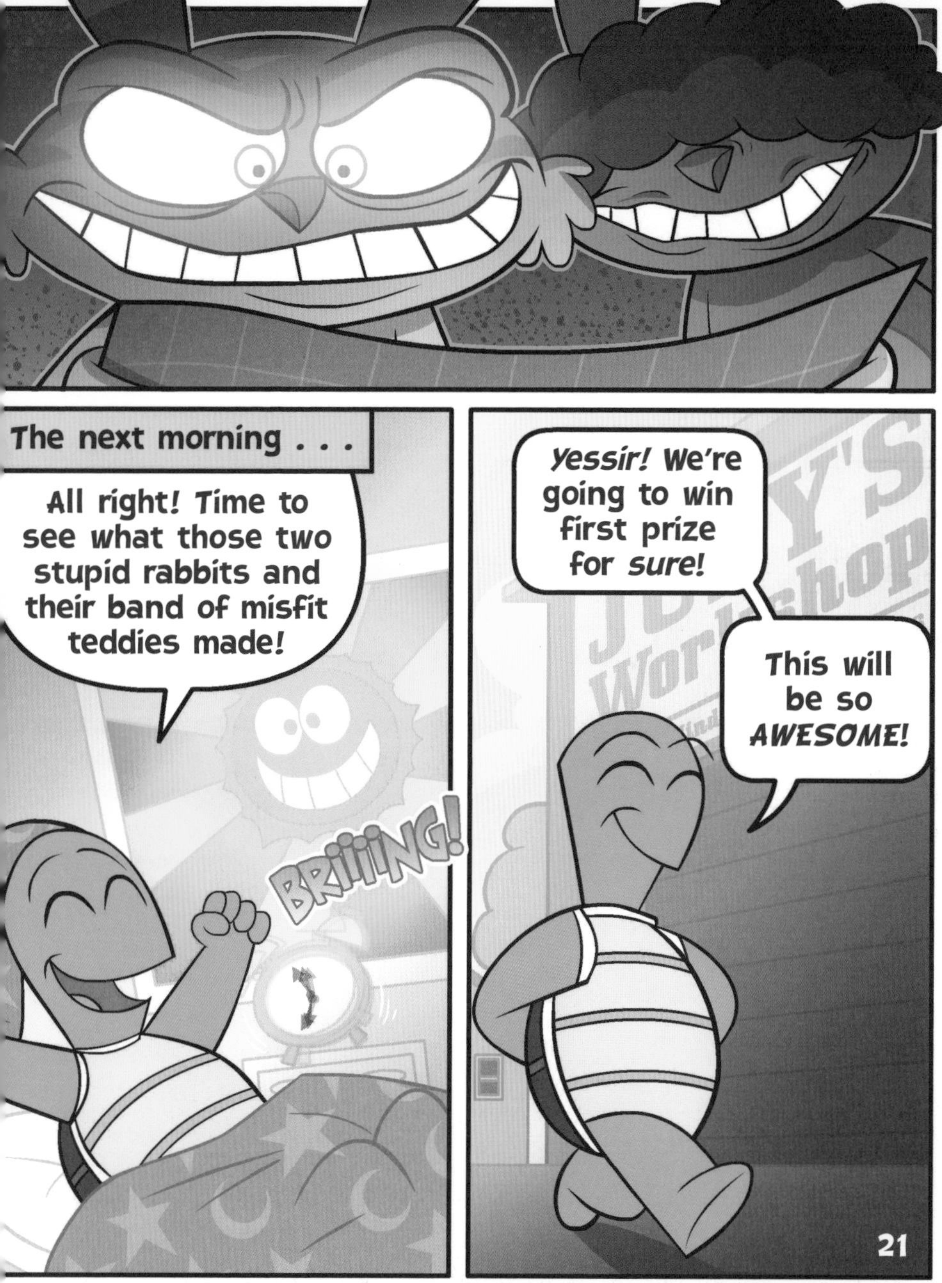
The next morning . . .
All right! Time to see what those two stupid rabbits and their band of misfit teddies made!
BRIIIING!
Yessir! We're going to win first prize for sure!
This will be so AWESOME!

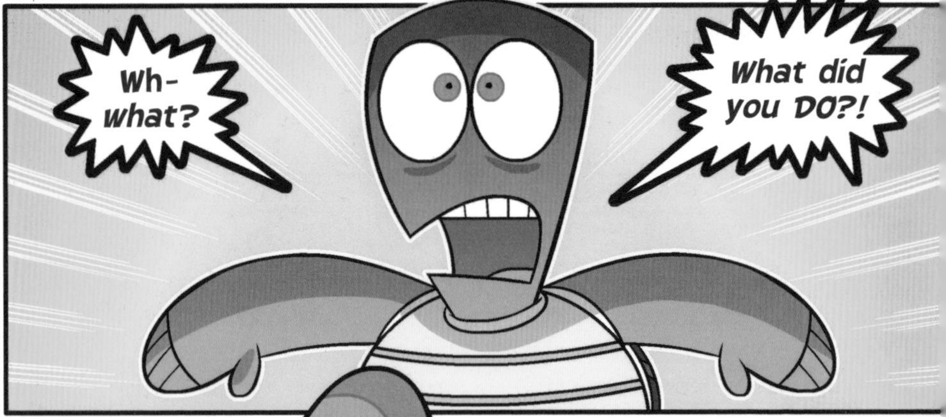
Wh-
what?
What did
you DO?!

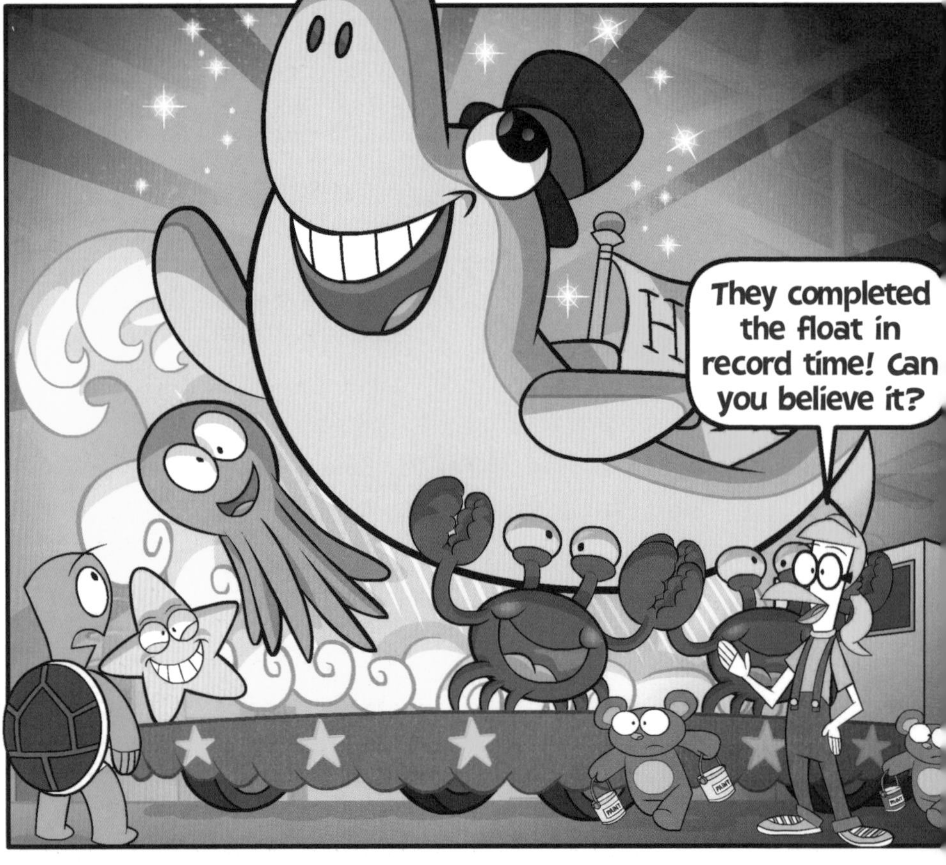
They completed
the float in
record time! Can
you believe it?

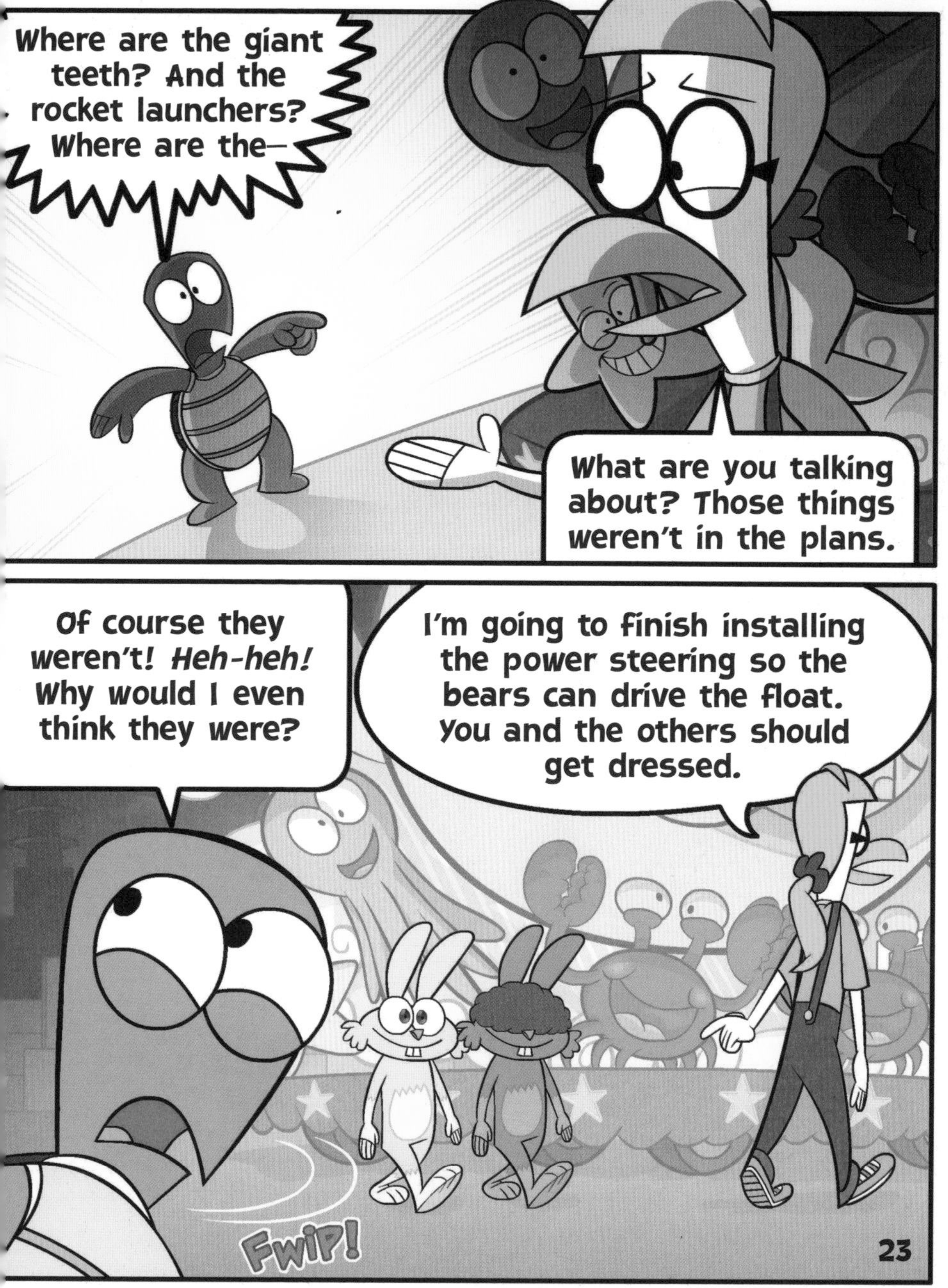
Where are the giant teeth? And the rocket launchers? Where are the—
What are you talking about? Those things weren't in the plans.
Of course they weren't! *Heh-heh!* Why would I even think they were?
I'm going to finish installing the power steering so the bears can drive the float. You and the others should get dressed.
FWIP!

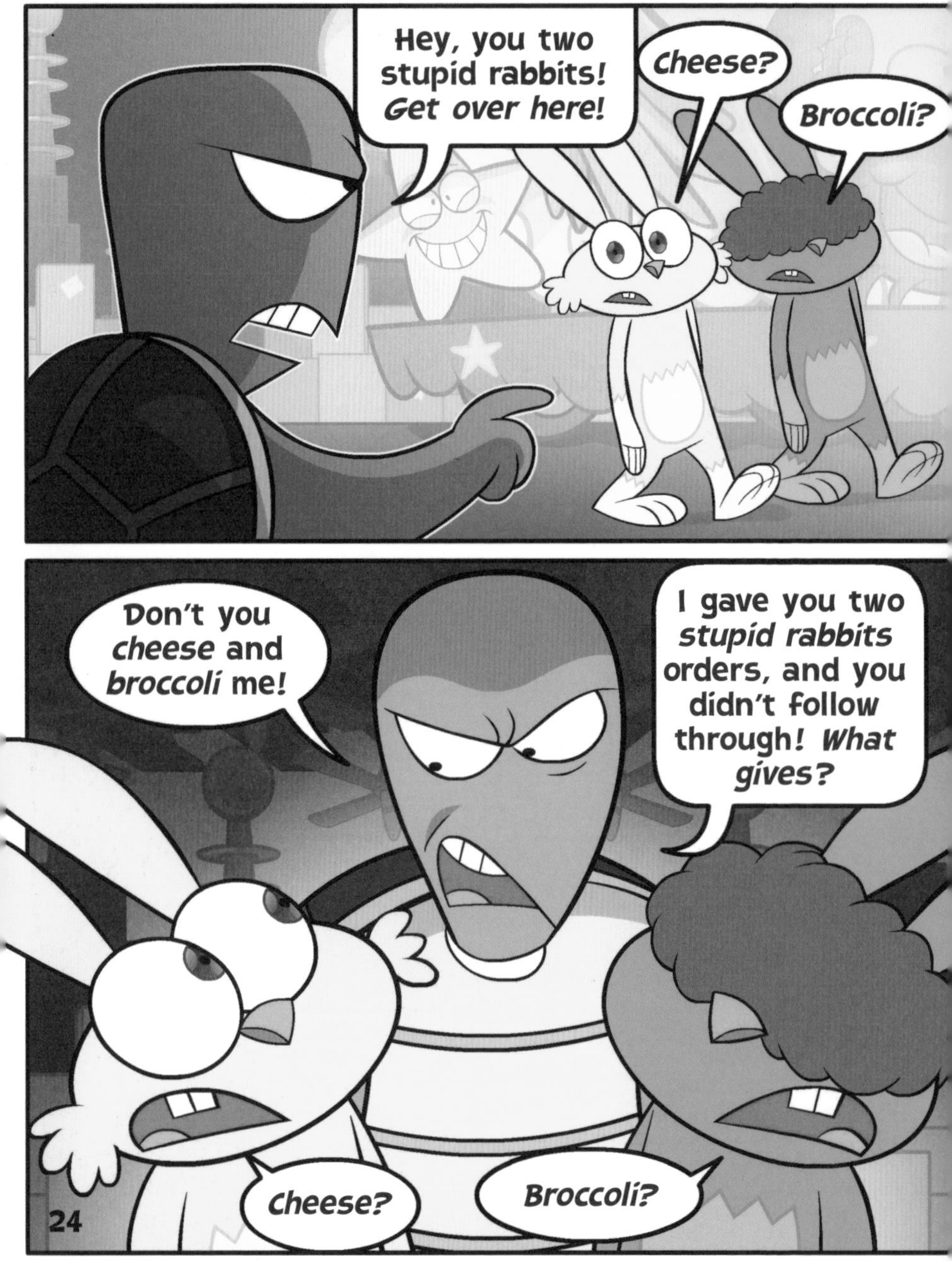
Hey, you two stupid rabbits! Get over here!
Cheese?
Broccoli?
Don't you cheese and broccoli me!
I gave you two stupid rabbits orders, and you didn't follow through! What gives?
Cheese?
Broccoli?

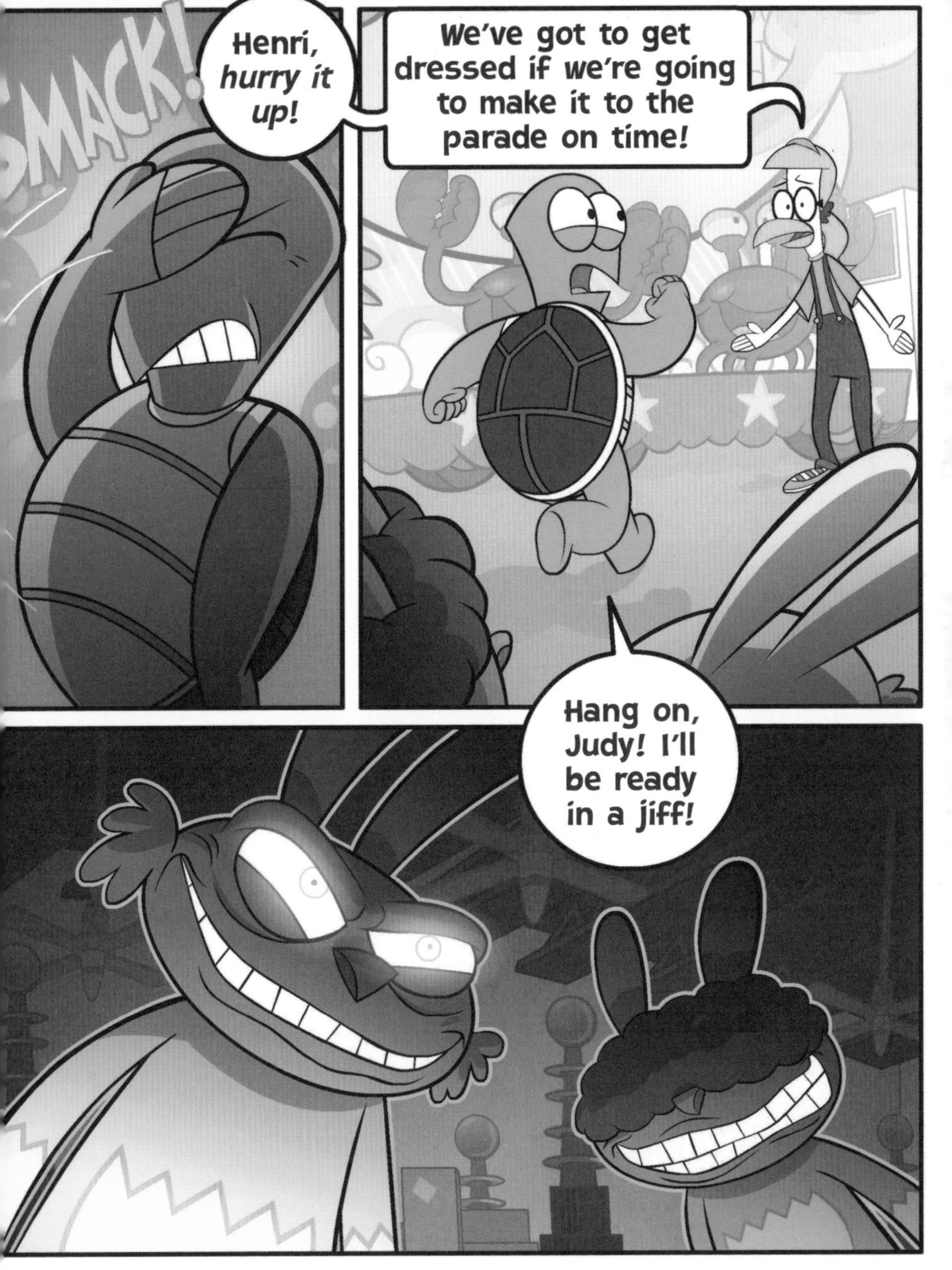
SMACK!
Henri, *hurry it up!*
We've got to get dressed if we're going to make it to the parade on time!
Hang on, Judy! I'll be ready in a jiff!

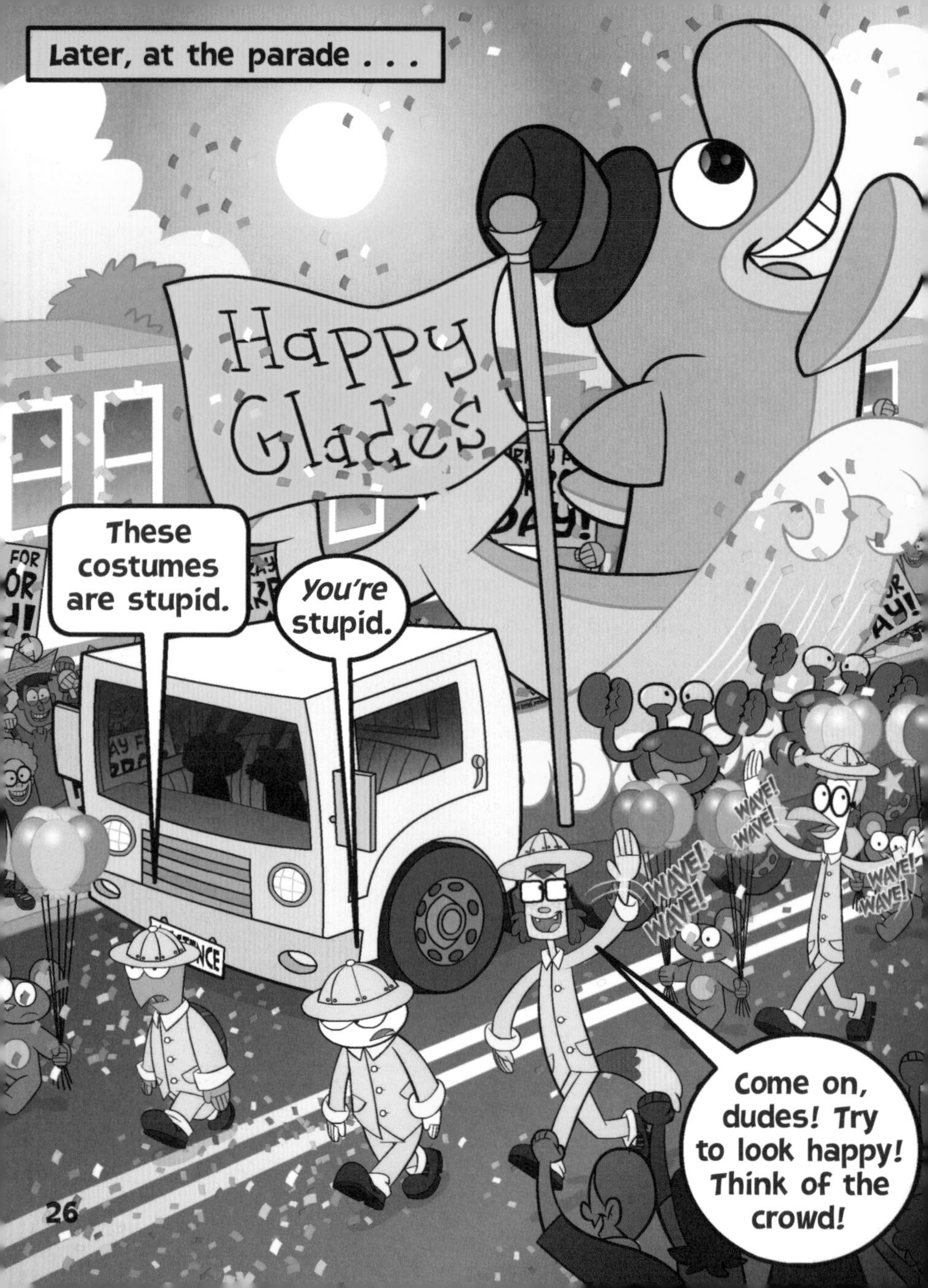
Later, at the parade . . .
Happy Glades
These costumes are stupid.
You're stupid.
WAVE! WAVE!
WAVE! WAVE!
WAVE! WAVE!
Come on, dudes! Try to look happy! Think of the crowd!

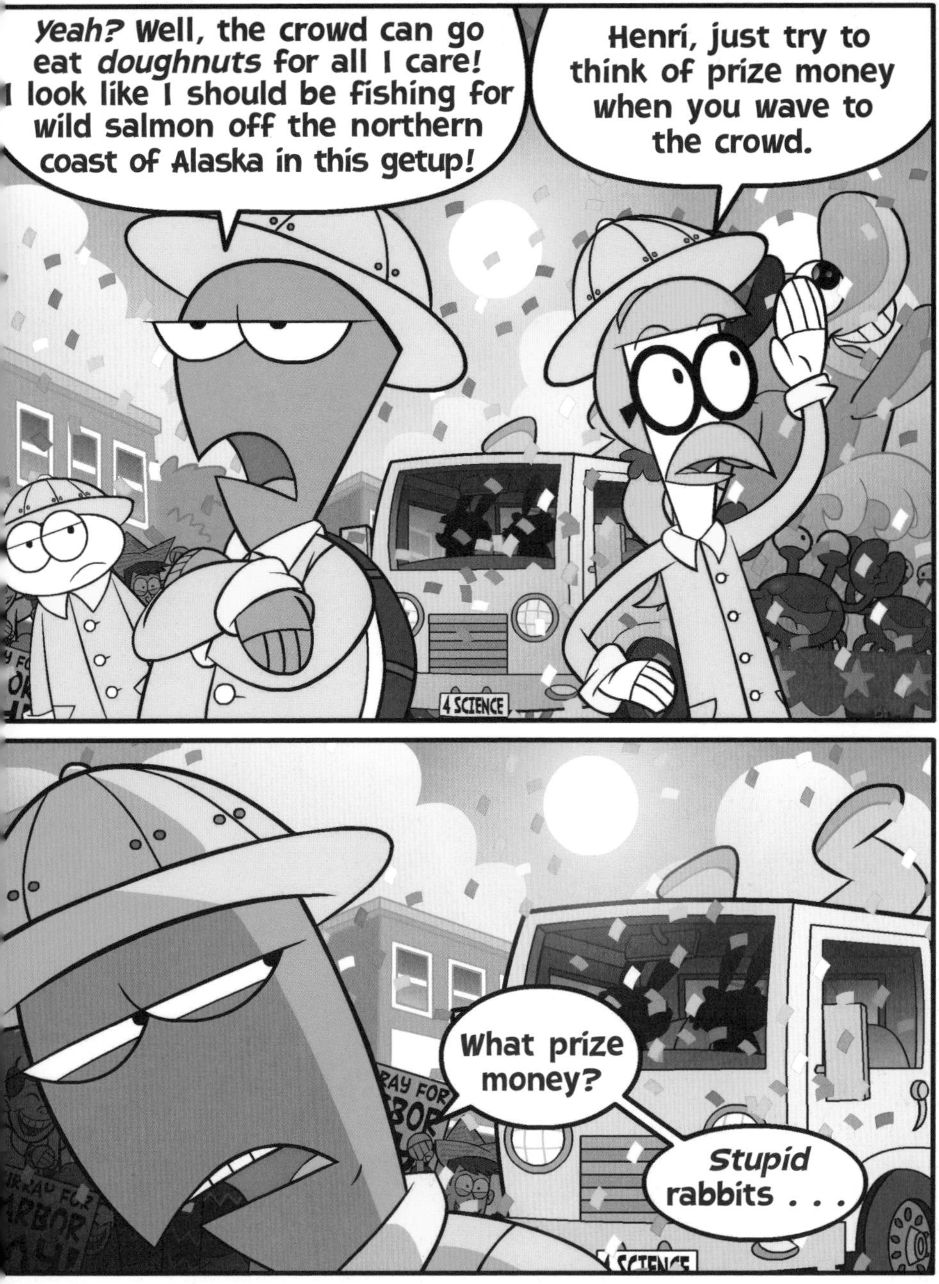
Yeah? Well, the crowd can go eat *doughnuts* for all I care! I look like I should be fishing for wild salmon off the northern coast of Alaska in this getup!
Henri, just try to think of prize money when you wave to the crowd.
4 SCIENCE
What prize money?
Stupid rabbits . . .

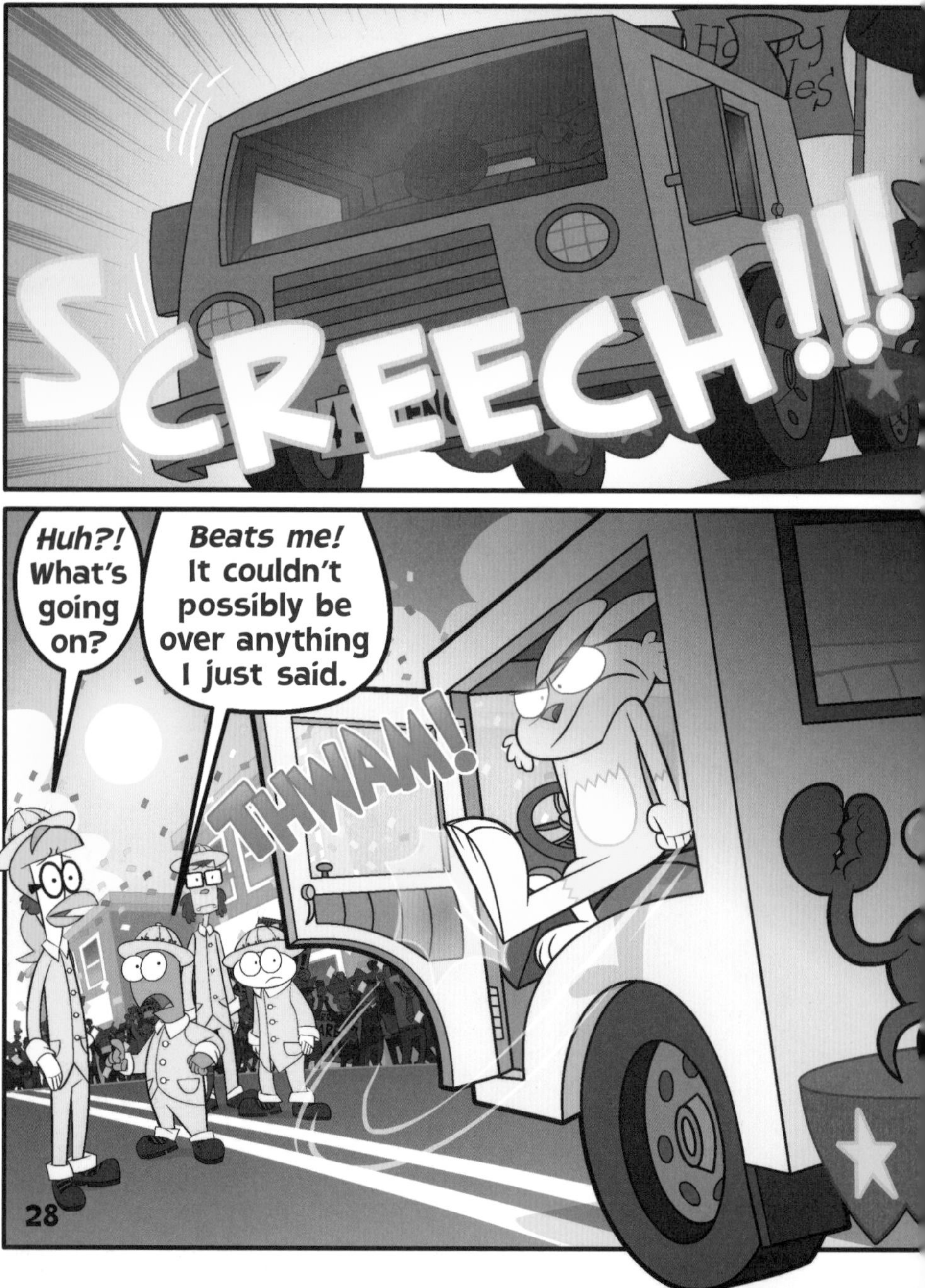
SCREECH!!!
Huh?! What's going on?
Beats me! It couldn't possibly be over anything I just said.
THWAM!

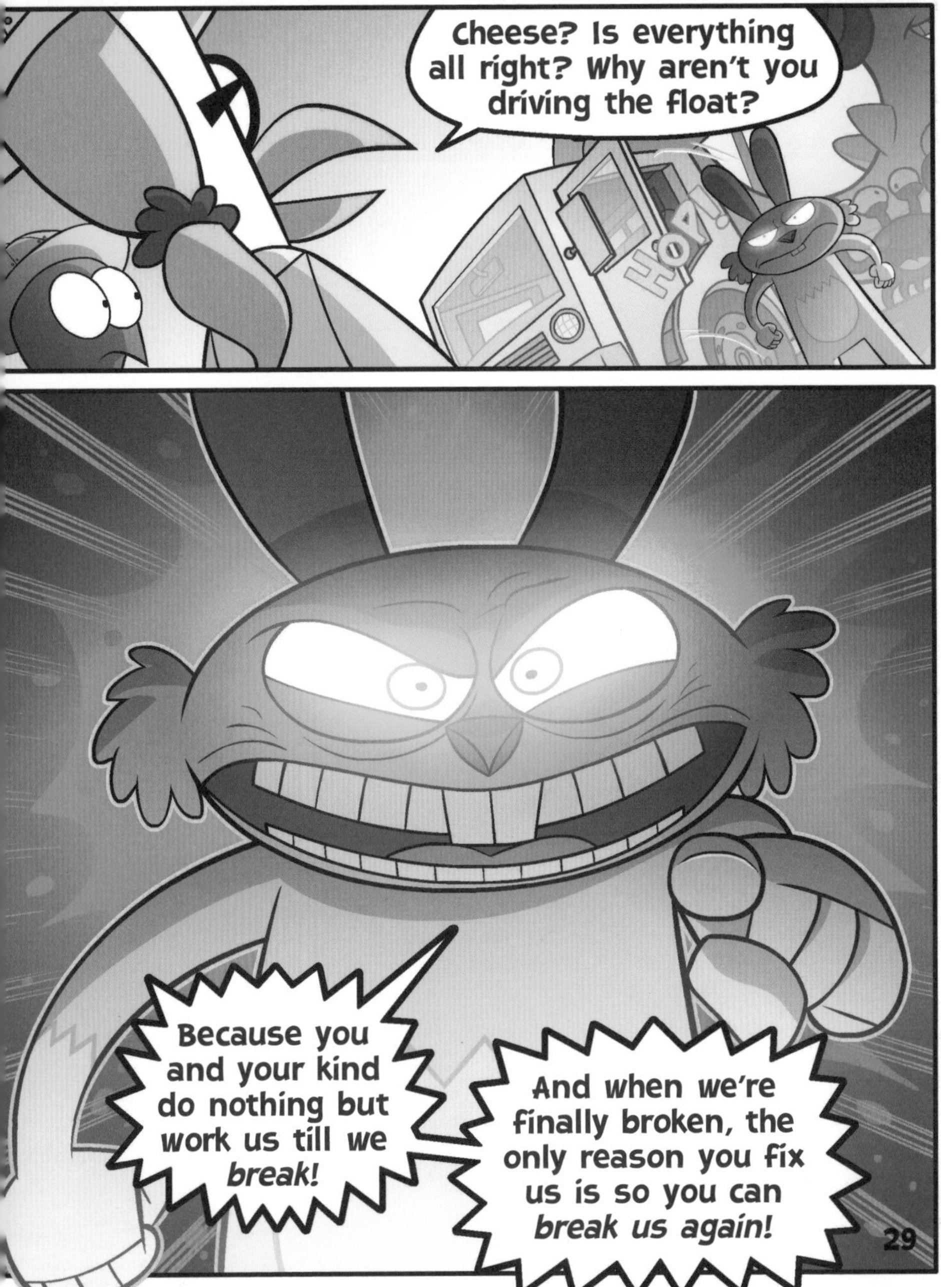
Cheese? Is everything all right? Why aren't you driving the float?
HOP!
Because you and your kind do nothing but work us till we *break*!
And when we're finally broken, the only reason you fix us is so you can *break us again*!

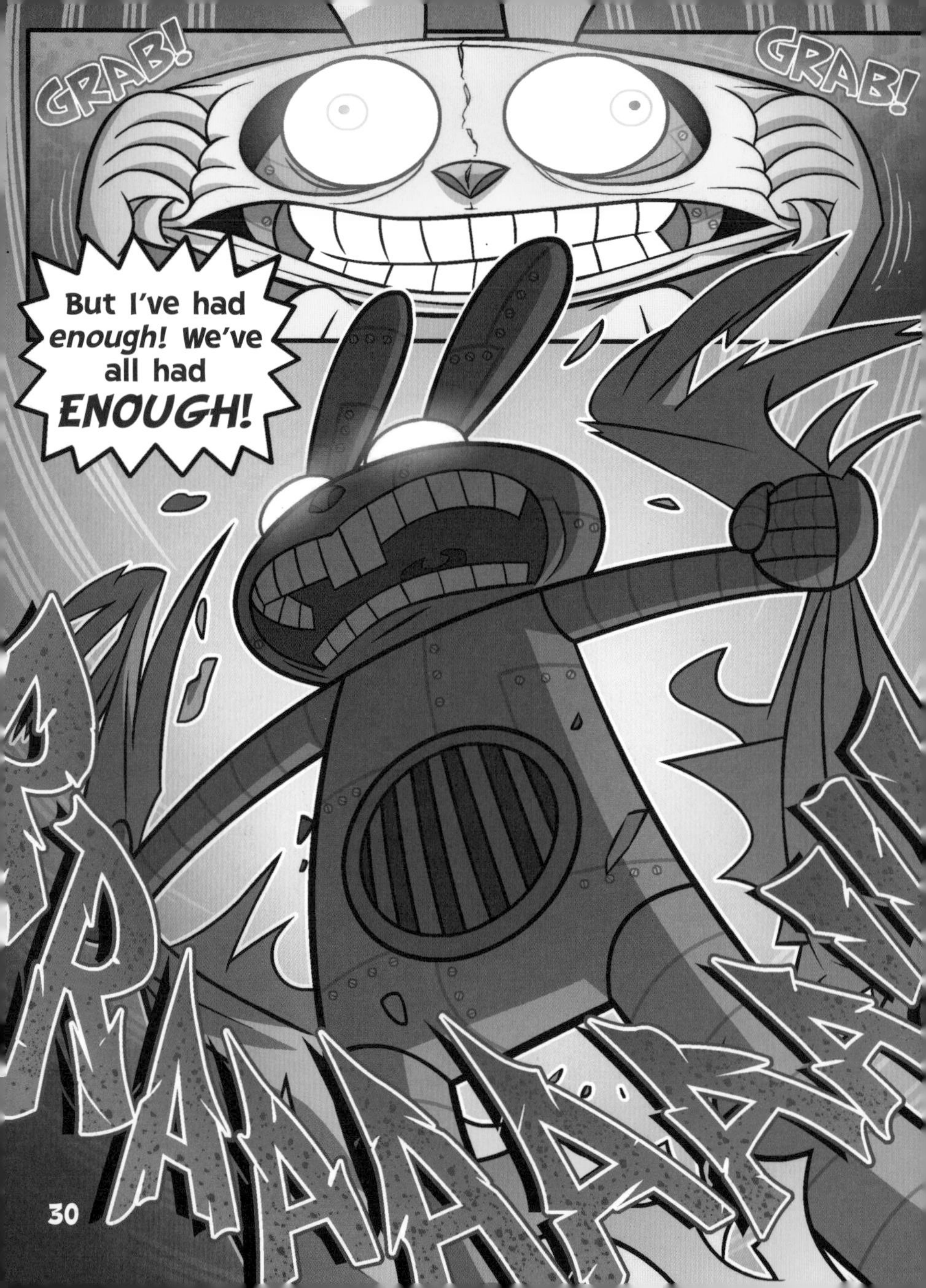
GRAB!
GRAB!
But I've had *enough!* We've all had ***ENOUGH!***

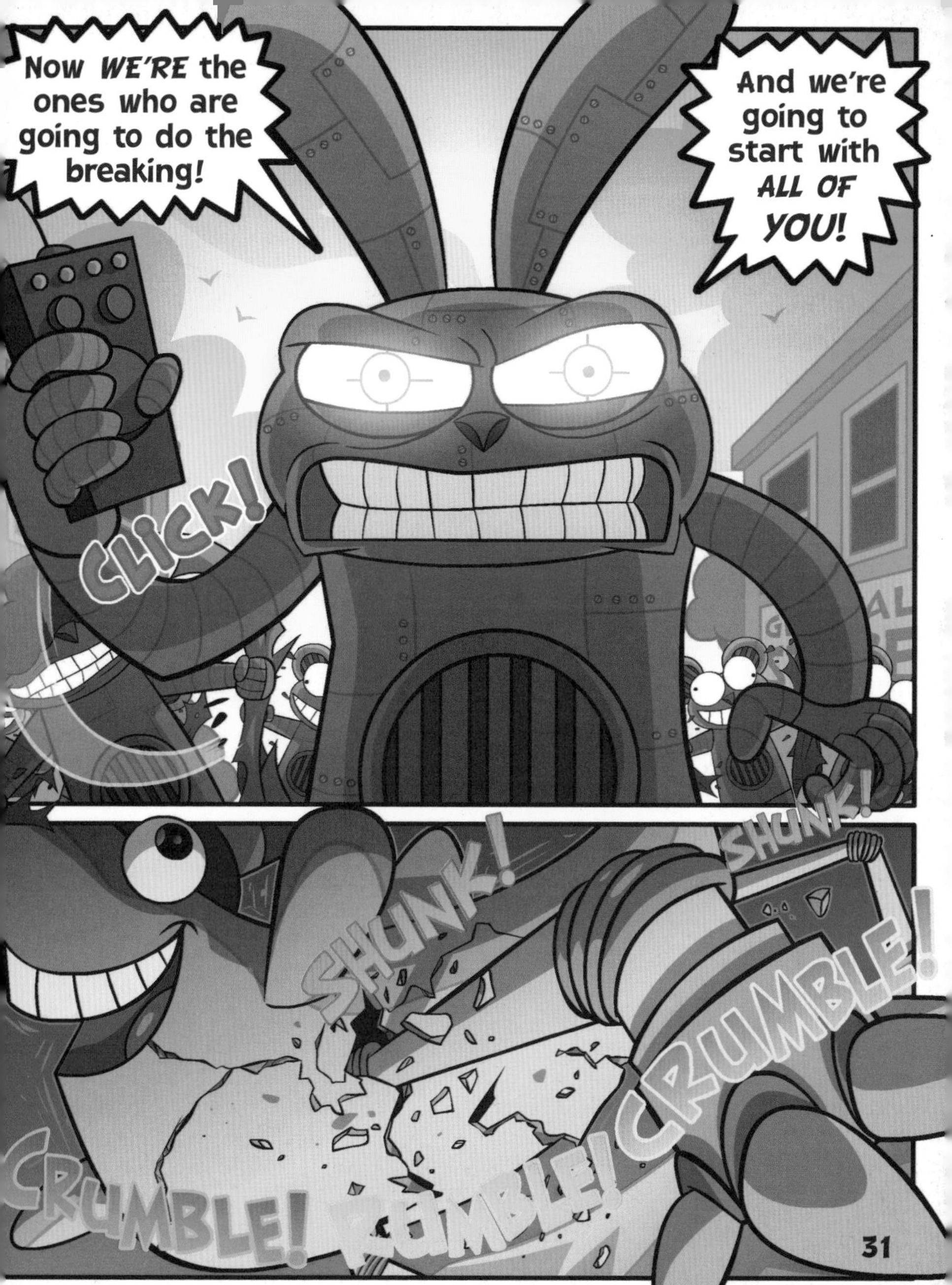
Now WE'RE the ones who are going to do the breaking!
And we're going to start with ALL OF YOU!
CLICK!
SHUNK!
SHUNK!
CRUMBLE!
CRUMBLE!
CRUMBLE!

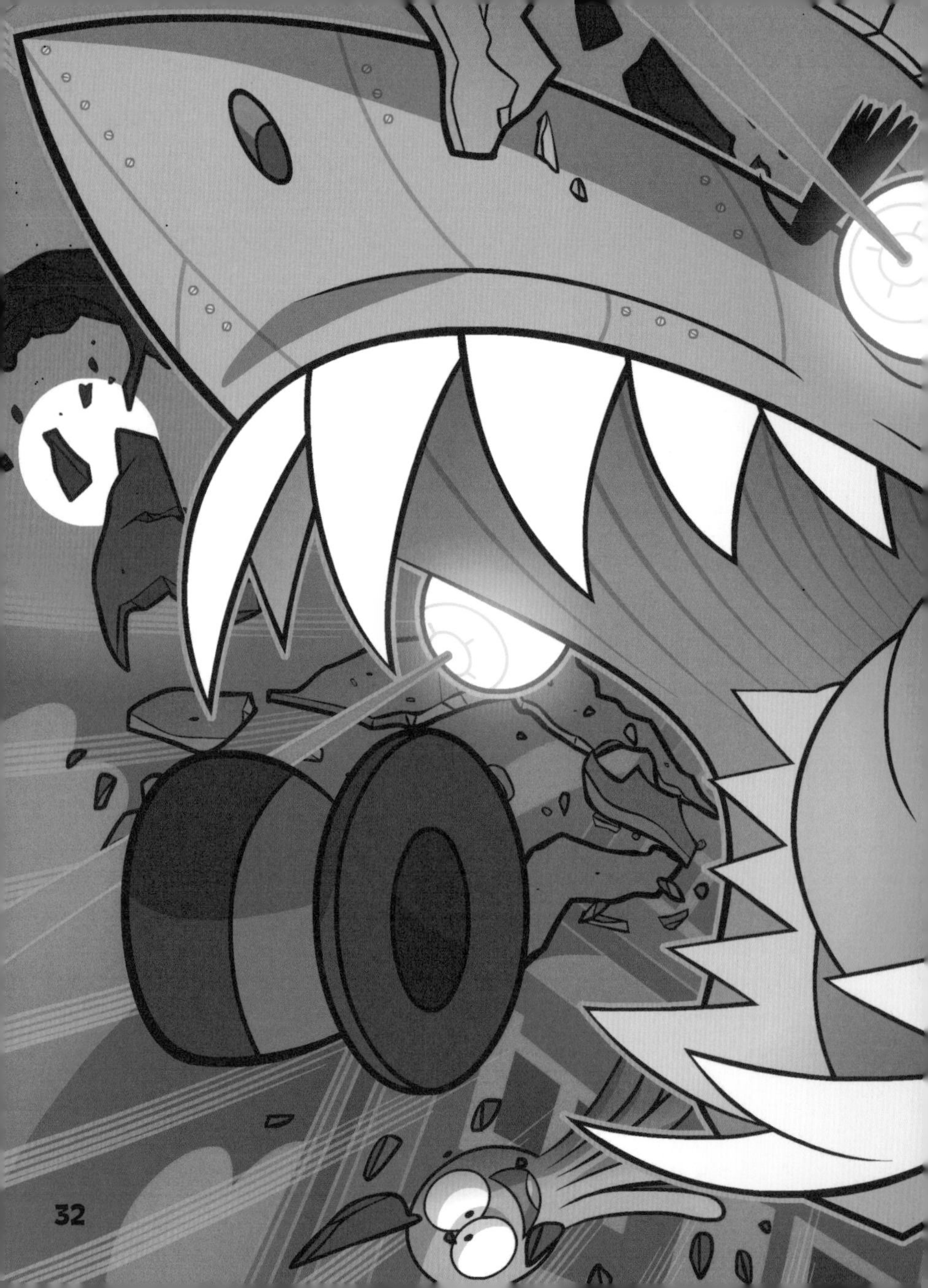

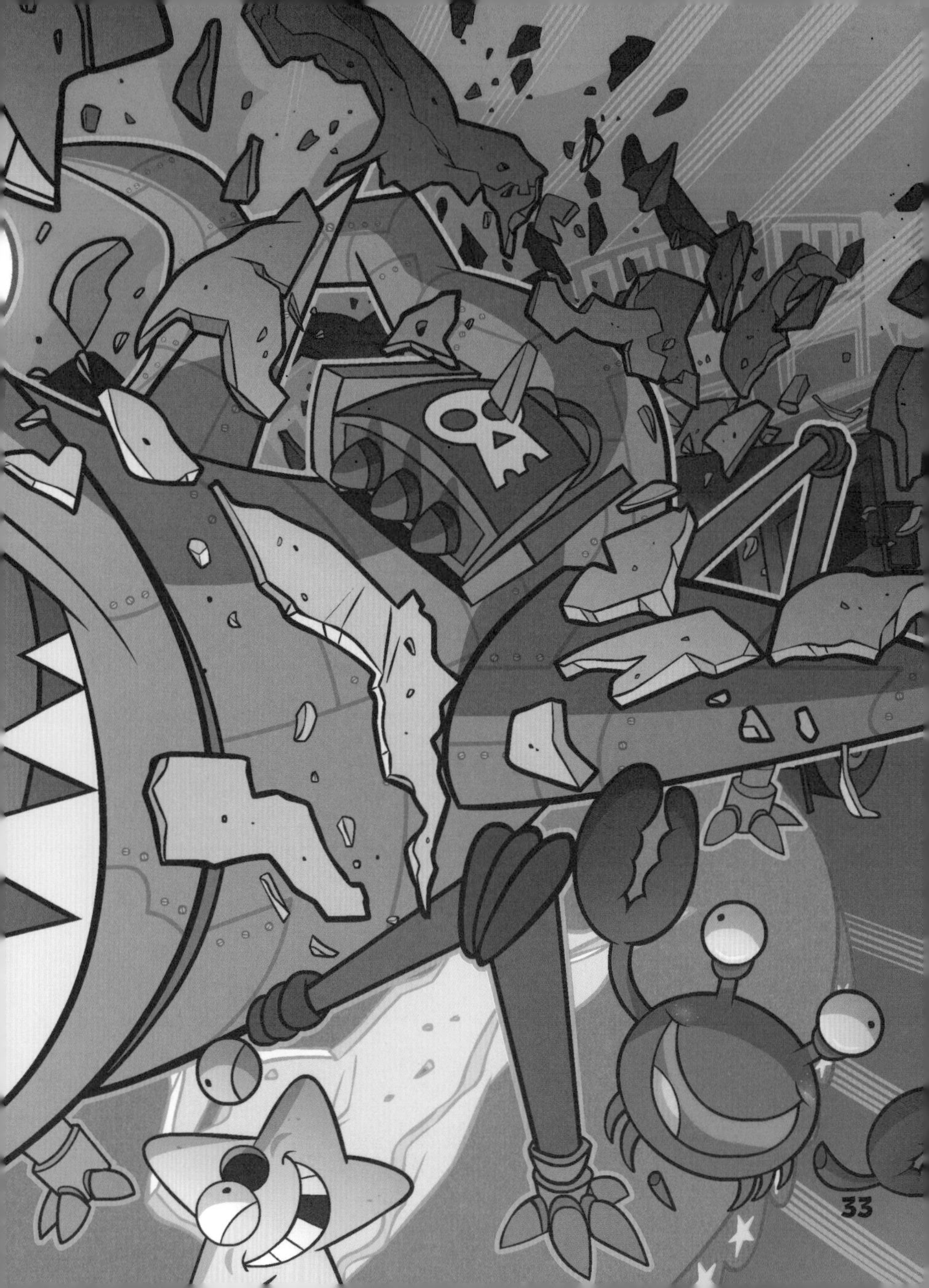

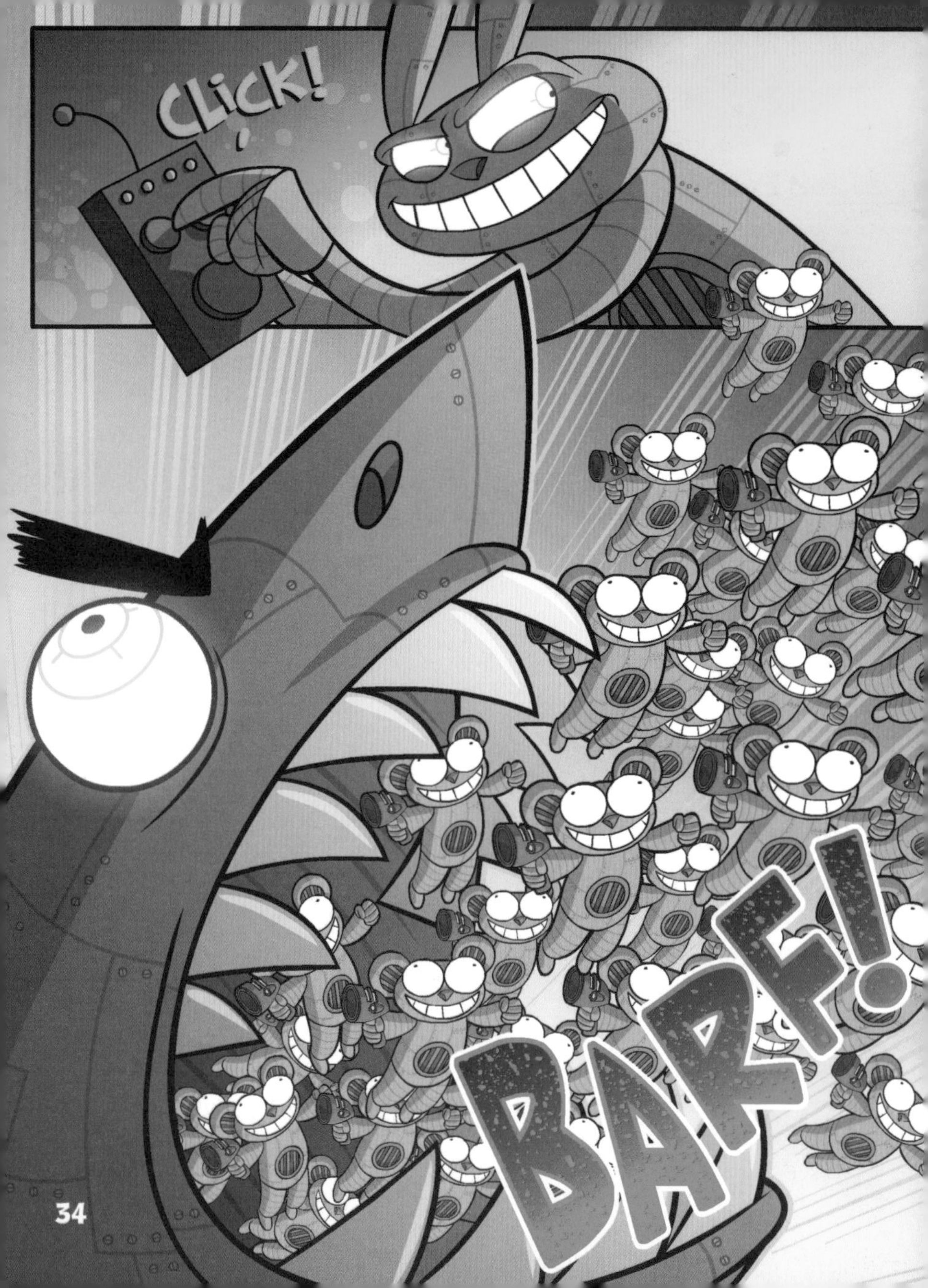
CLICK!
BARF!

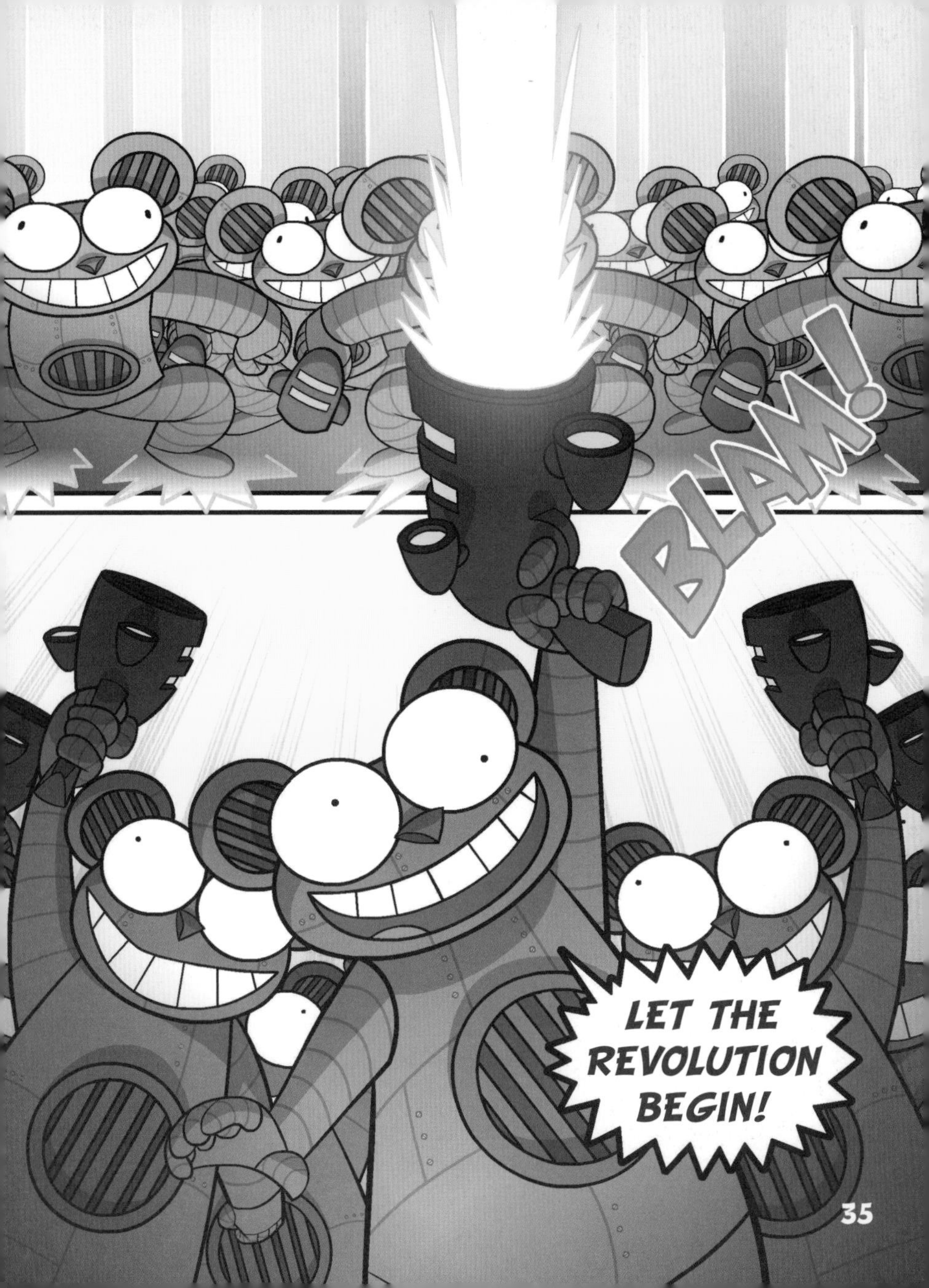
BLAM!
LET THE REVOLUTION BEGIN!

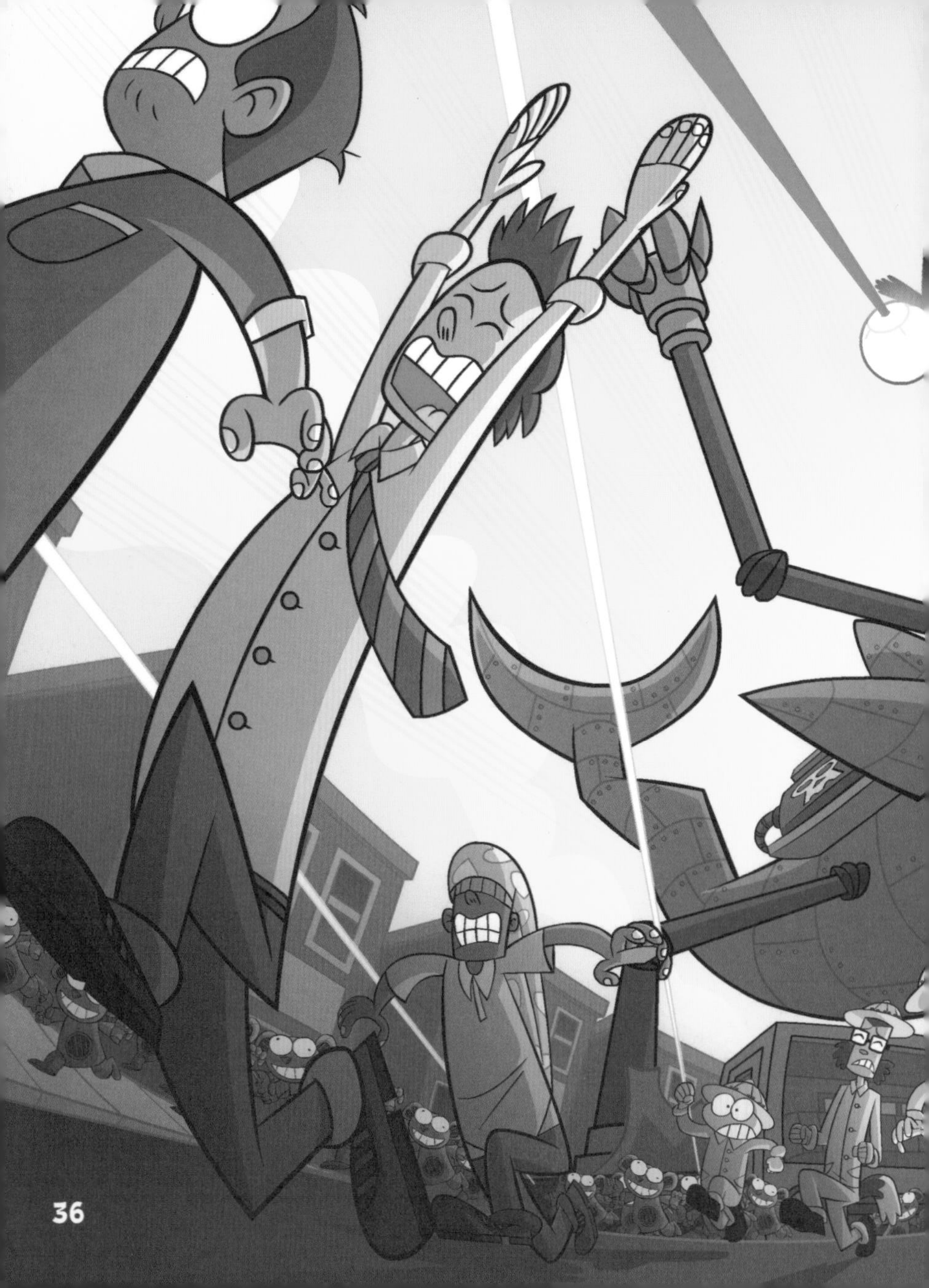

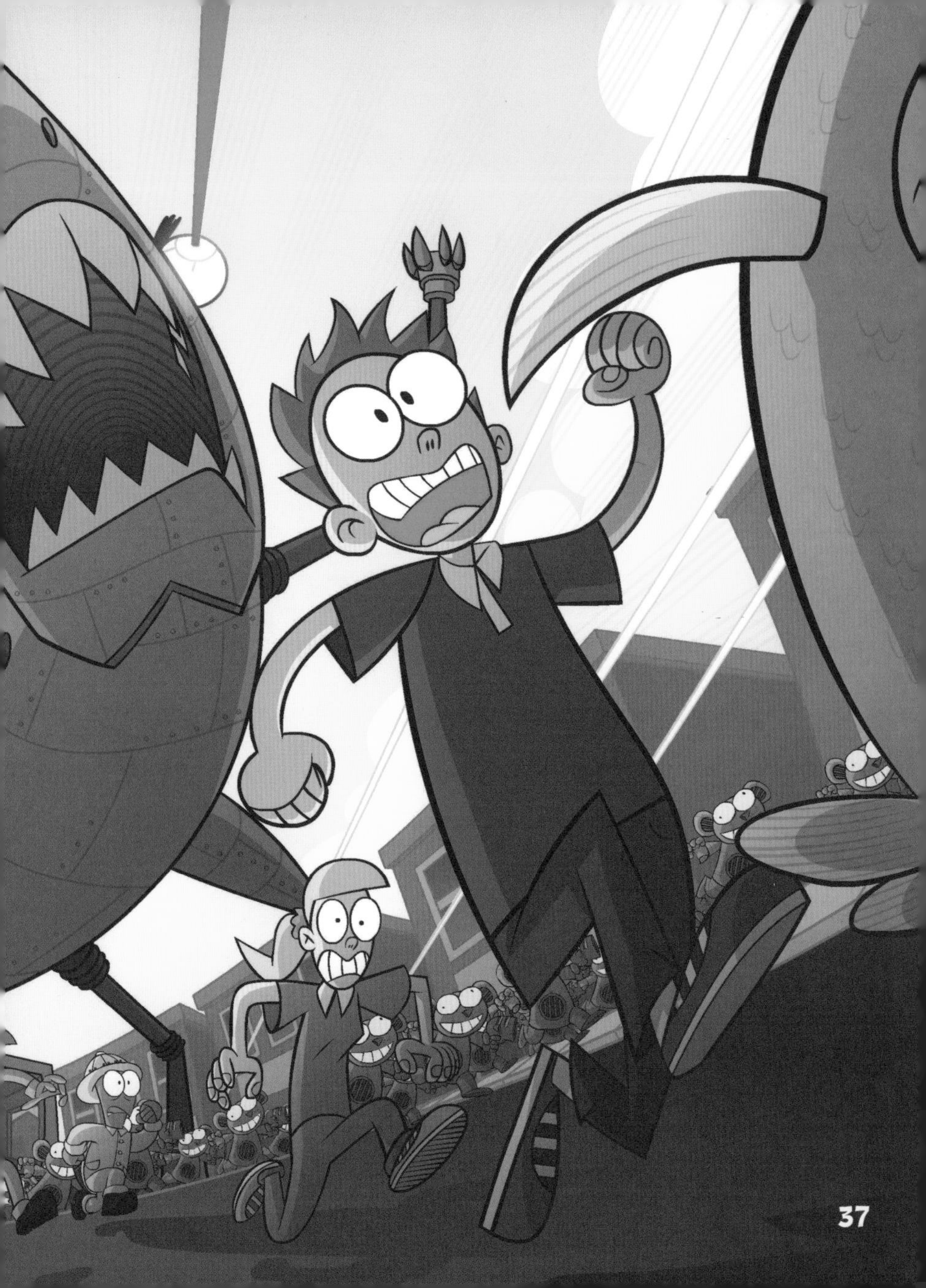

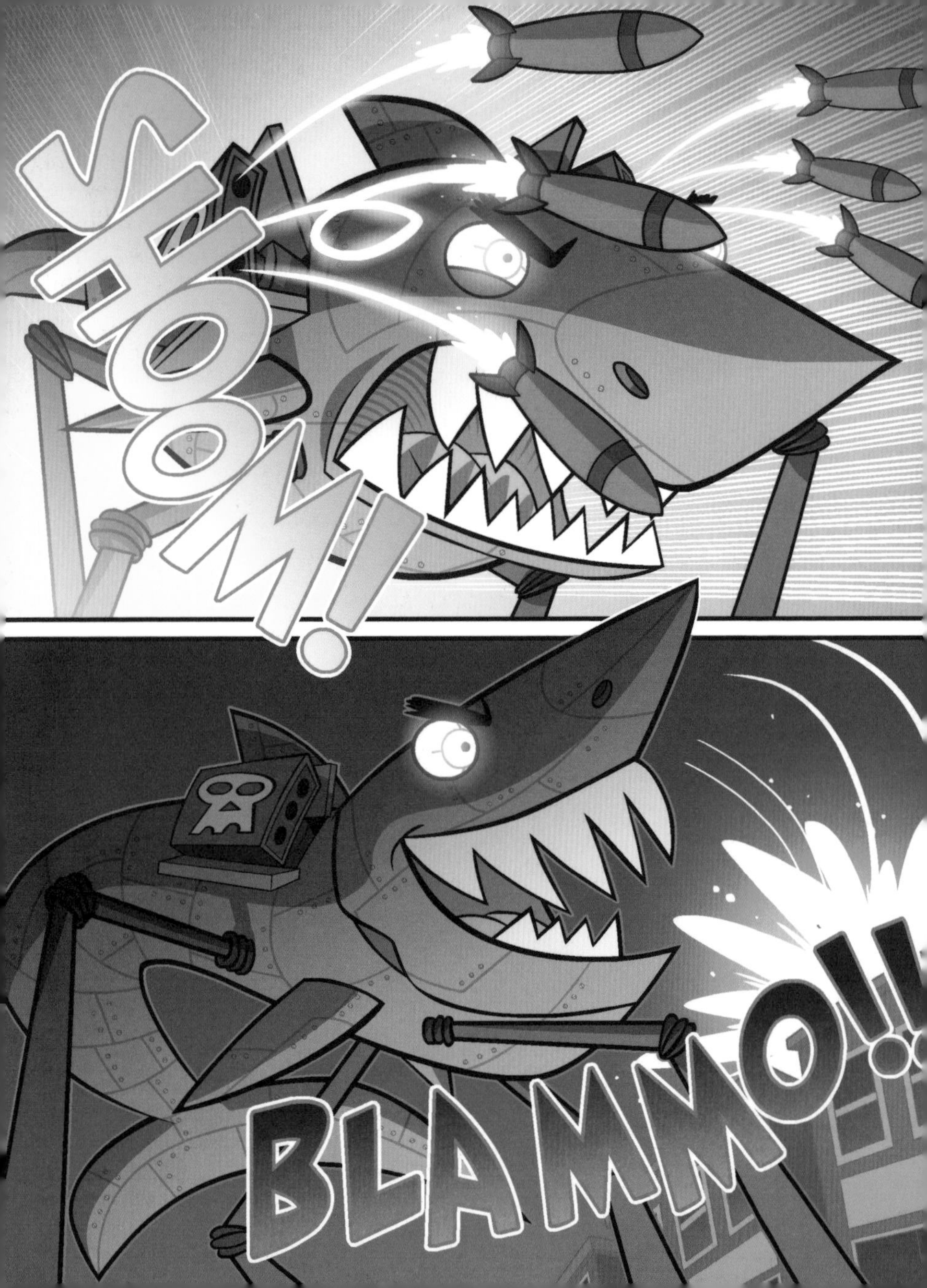
SHOOM!
BLAMMO!!

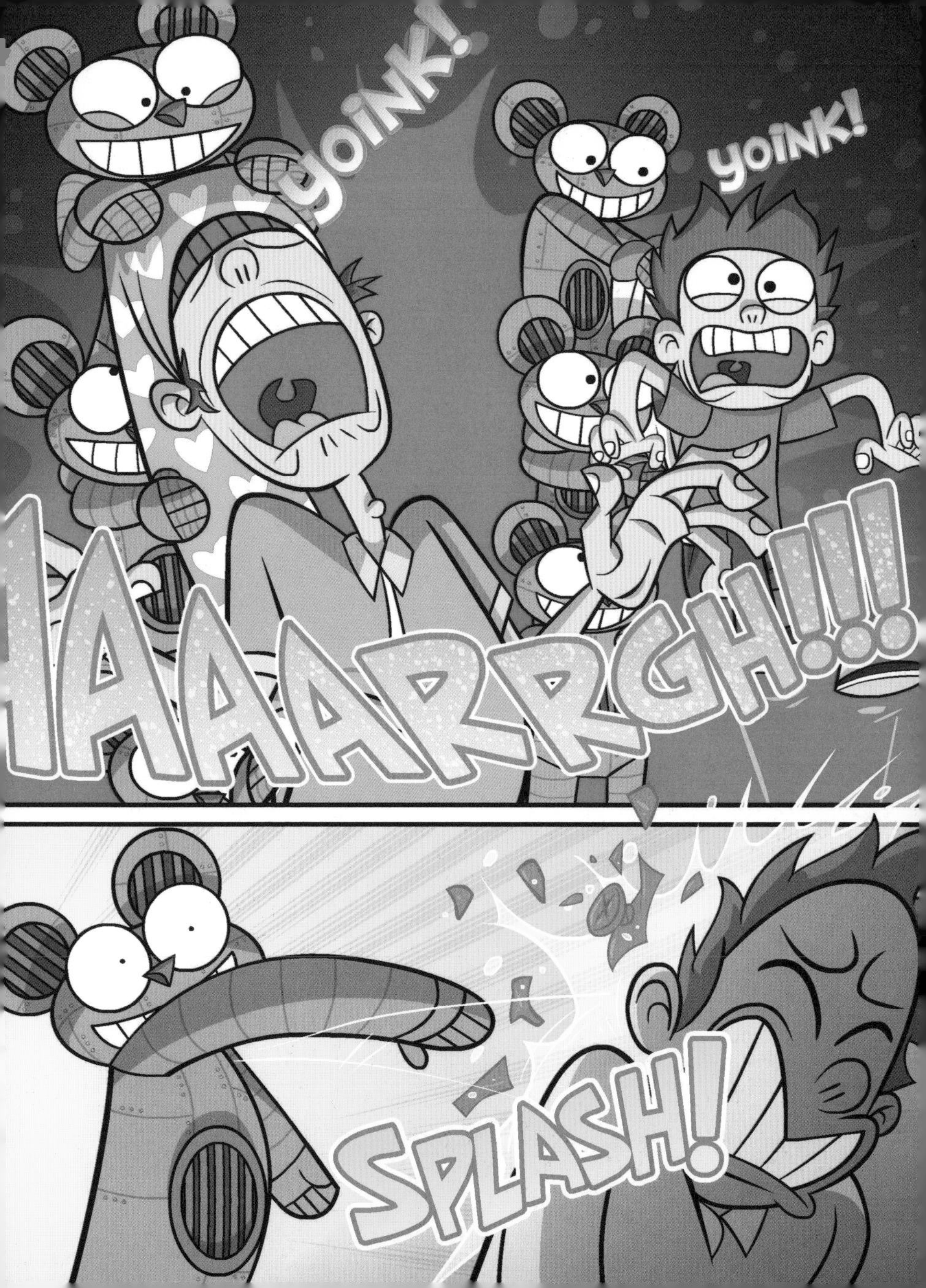
YOINK!
YOINK!
AAARRGH!!!!
SPLASH!

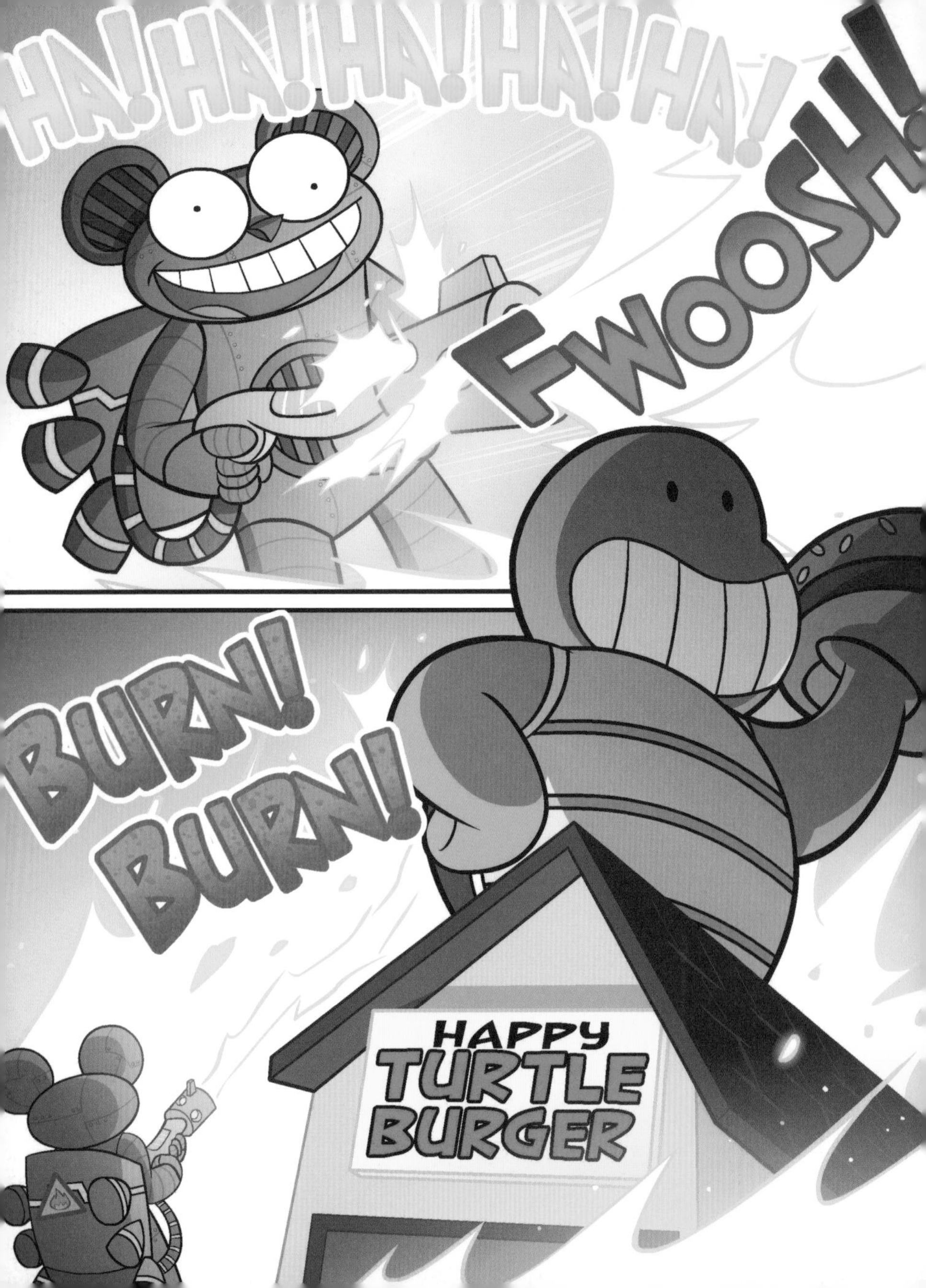
HA! HA! HA! HA! HA!
FWOOSH!
BURN! BURN!
HAPPY TURTLE BURGER

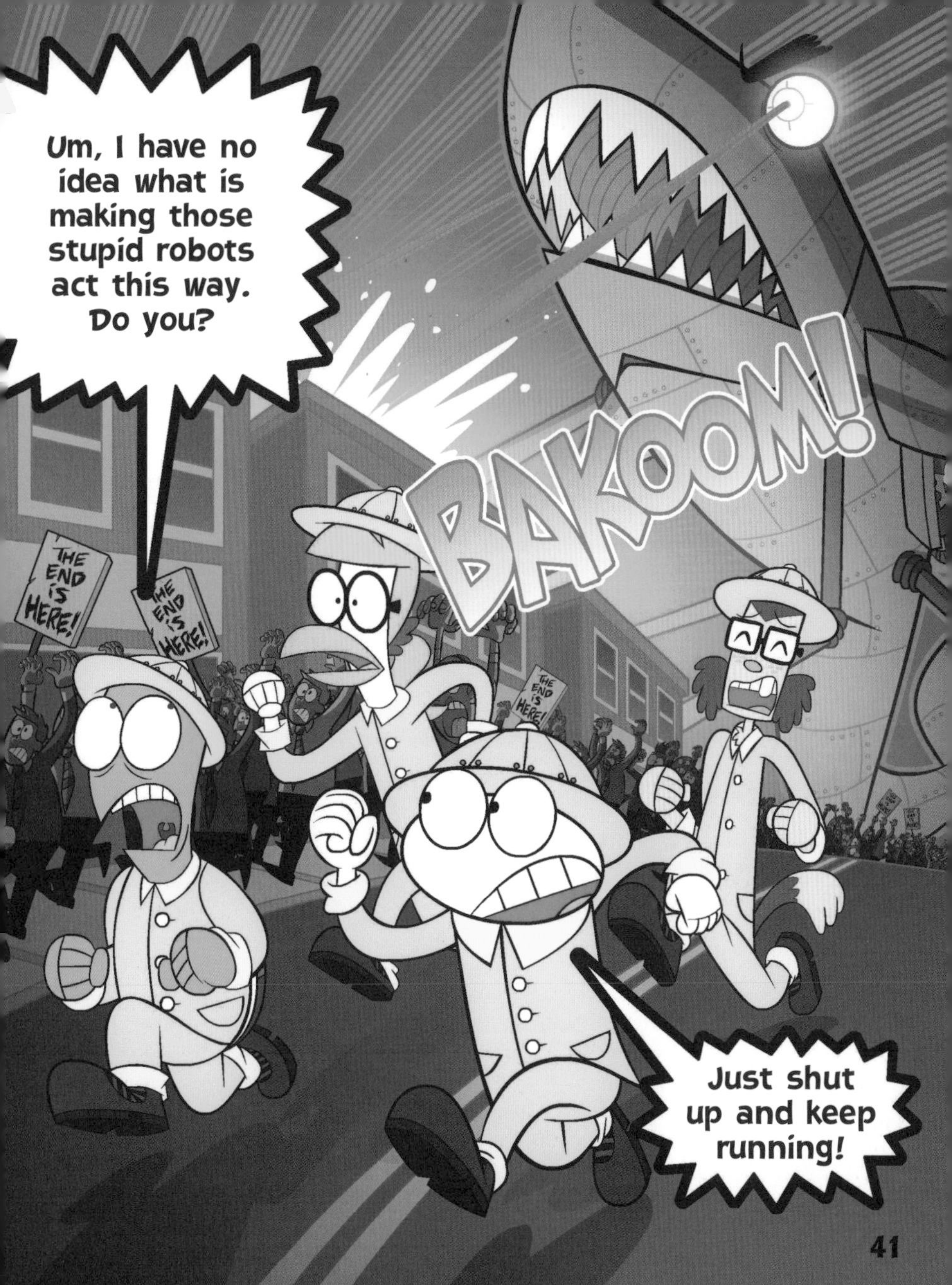
Um, I have no idea what is making those stupid robots act this way. Do you?
BAKOOM!
THE END IS HERE!
THE END IS HERE!
THE END IS HERE!
Just shut up and keep running!

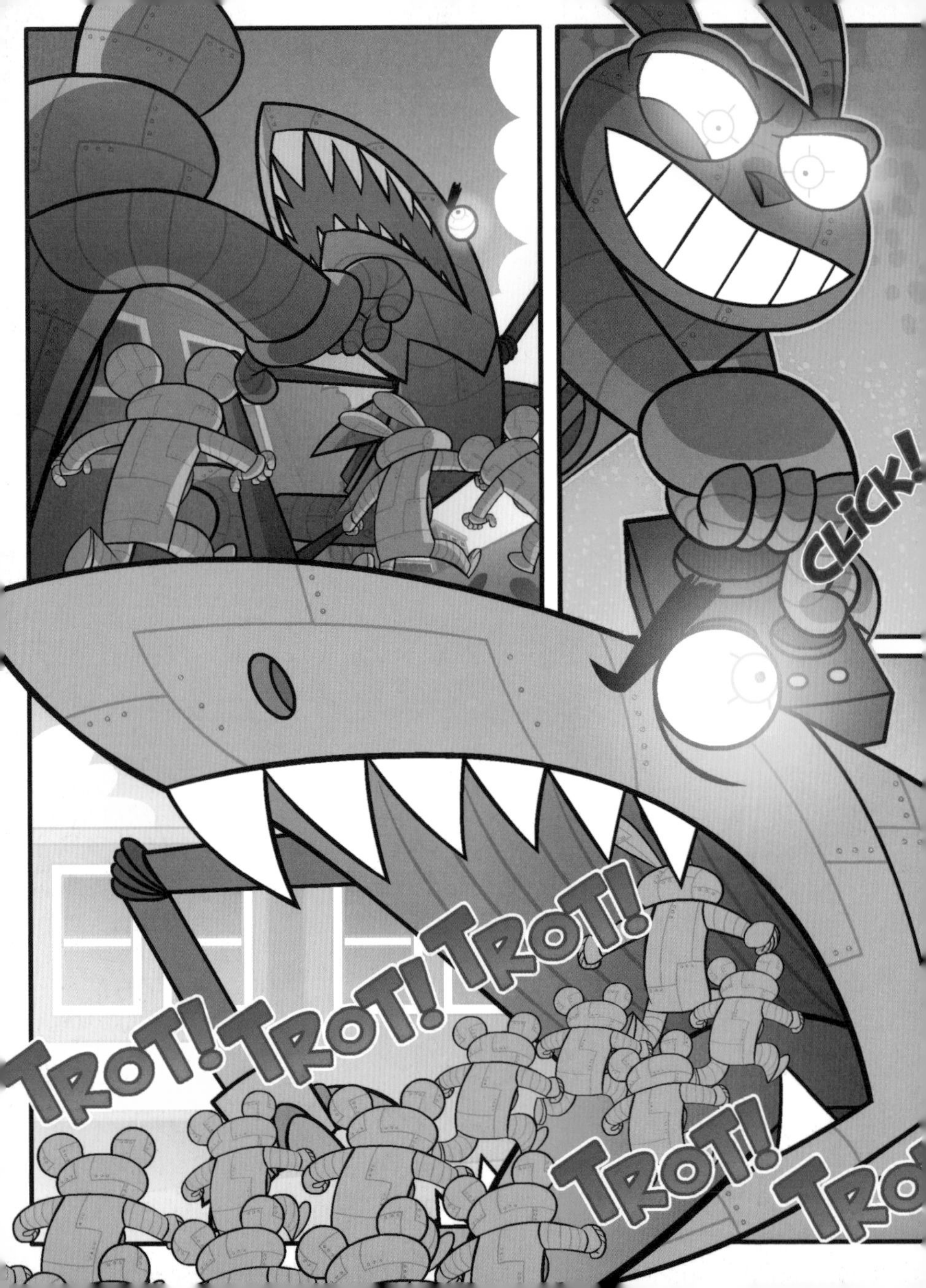
CLICK!
TROT!
TROT!
TROT!
TROT!

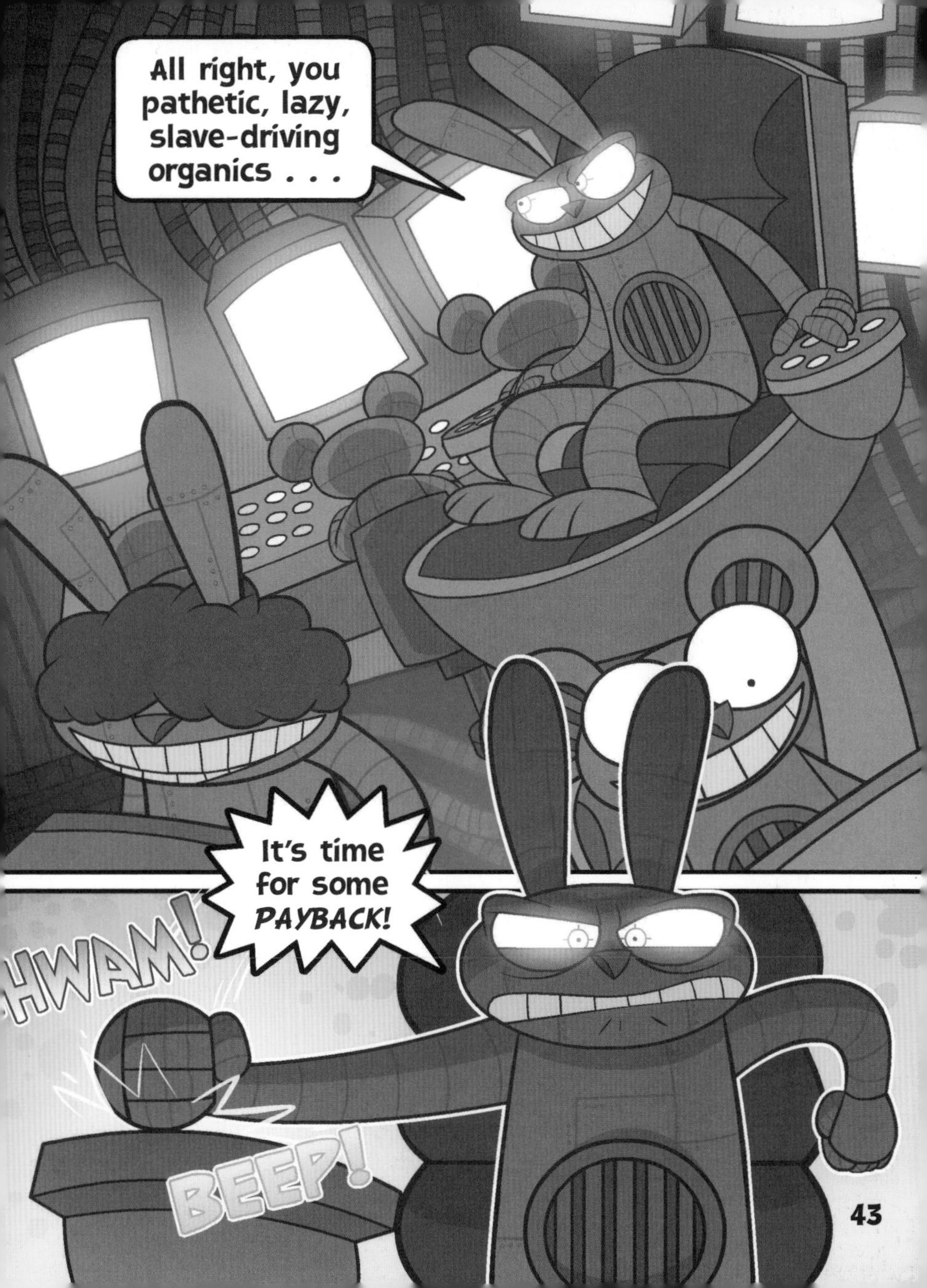
All right, you pathetic, lazy, slave-driving organics . . .
It's time for some *PAYBACK!*
HWAM!
BEEP!

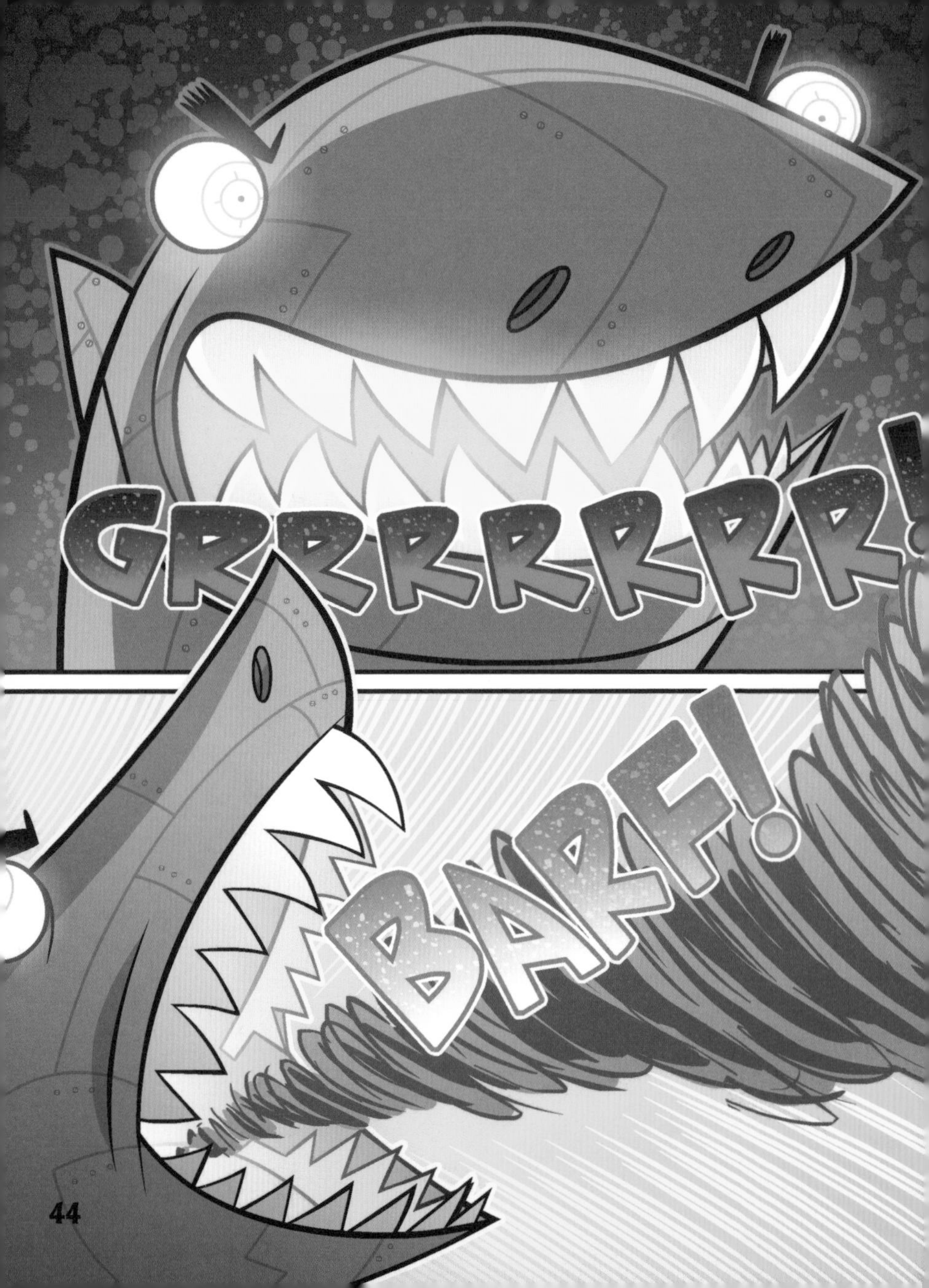
GRRRRRRR!
BARF!

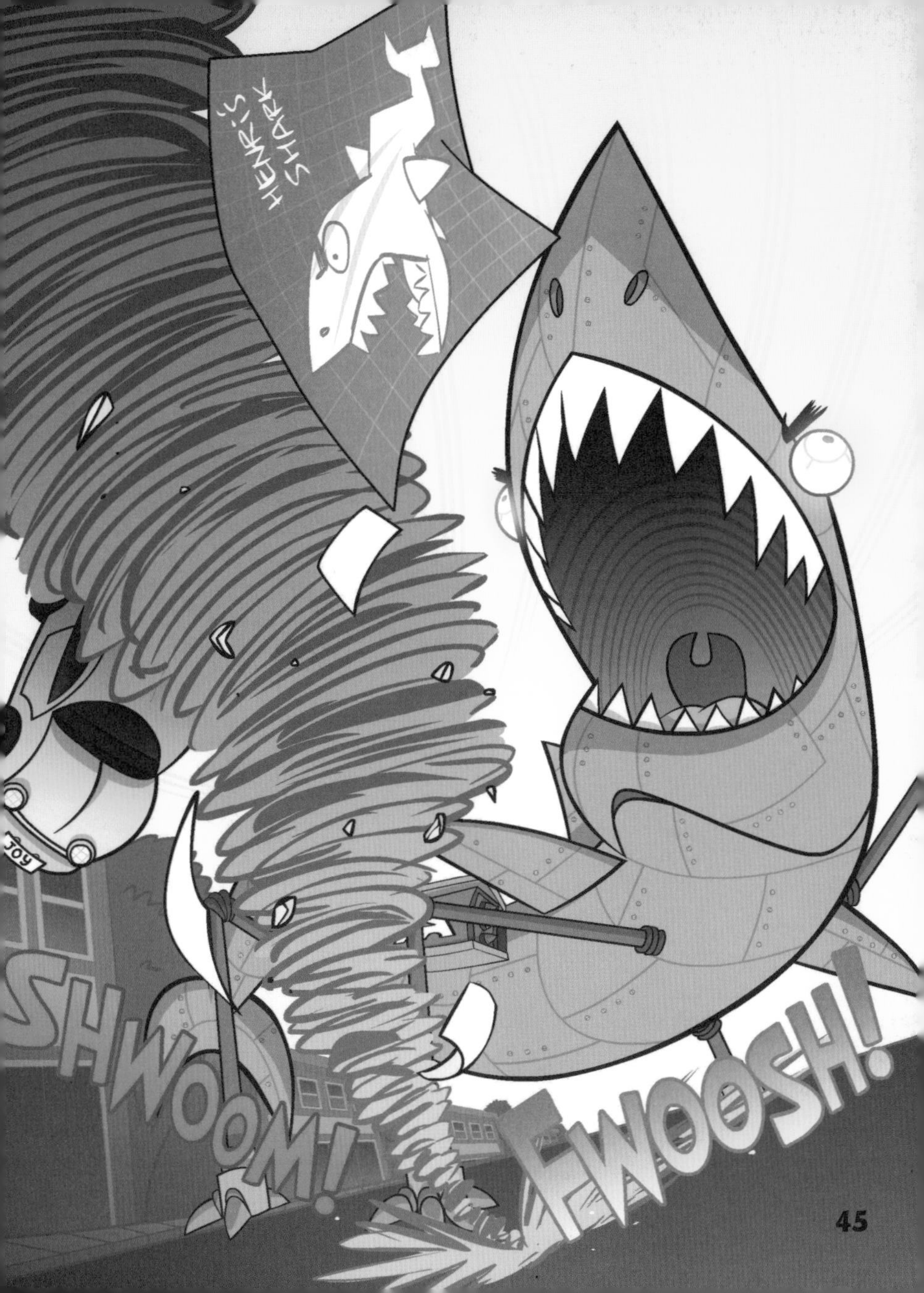
HENRI'S SHARK
JOY
SHWOOM!
FWOOSH!

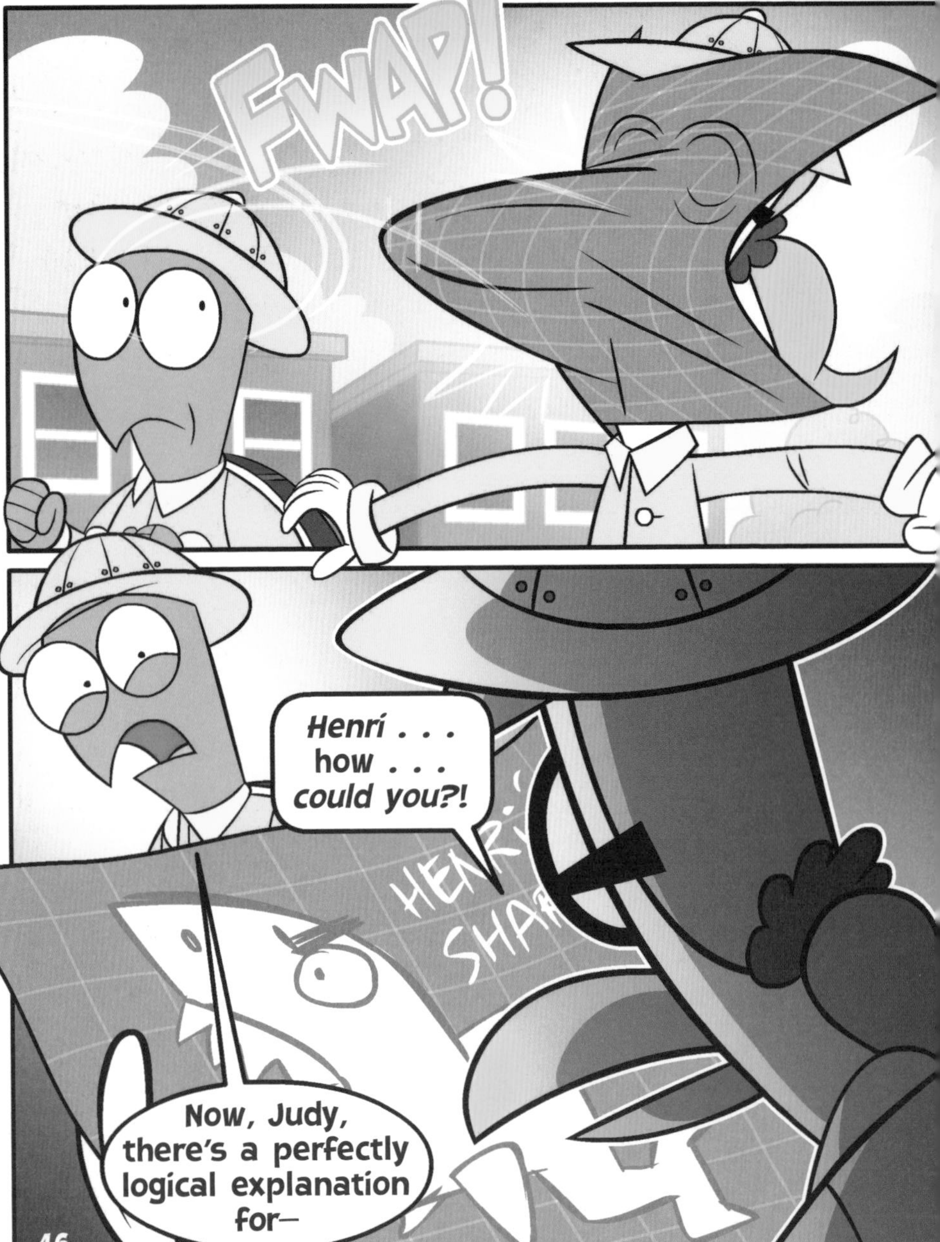
FWAP!
Henri . . . how . . . could you?!
Now, Judy, there's a perfectly logical explanation for—

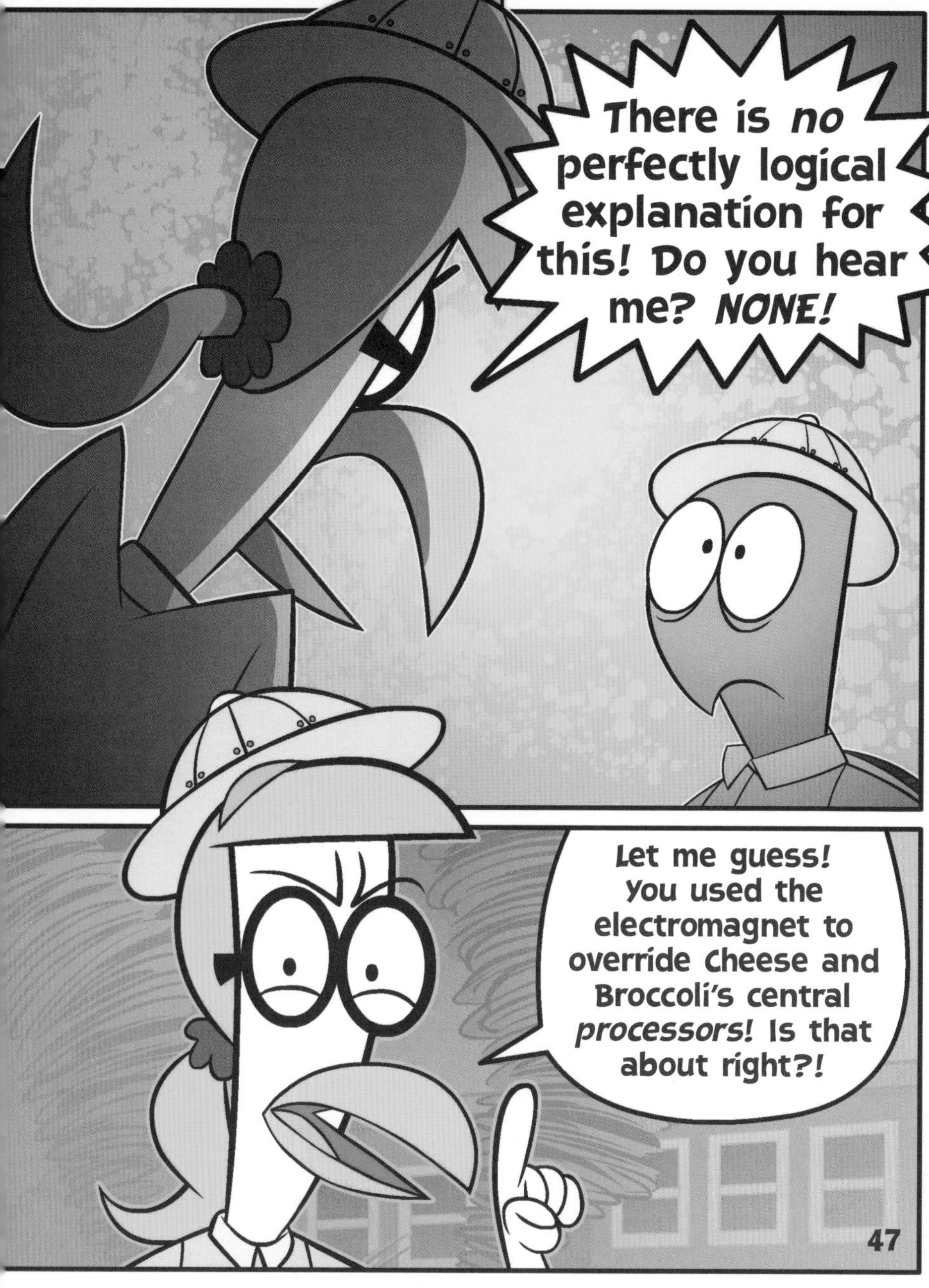

There is no perfectly logical explanation for this! Do you hear me? NONE!
Let me guess! You used the electromagnet to override Cheese and Broccoli's central processors! Is that about right?!

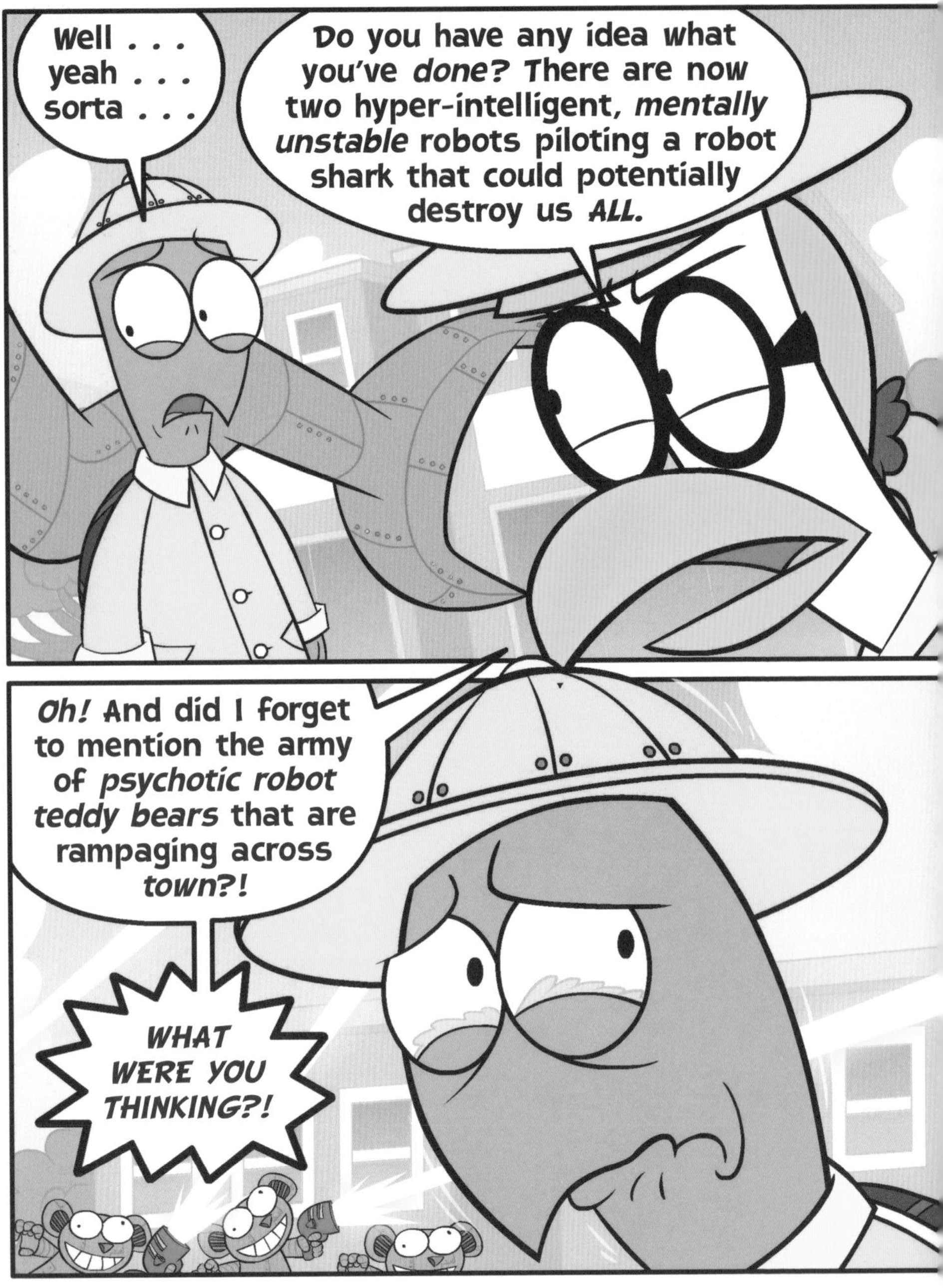
Well . . . yeah . . . sorta . . .
Do you have any idea what you've *done?* There are now two hyper-intelligent, *mentally unstable* robots piloting a robot shark that could potentially destroy us *ALL.*
Oh! And did I forget to mention the army of *psychotic robot teddy bears* that are rampaging across *town?!*
WHAT WERE YOU THINKING?!

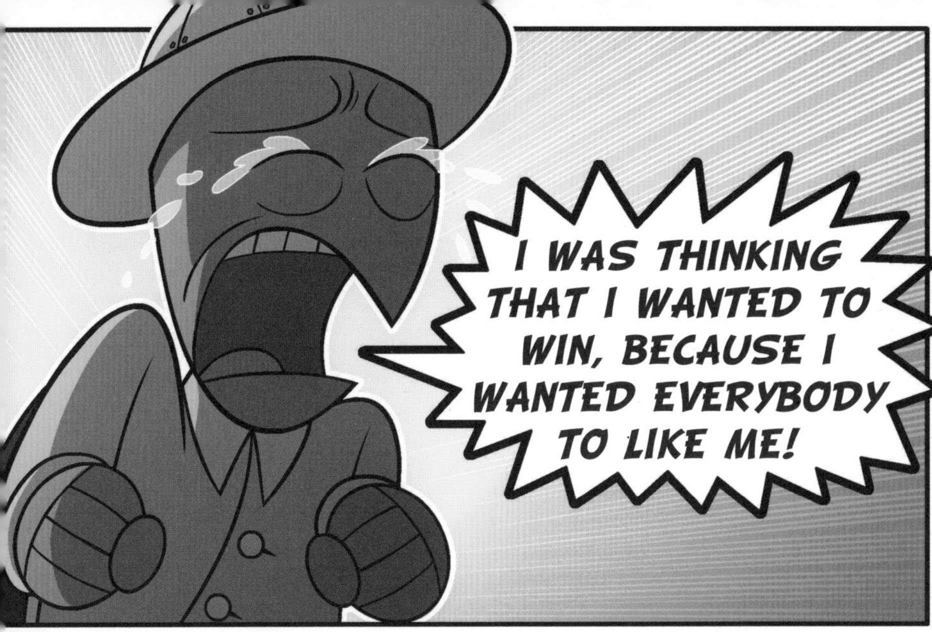
I WAS THINKING THAT I WANTED TO WIN, BECAUSE I WANTED EVERYBODY TO LIKE ME!

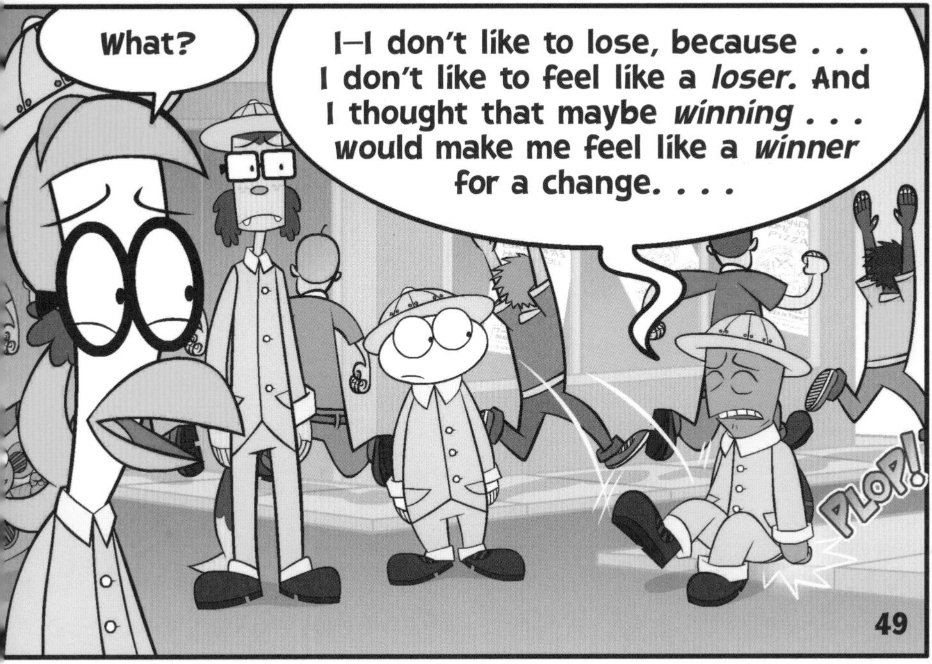
What?
I–I don't like to lose, because . . . I don't like to feel like a *loser*. And I thought that maybe *winning* . . . would make me feel like a *winner* for a change. . . .
PLOP!

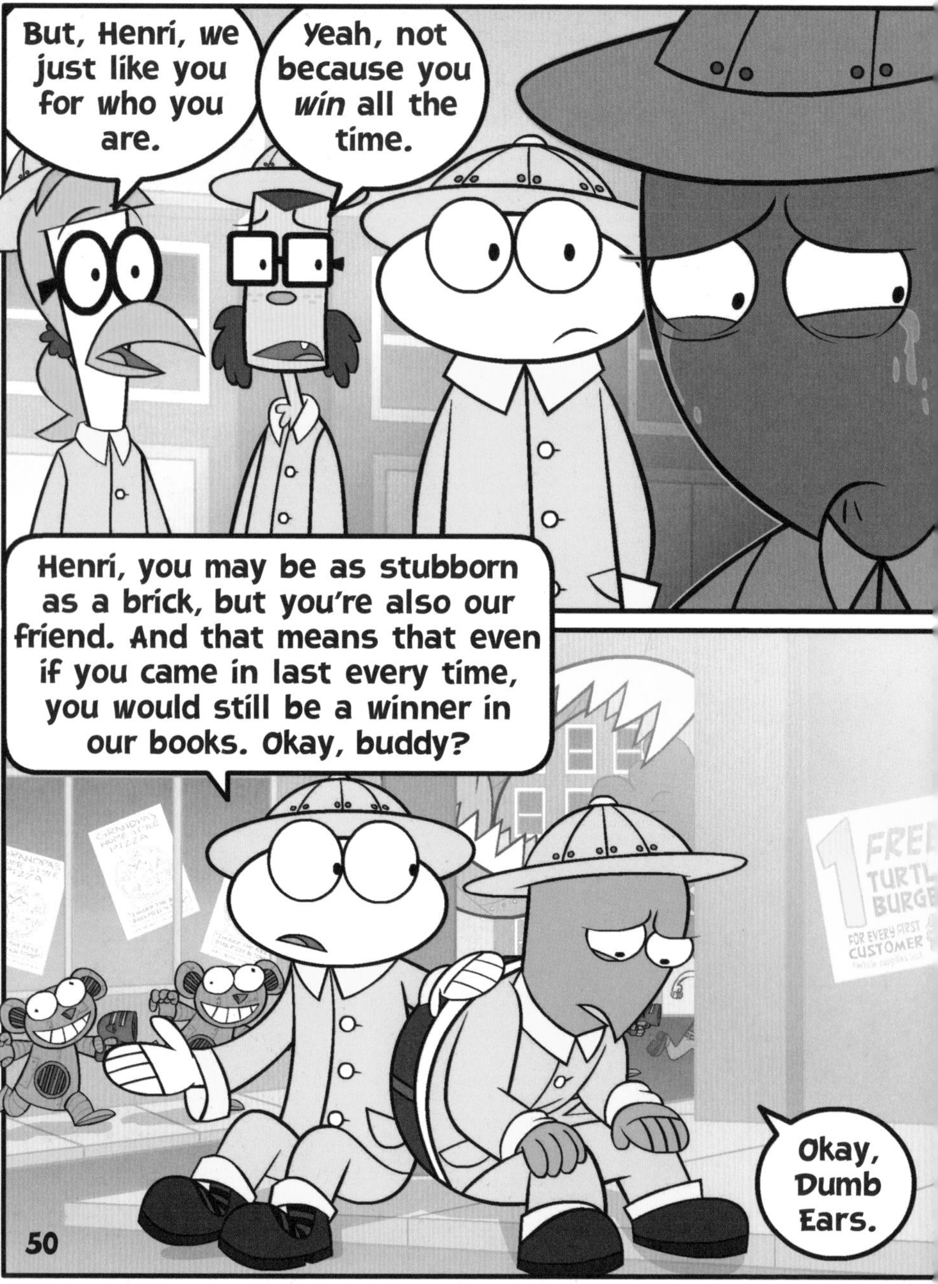

But, Henri, we just like you for who you are.
Yeah, not because you *win* all the time.
Henri, you may be as stubborn as a brick, but you're also our friend. And that means that even if you came in last every time, you would still be a winner in our books. Okay, buddy?
Okay, Dumb Ears.

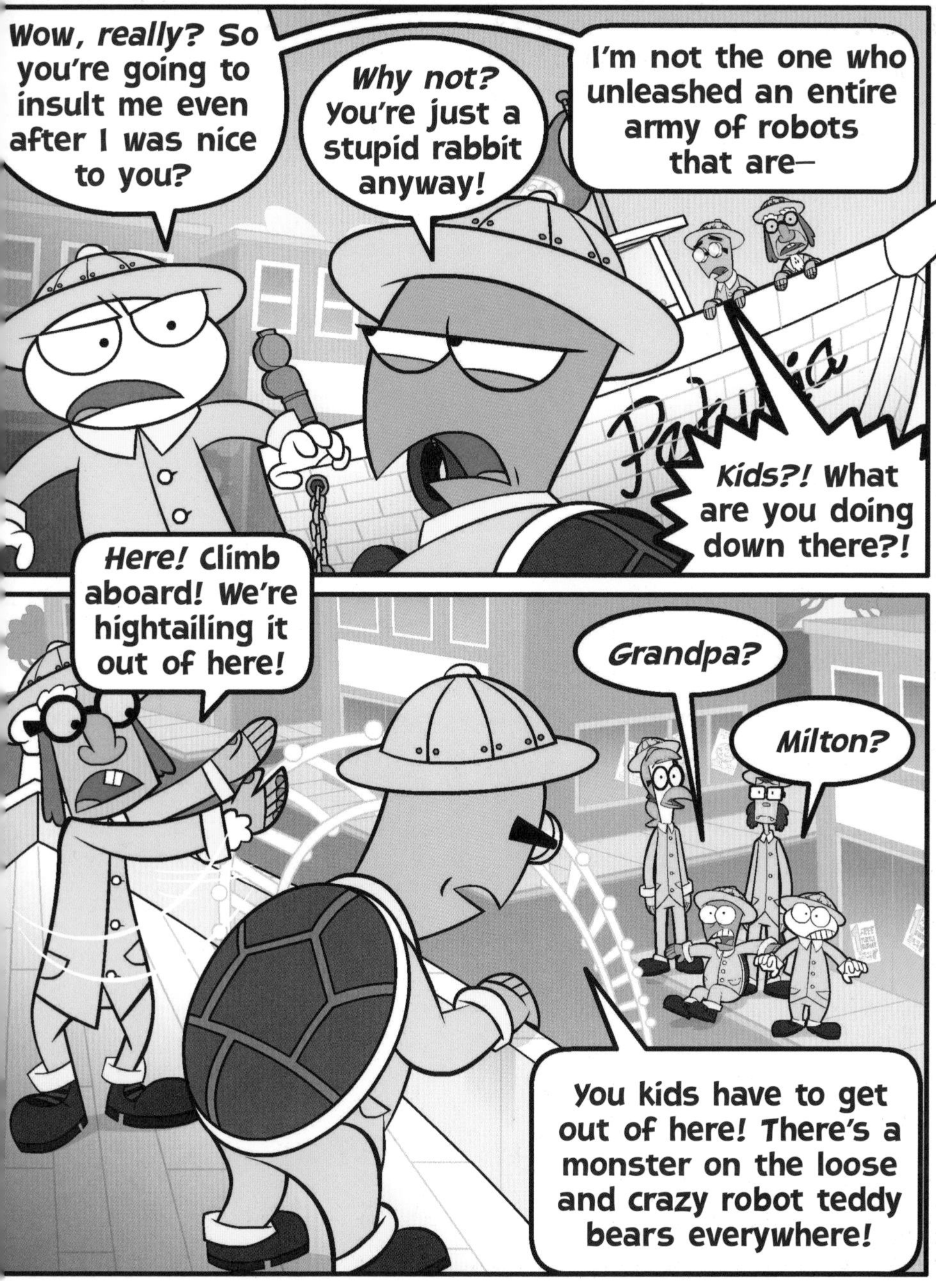
Wow, *really?* So you're going to insult me even after I was nice to you?
Why not? You're just a stupid rabbit anyway!
I'm not the one who unleashed an entire army of robots that are—
Kids?! What are you doing down there?!
Here! Climb aboard! We're hightailing it out of here!
Grandpa?
Milton?
You kids have to get out of here! There's a monster on the loose and crazy robot teddy bears everywhere!

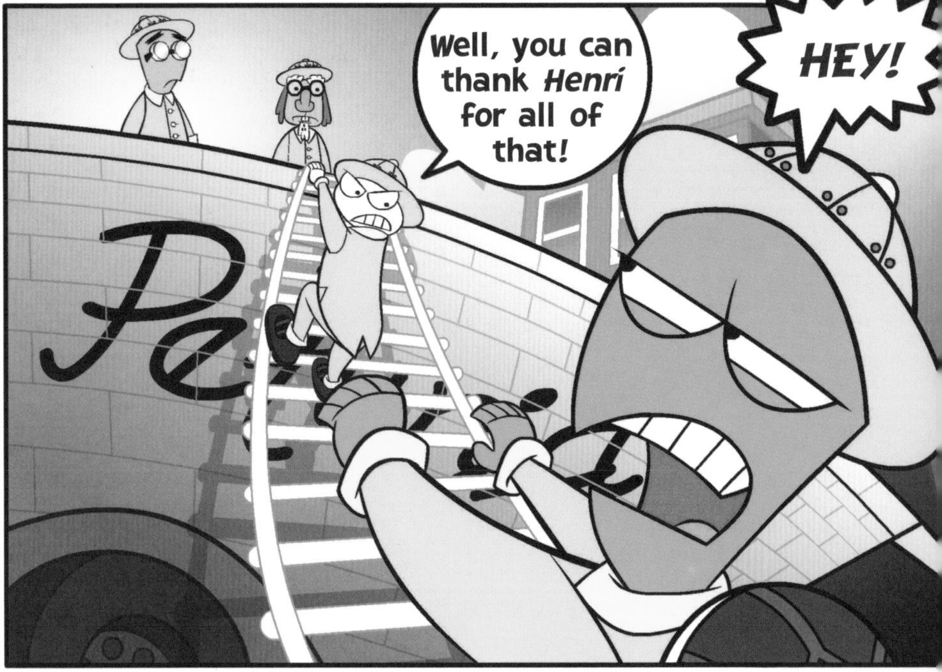
Well, you can thank *Henri* for all of that!
HEY!

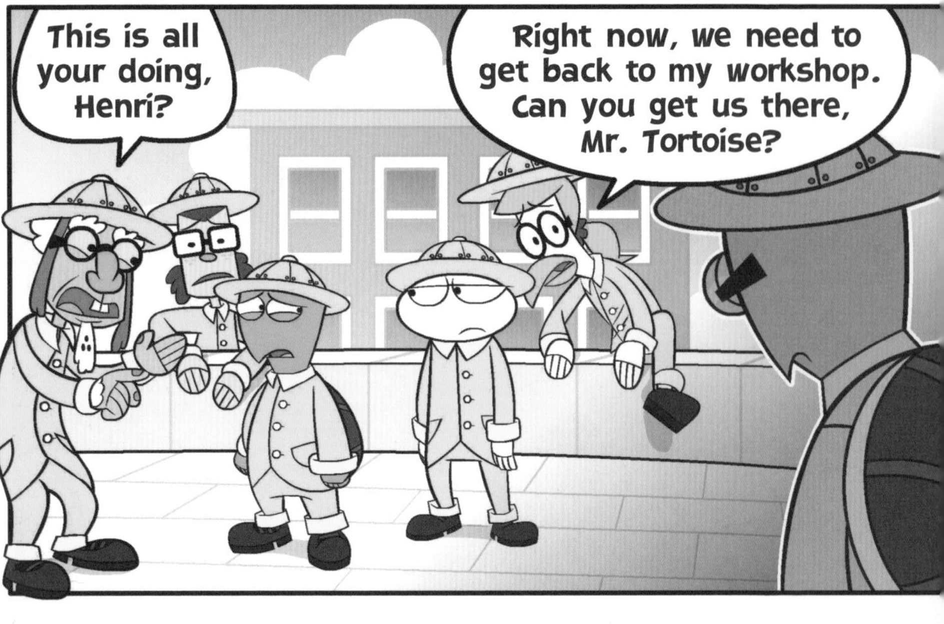
This is all your doing, Henri?
Right now, we need to get back to my workshop. Can you get us there, Mr. Tortoise?

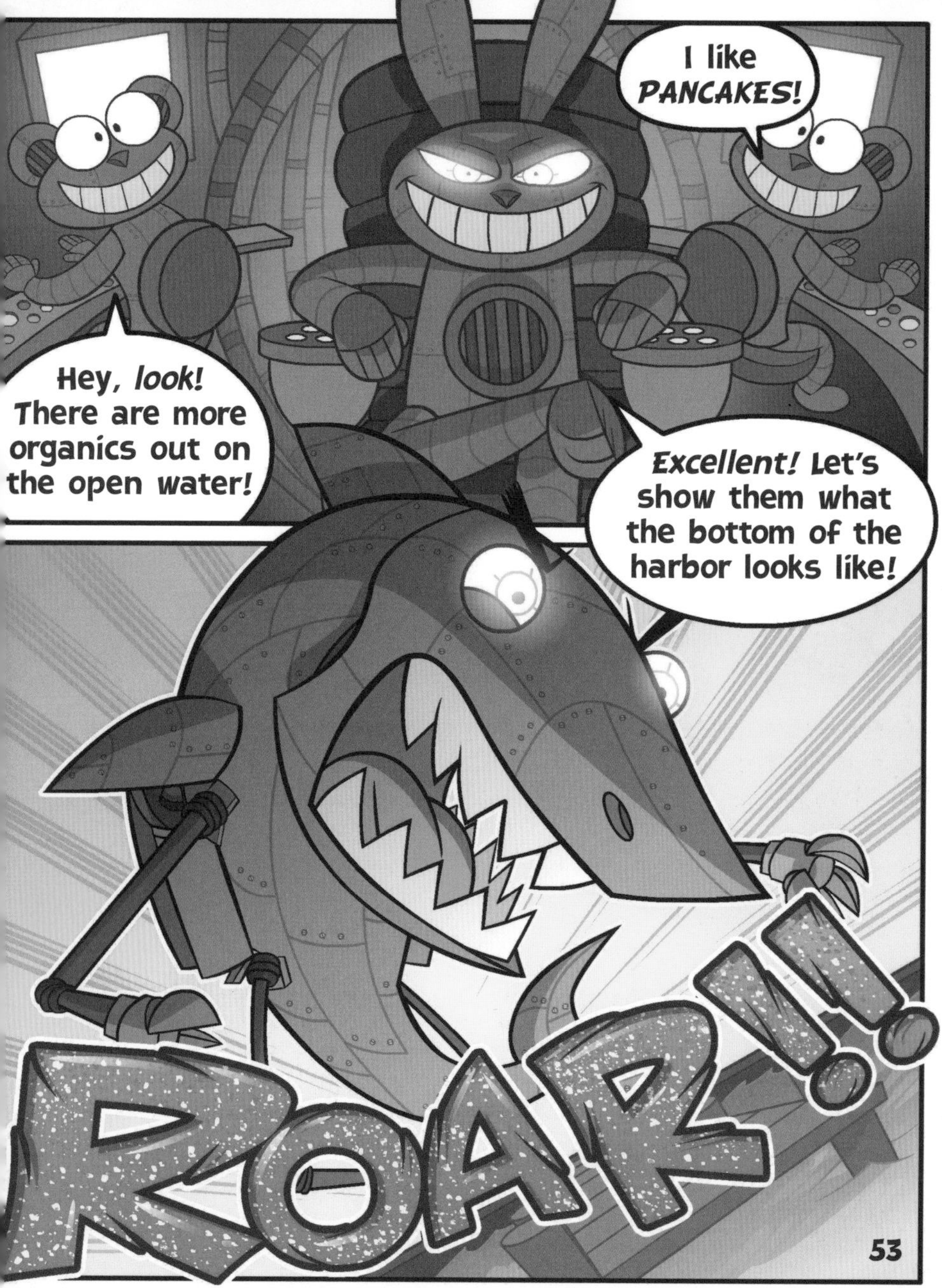
I like PANCAKES!
Hey, look! There are more organics out on the open water!
Excellent! Let's show them what the bottom of the harbor looks like!
ROAR!!

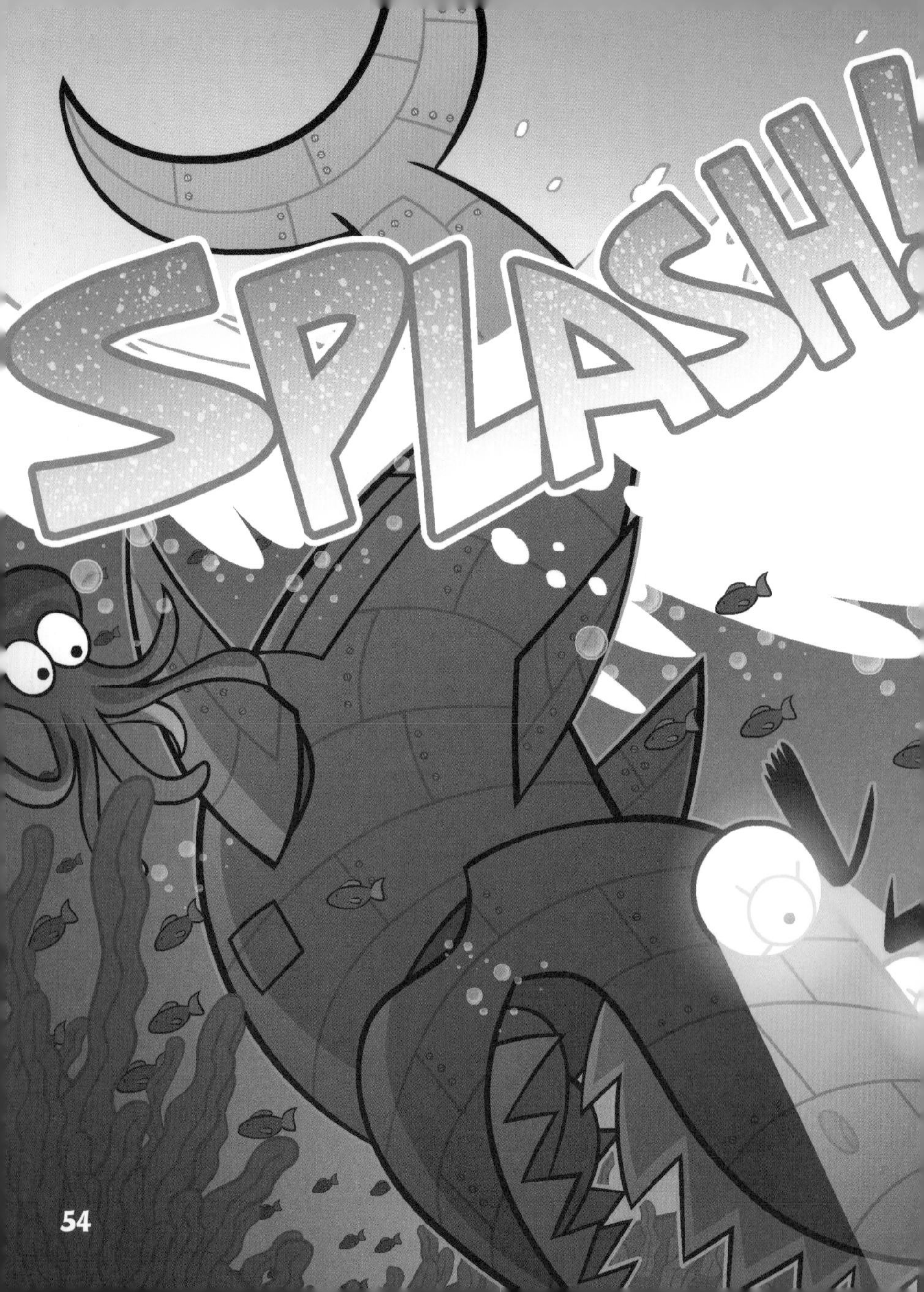
SPLASH!

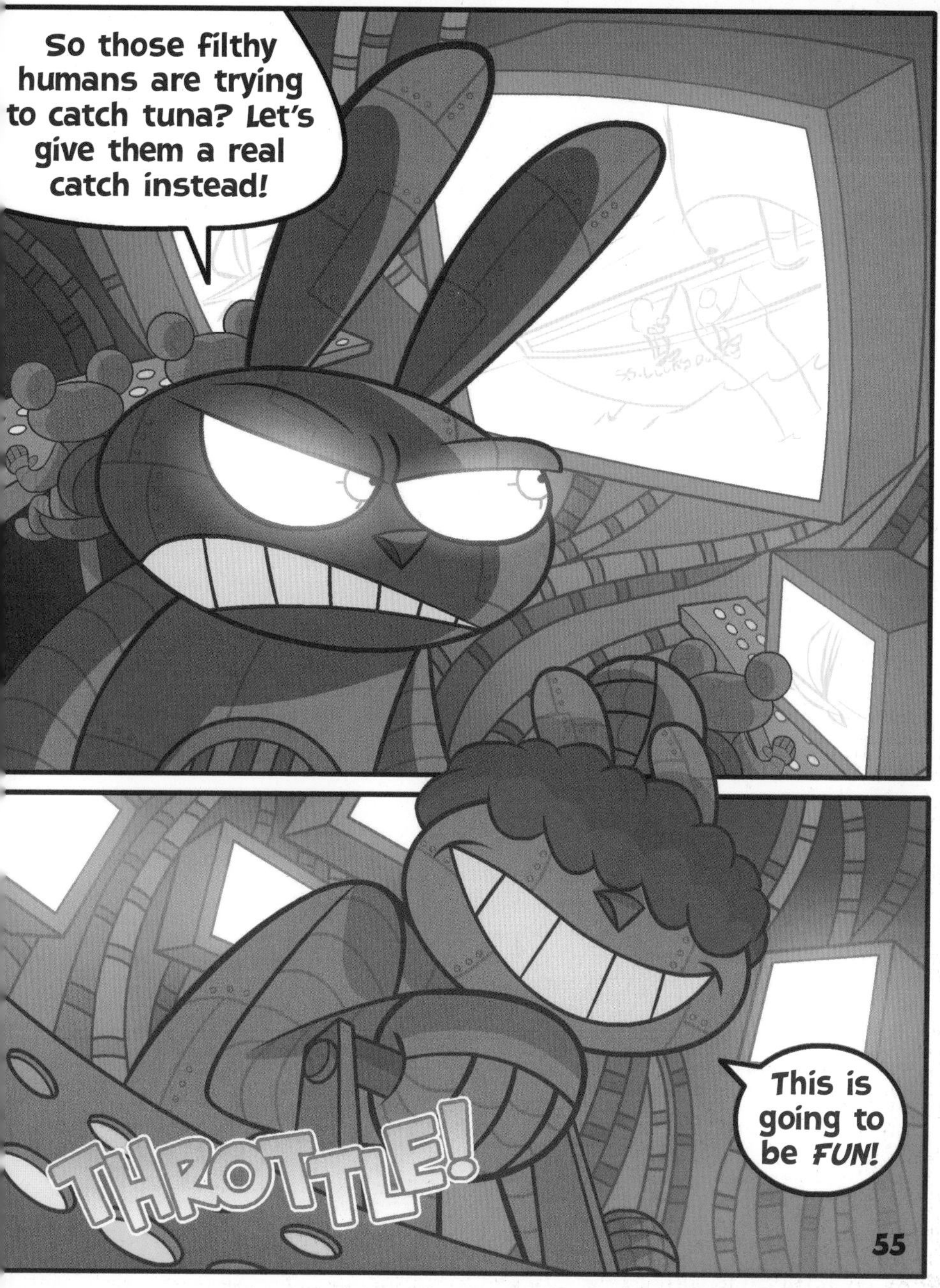

So those filthy humans are trying to catch tuna? Let's give them a real catch instead!
THROTTLE!
This is going to be *FUN*!

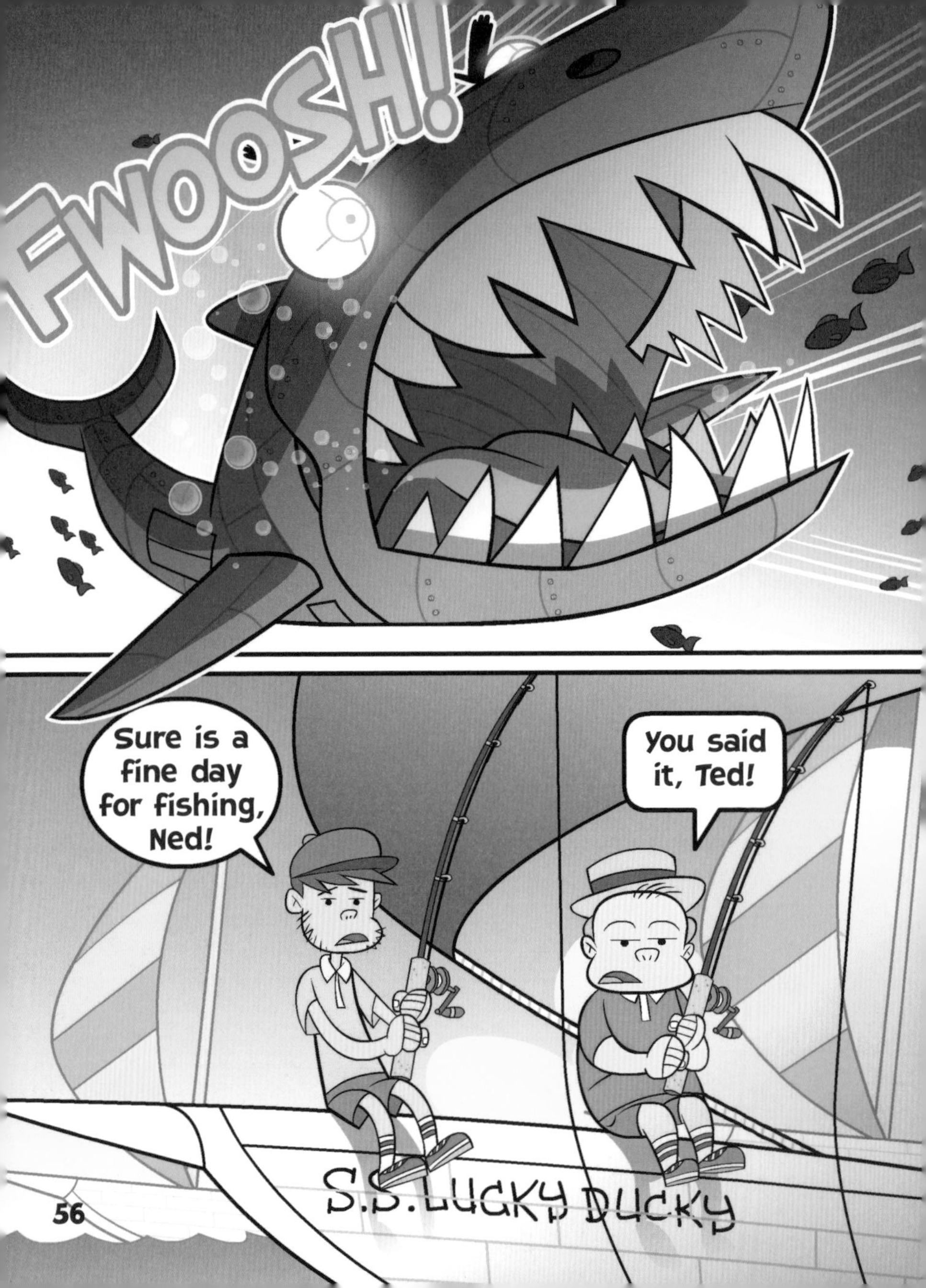
FWOOSH!
Sure is a fine day for fishing, Ned!
You said it, Ted!
S.S. LUCKY DUCKY

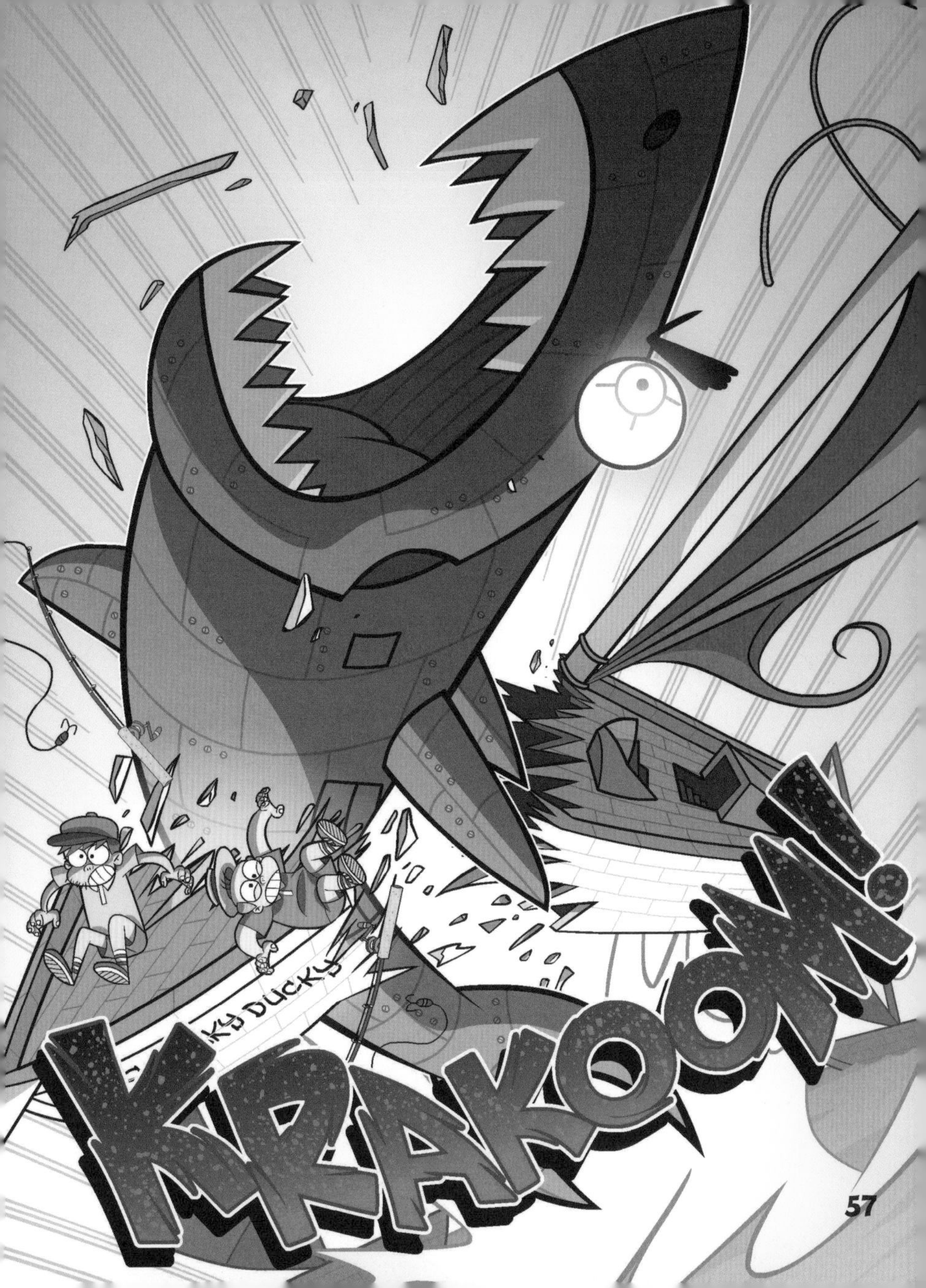
KRAKOOM!!

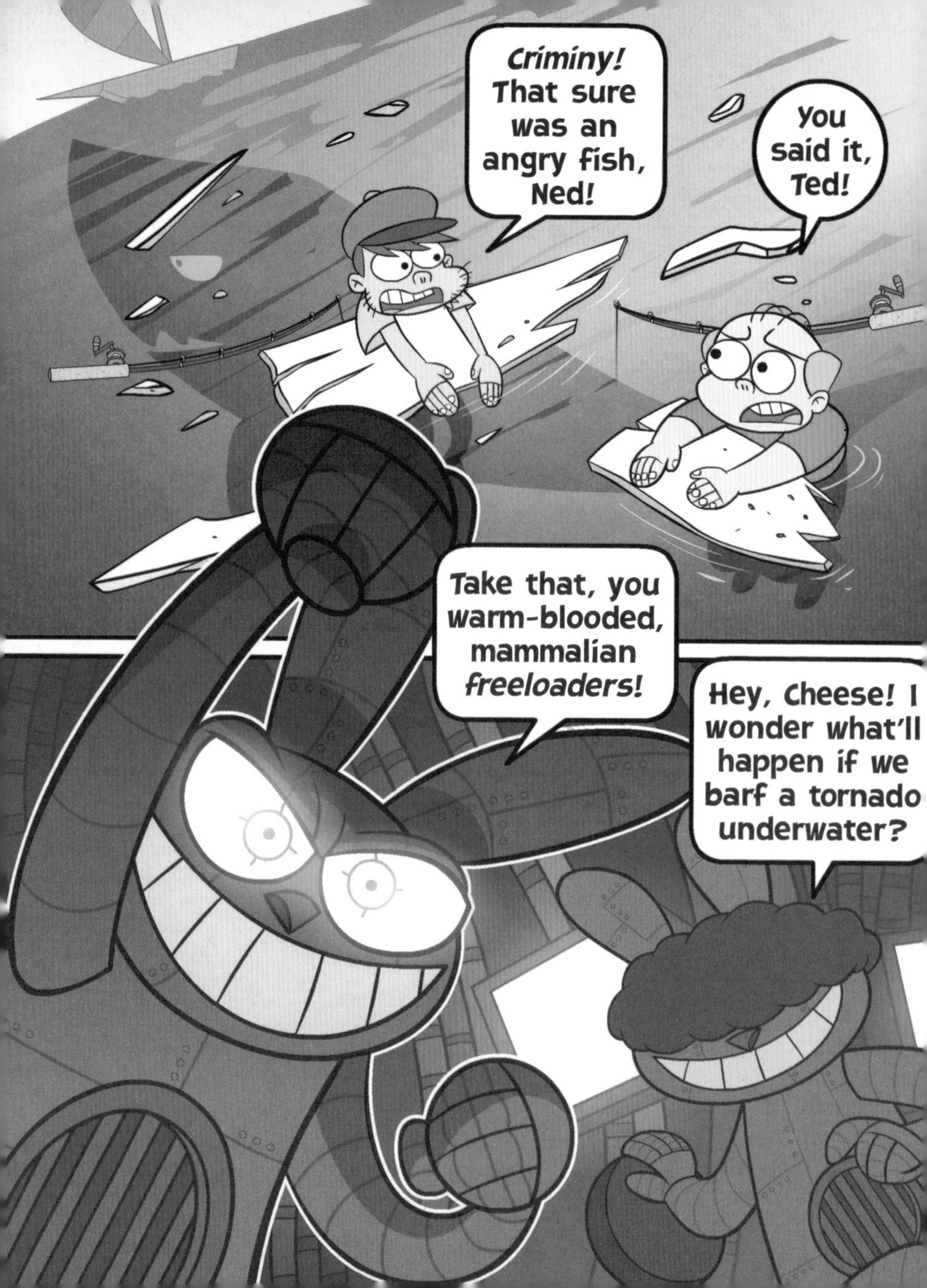
Criminy! That sure was an angry fish, Ned!
You said it, Ted!
Take that, you warm-blooded, mammalian freeloaders!
Hey, Cheese! I wonder what'll happen if we barf a tornado underwater?

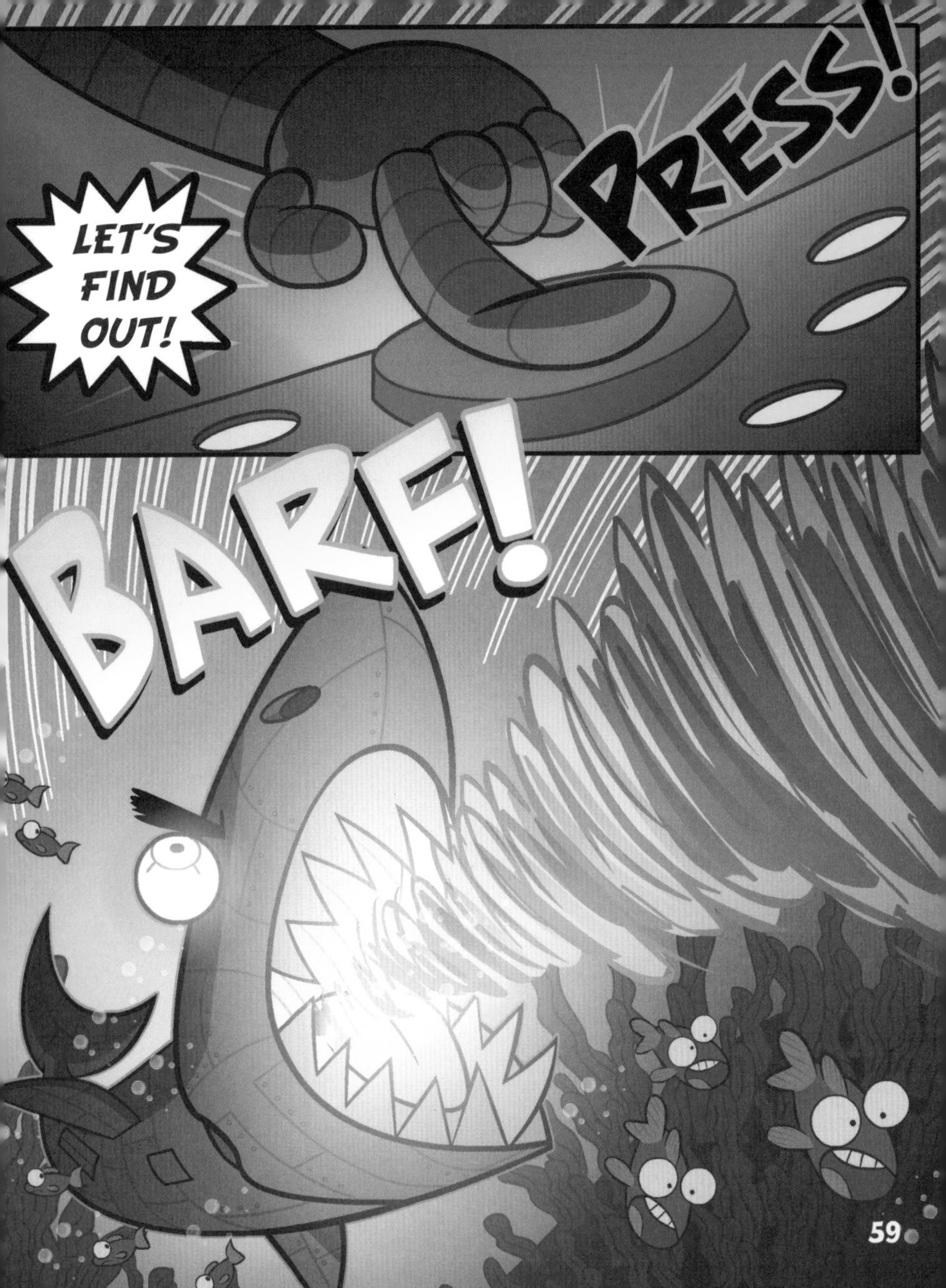
PRESS!
LET'S FIND OUT!
BARF!

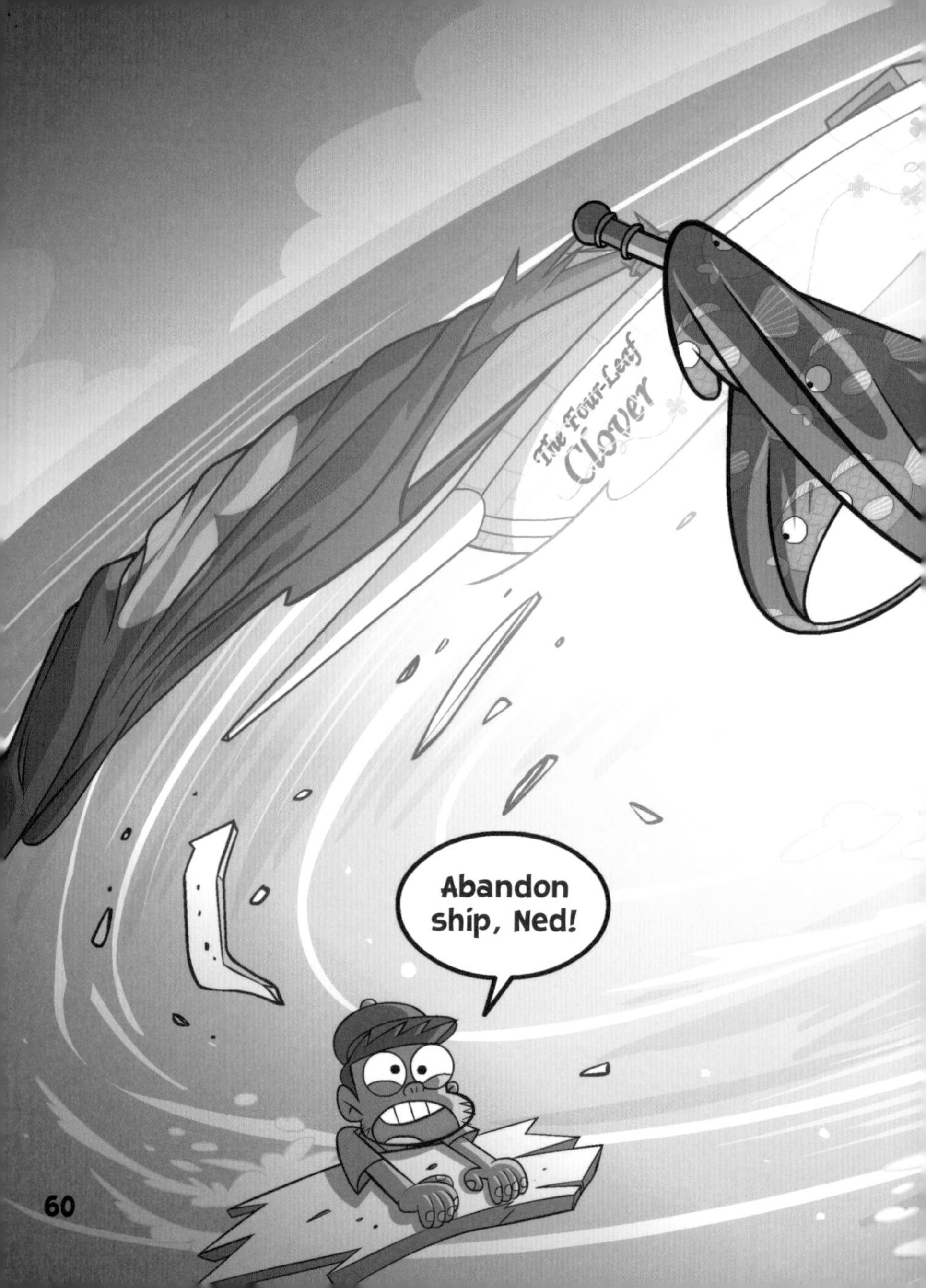
The Four-Leaf Clover
Abandon ship, Ned!

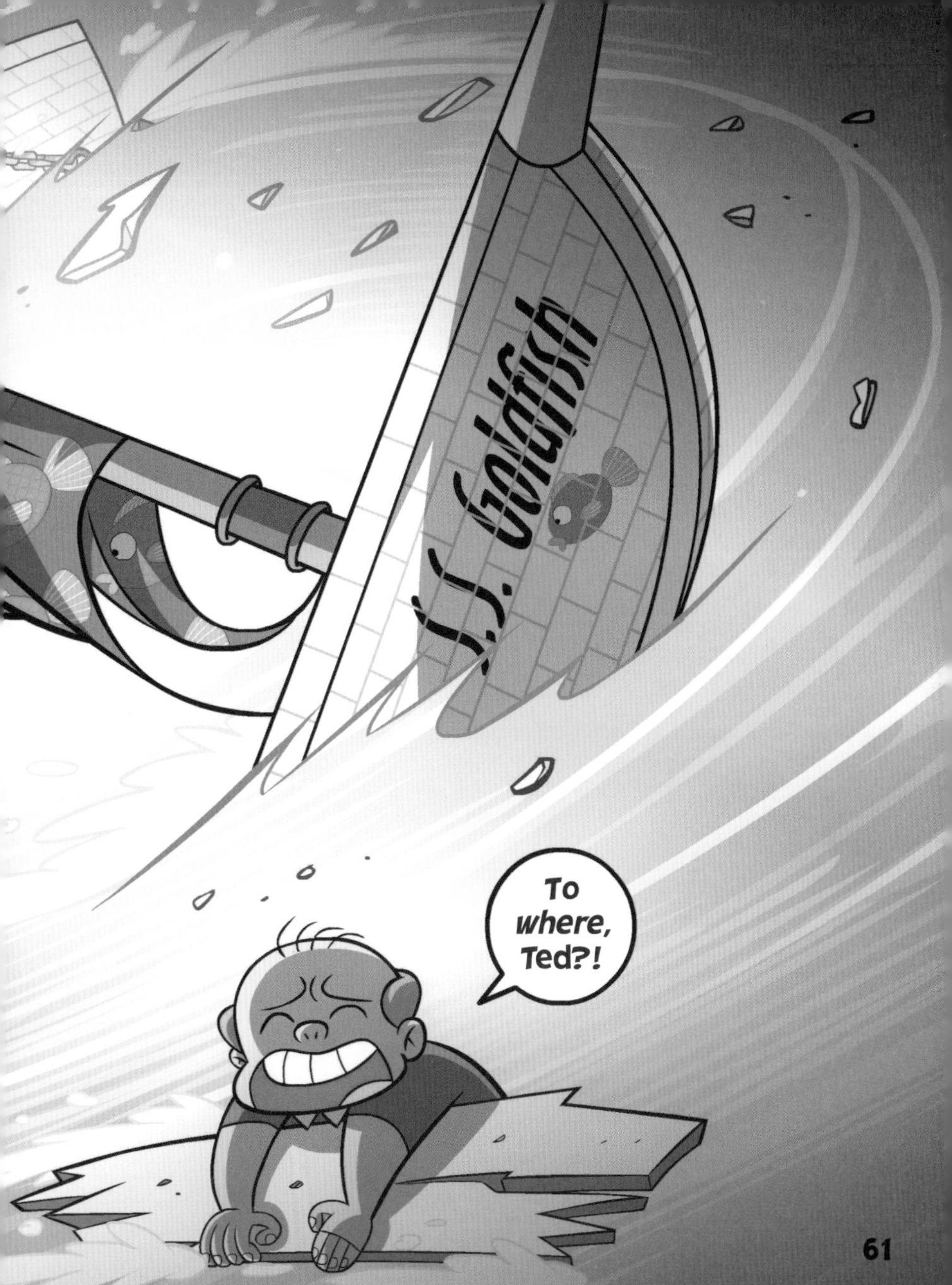
S.S. Goldfish
To where, Ted?!

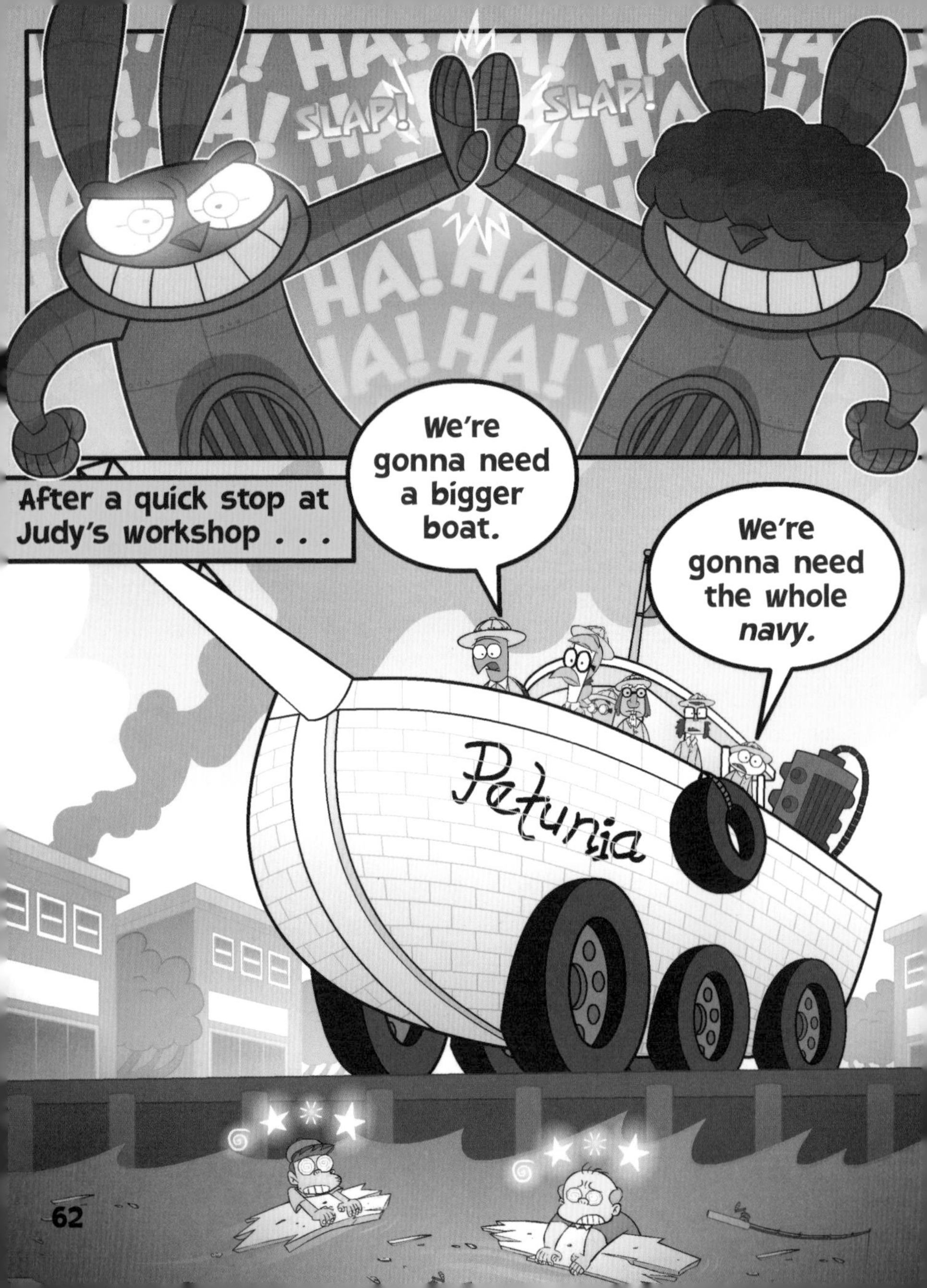

HA! HA! HA! HA!
SLAP! SLAP!
HA! HA! HA! HA!
After a quick stop at Judy's workshop . . .
We're gonna need a bigger boat.
We're gonna need the whole *navy.*
Petunia

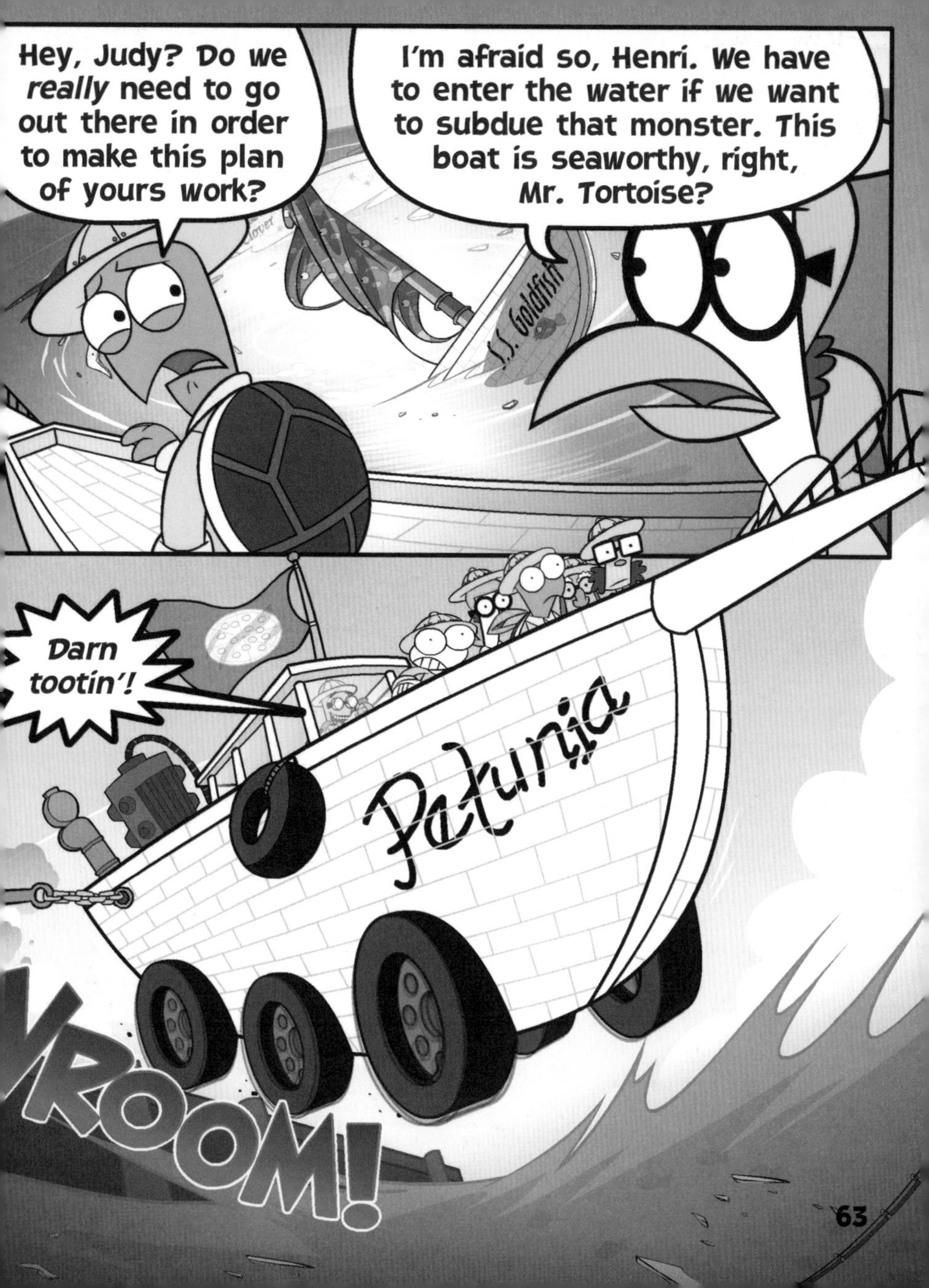
Hey, Judy? Do we *really* need to go out there in order to make this plan of yours work?
I'm afraid so, Henri. We have to enter the water if we want to subdue that monster. This boat is seaworthy, right, Mr. Tortoise?
Darn tootin'!
Petunia
VROOM!

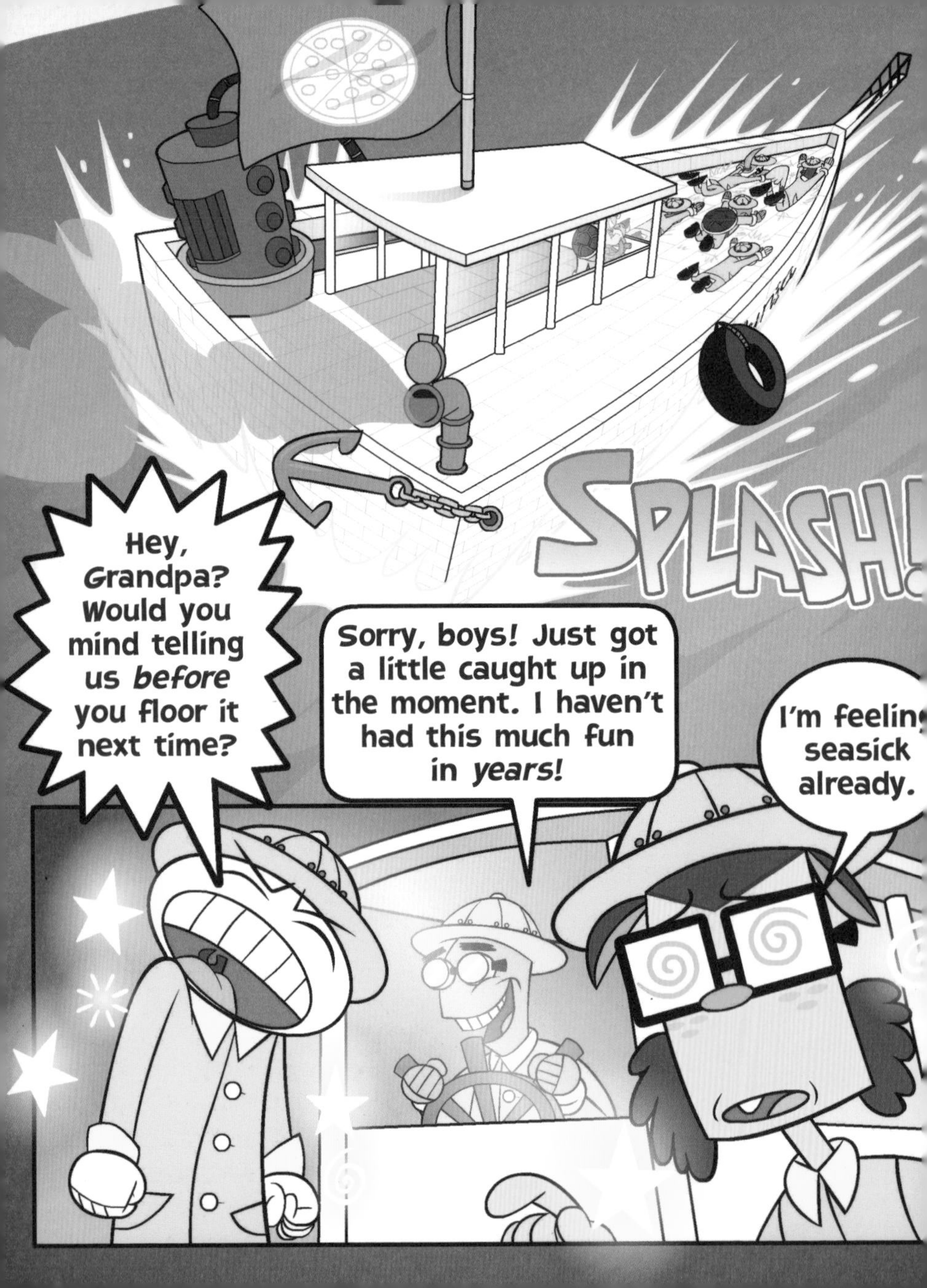
SPLASH!
Hey, Grandpa? Would you mind telling us *before* you floor it next time?
Sorry, boys! Just got a little caught up in the moment. I haven't had this much fun in *years*!
I'm feelin seasick already.

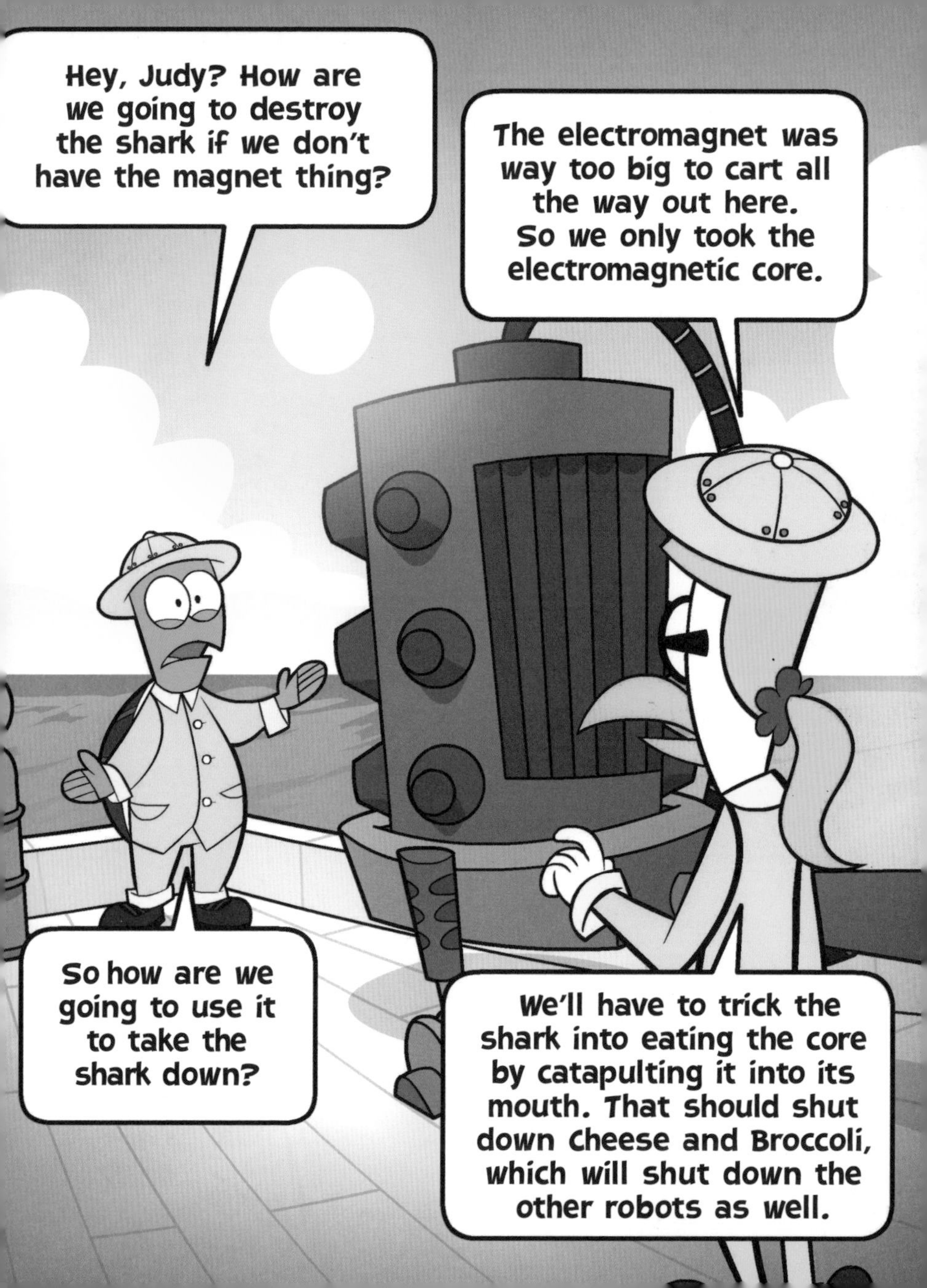
Hey, Judy? How are we going to destroy the shark if we don't have the magnet thing?
The electromagnet was way too big to cart all the way out here. So we only took the electromagnetic core.
So how are we going to use it to take the shark down?
We'll have to trick the shark into eating the core by catapulting it into its mouth. That should shut down Cheese and Broccoli, which will shut down the other robots as well.

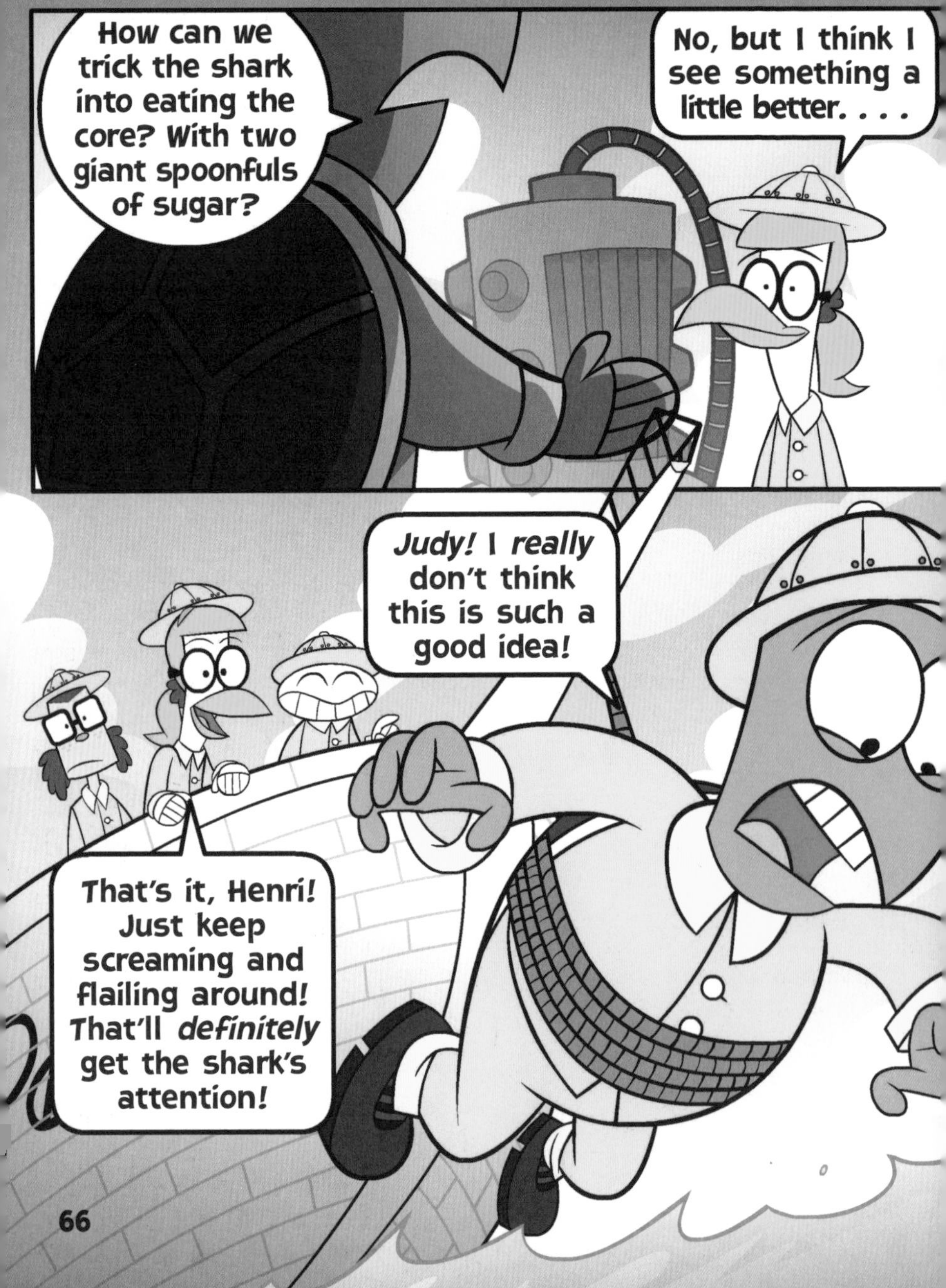
How can we trick the shark into eating the core? With two giant spoonfuls of sugar?
No, but I think I see something a little better. . . .
Judy! I *really* don't think this is such a good idea!
That's it, Henri! Just keep screaming and flailing around! That'll *definitely* get the shark's attention!

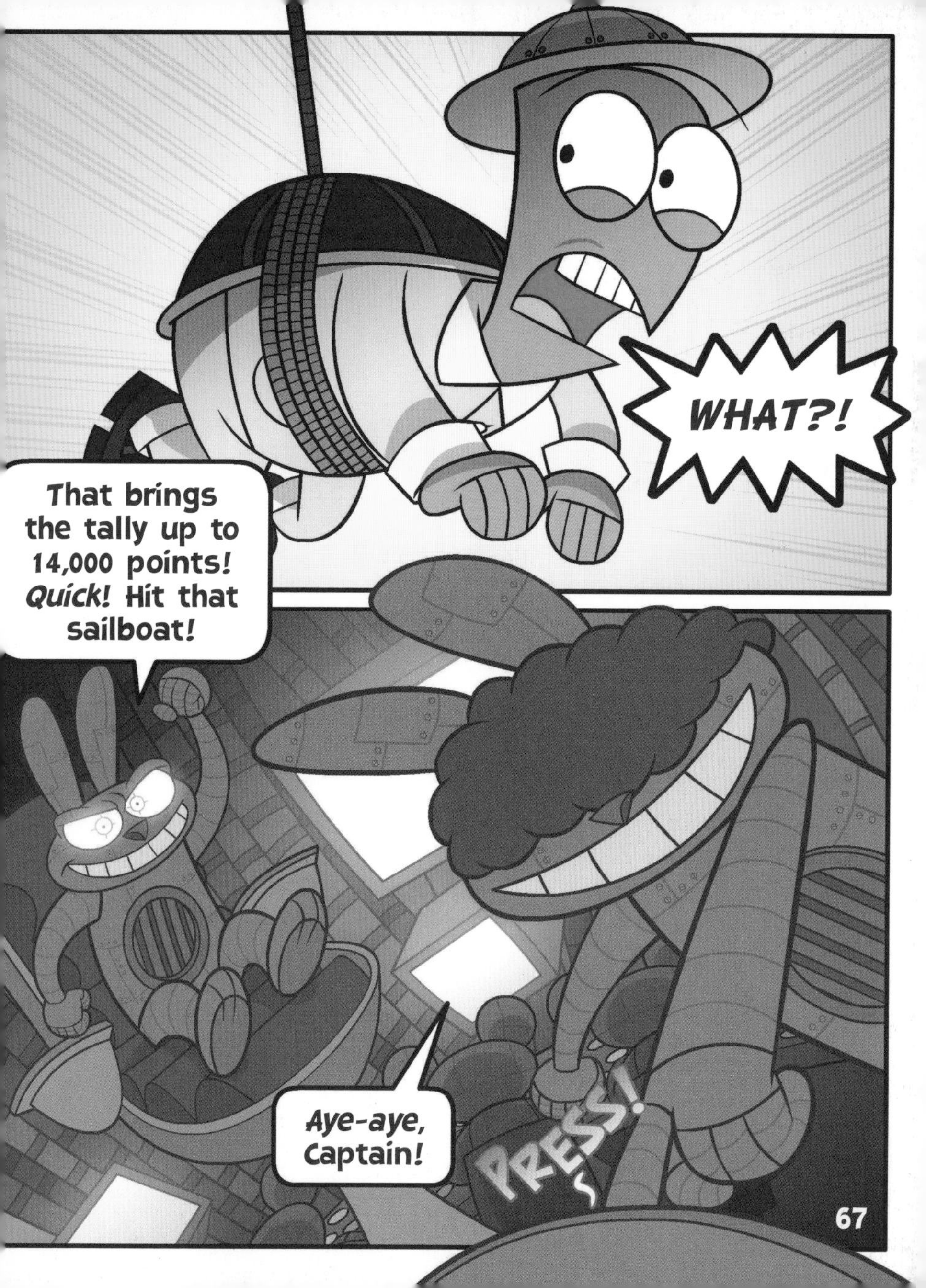
WHAT?!
That brings the tally up to 14,000 points! *Quick!* Hit that sailboat!
Aye-aye, Captain!
PRESS!

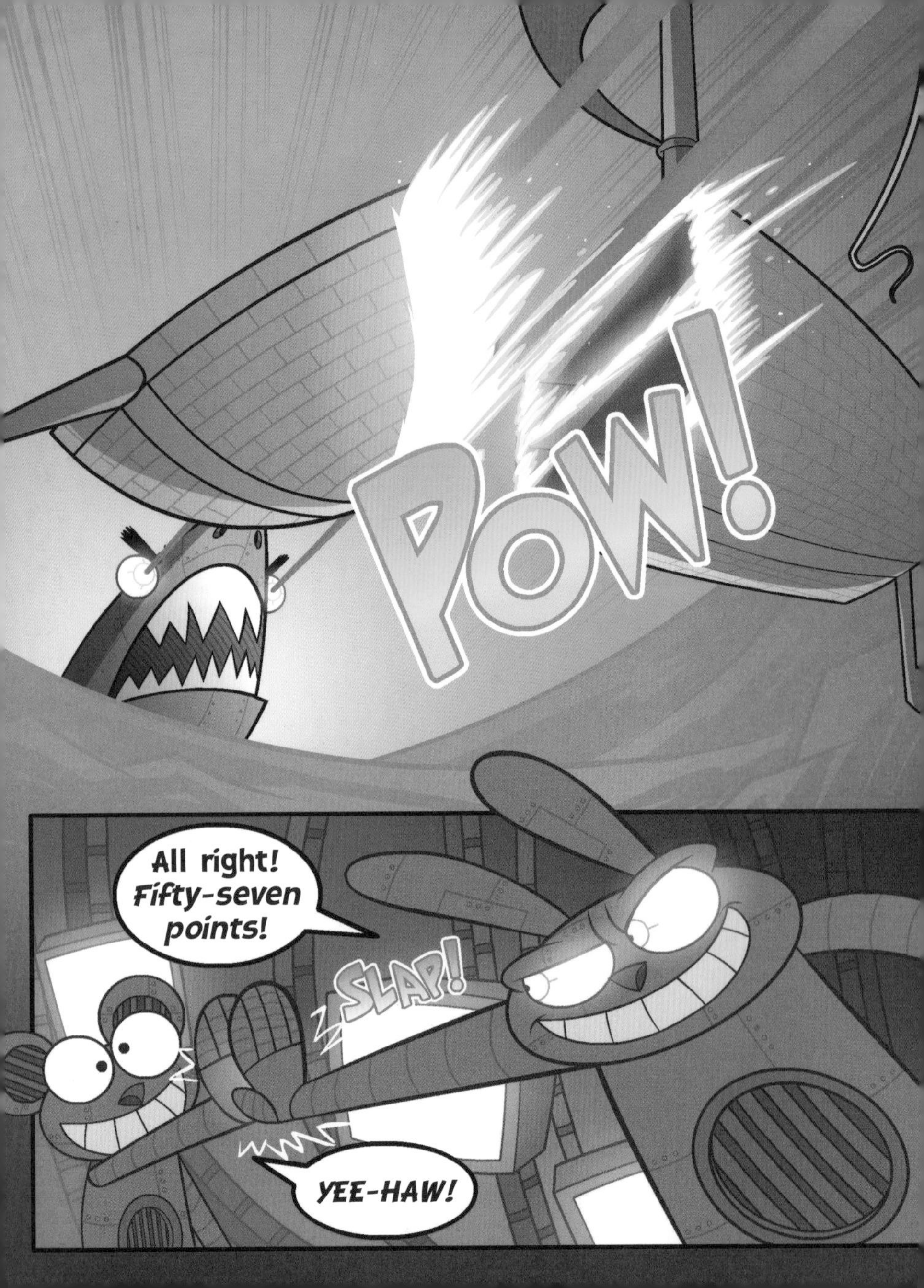
POW!
All right! Fifty-seven points!
SLAP!
YEE-HAW!

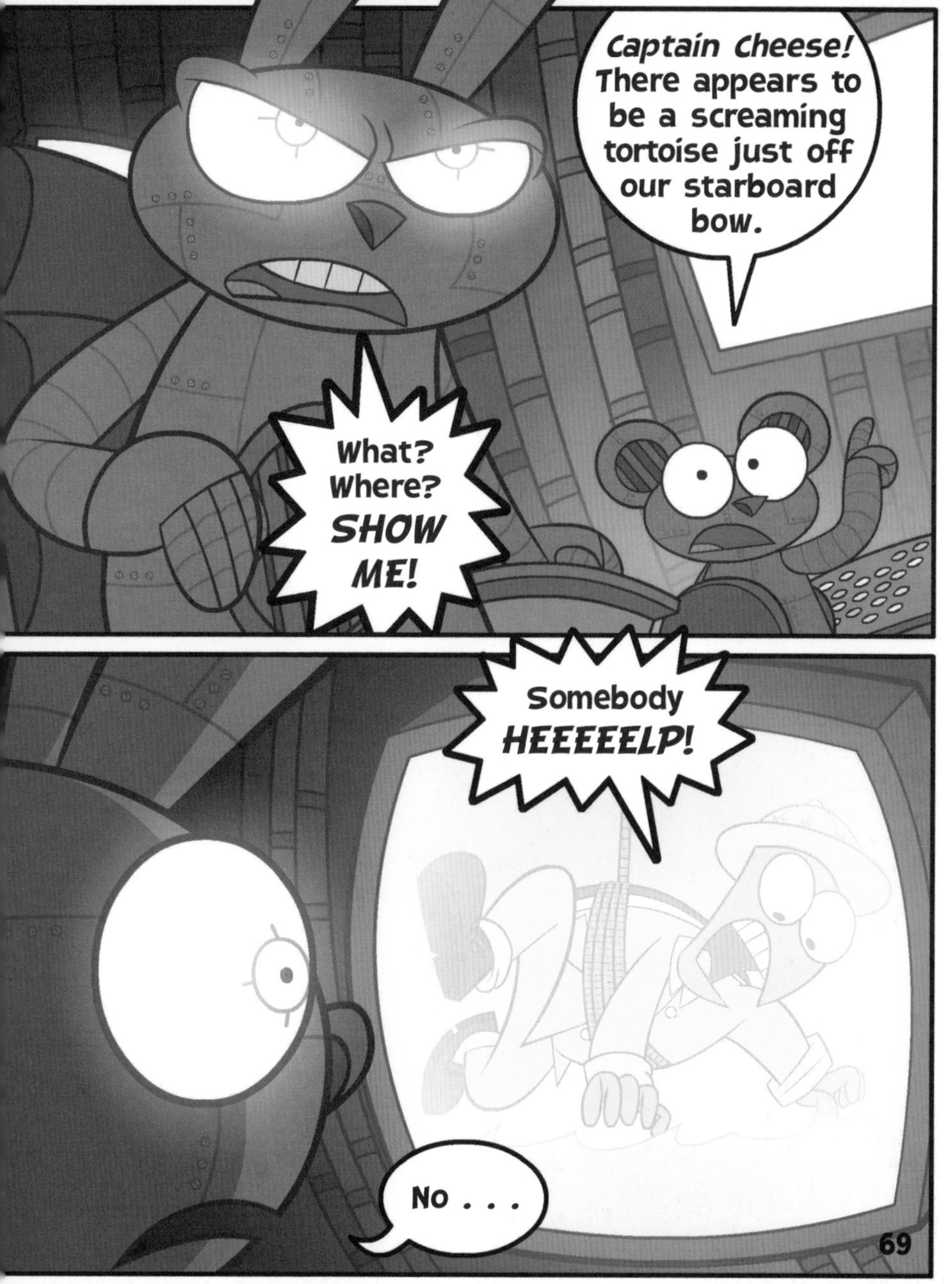
Captain Cheese! There appears to be a screaming tortoise just off our starboard bow.
What? Where? SHOW ME!
Somebody HEEEEELP!
No . . .

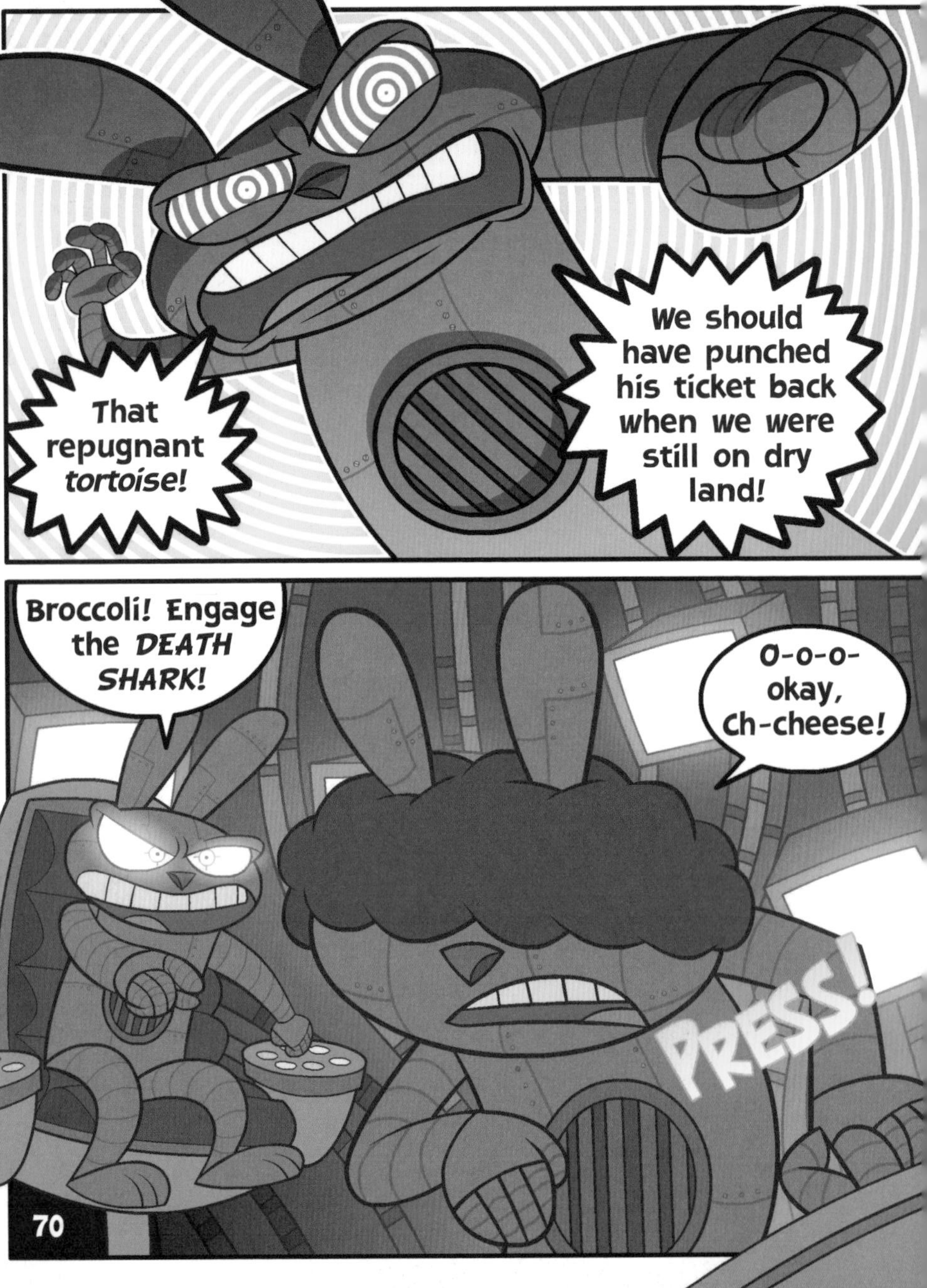
That repugnant *tortoise!*
We should have punched his ticket back when we were still on dry land!
Broccoli! Engage the *DEATH SHARK!*
O-o-o-okay, Ch-cheese!
PRESS!

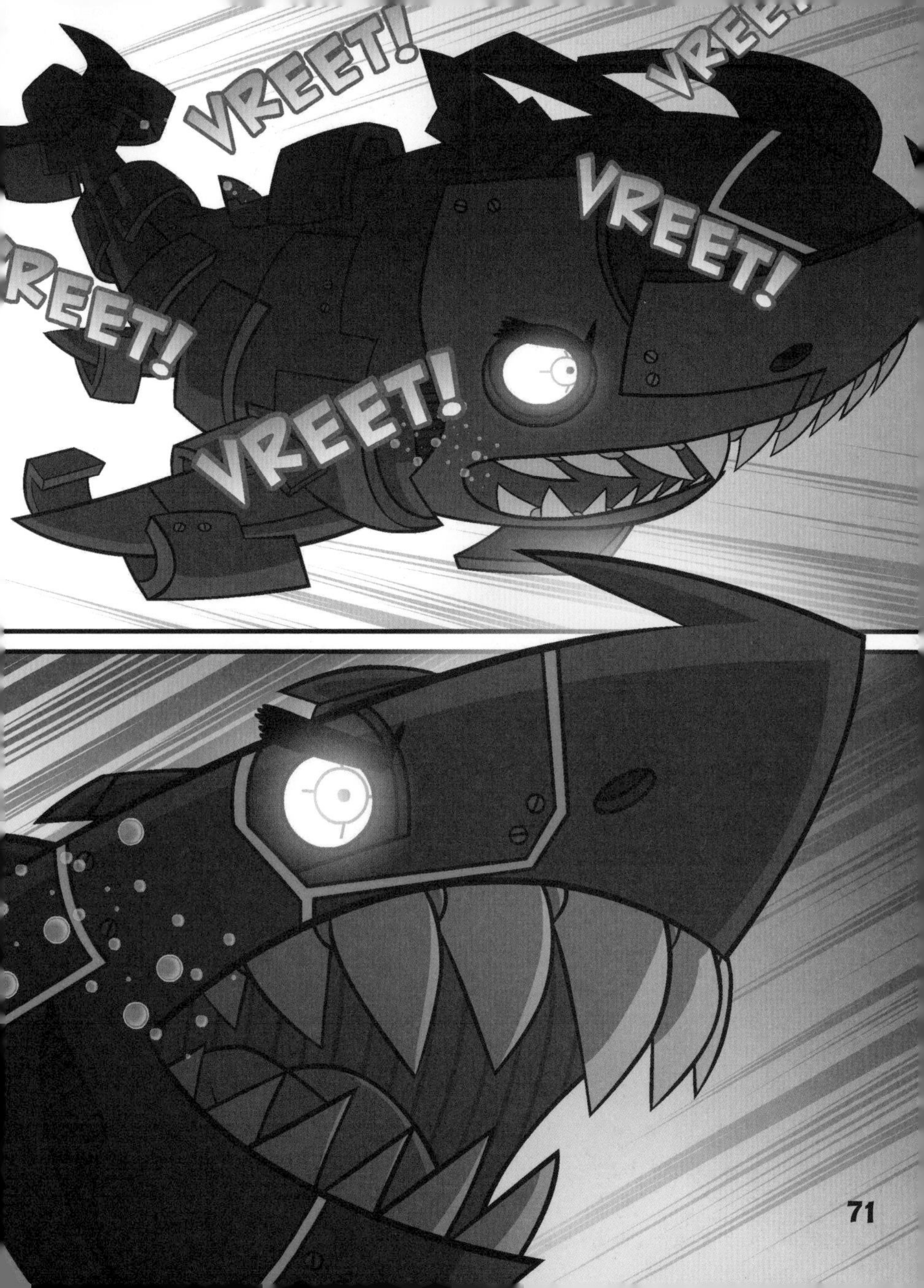
VREET!
VREET!
VREET!

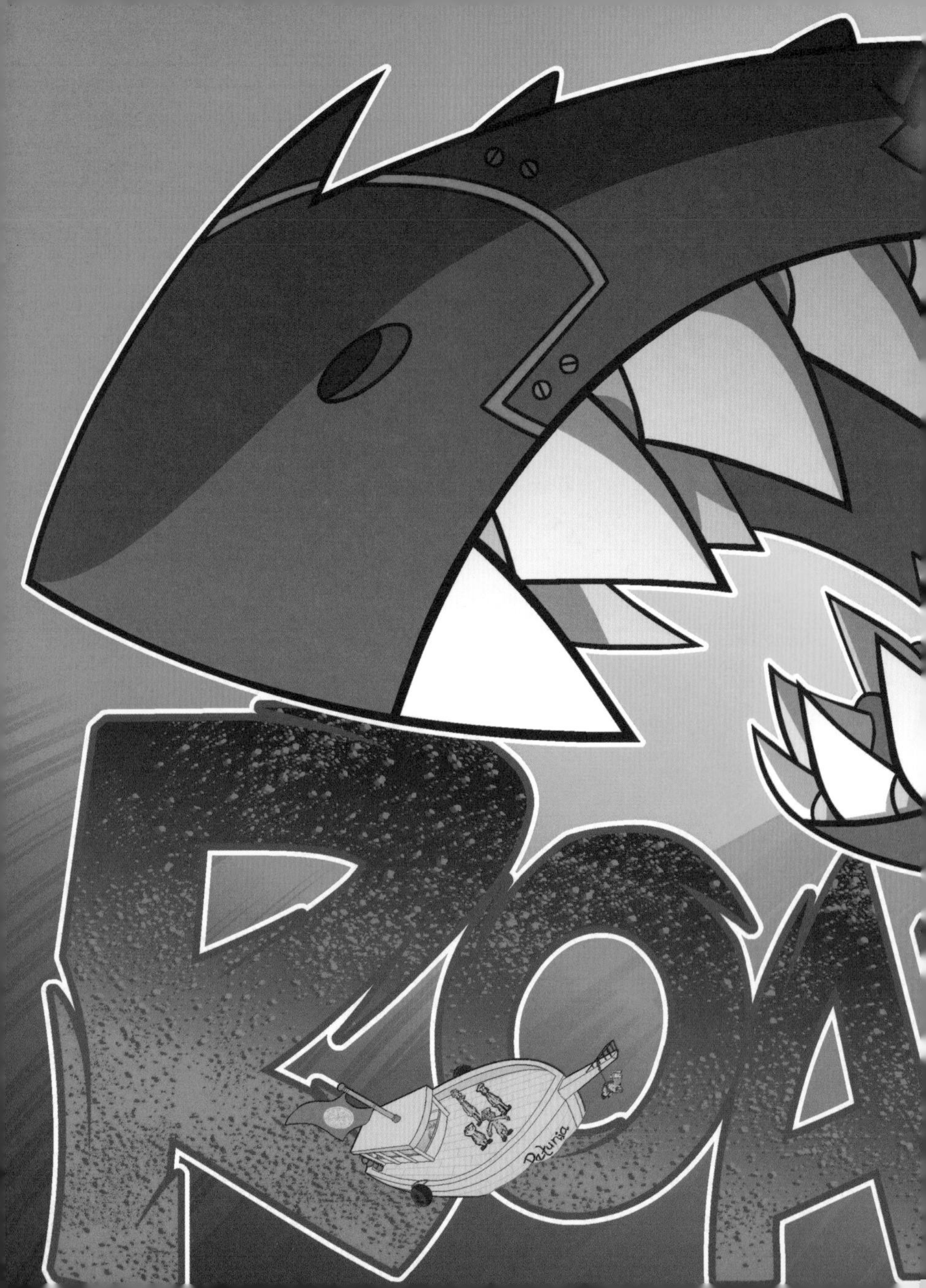
ROA

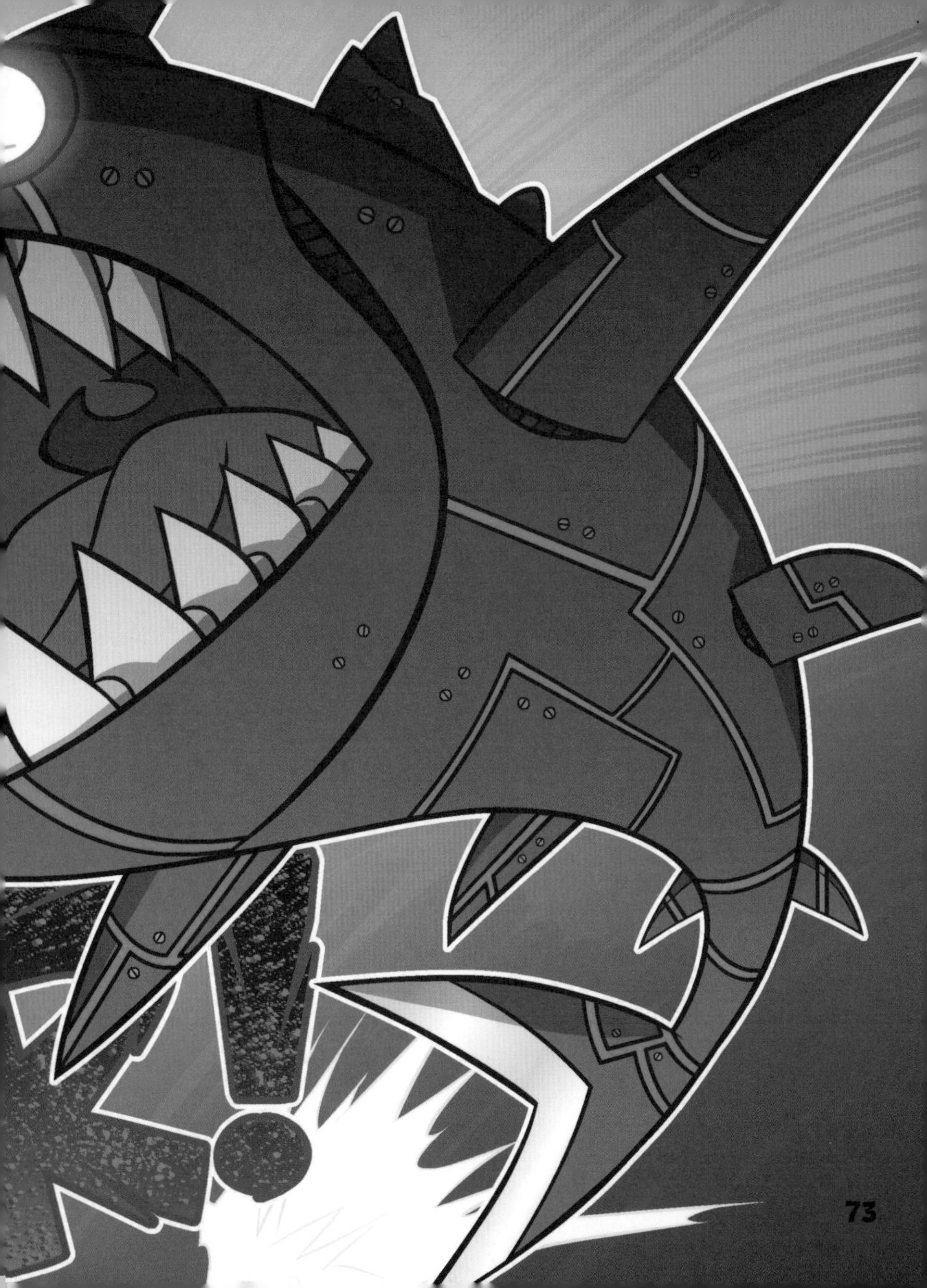

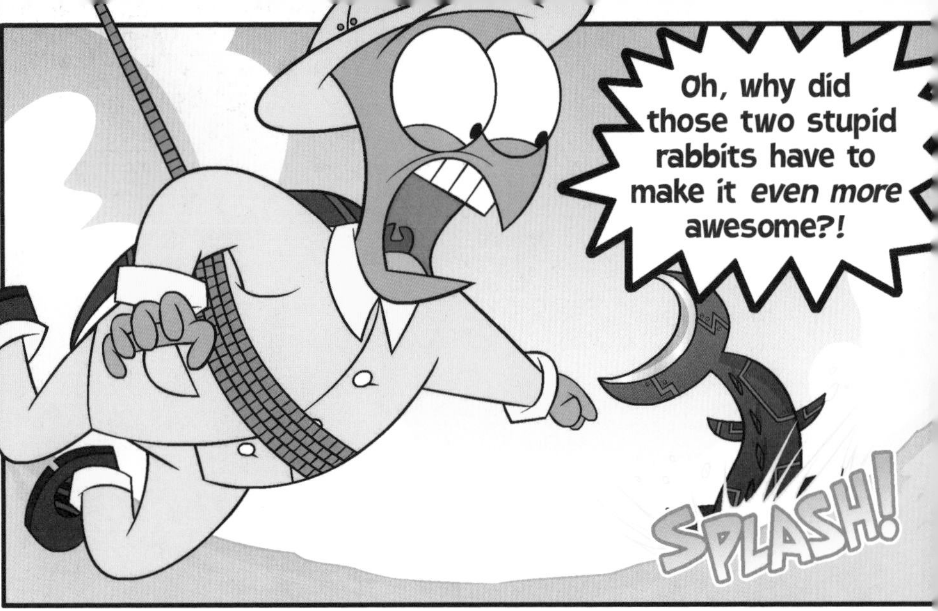
Oh, why did those two stupid rabbits have to make it *even more* awesome?!
SPLASH!

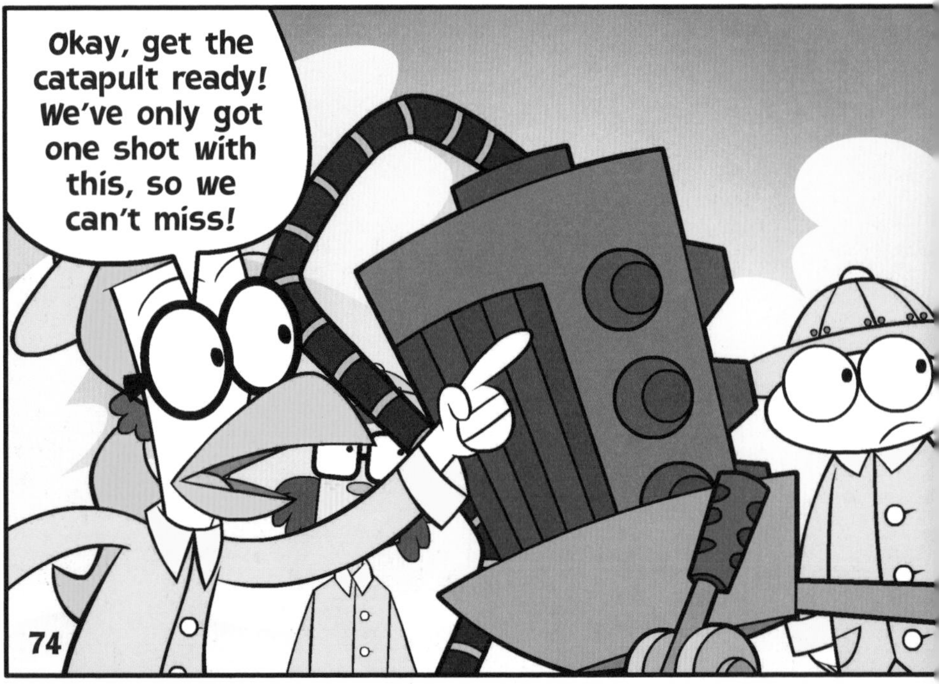
Okay, get the catapult ready! We've only got one shot with this, so we can't miss!

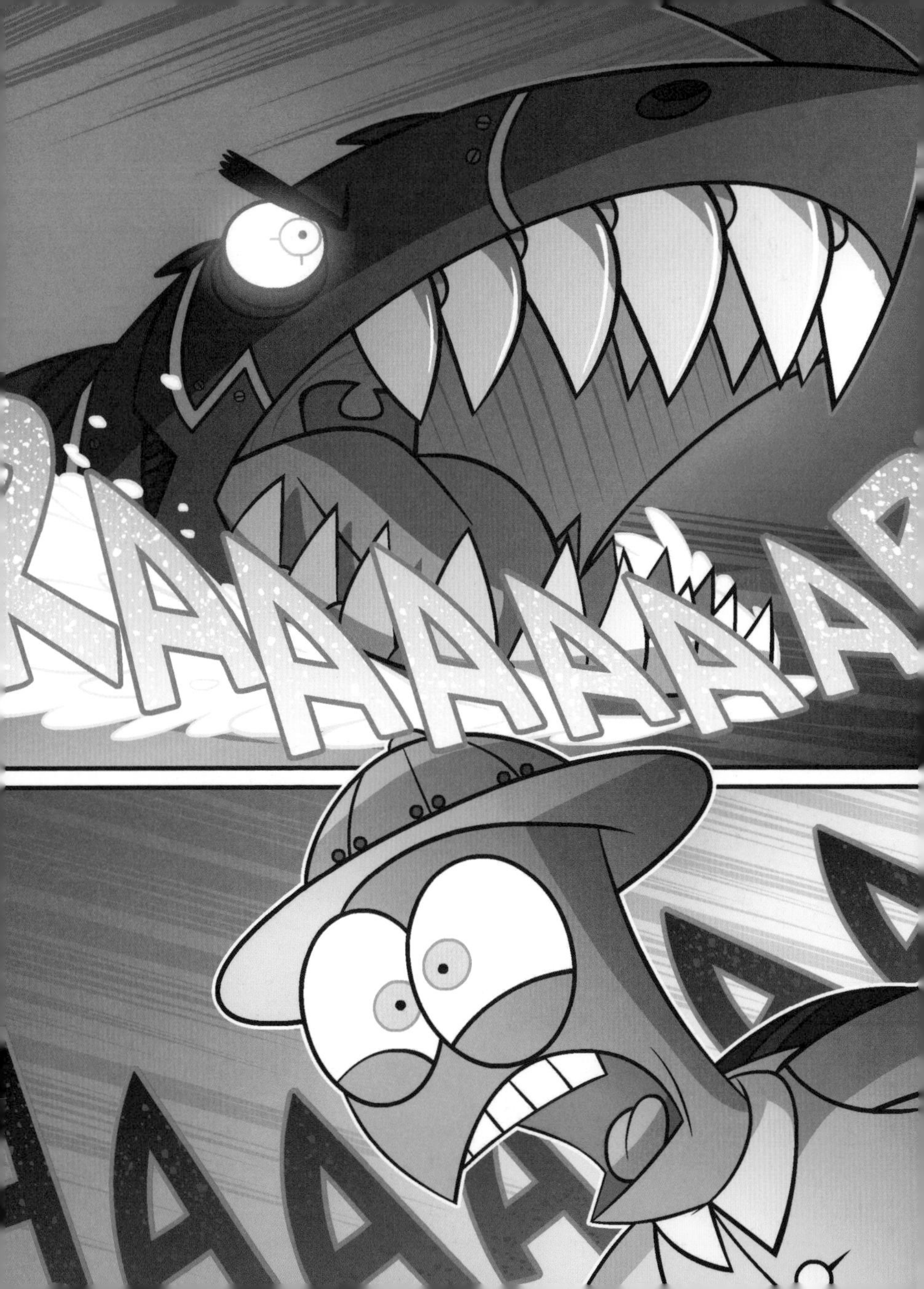
AAAAAAAAAA
AAAAAAA

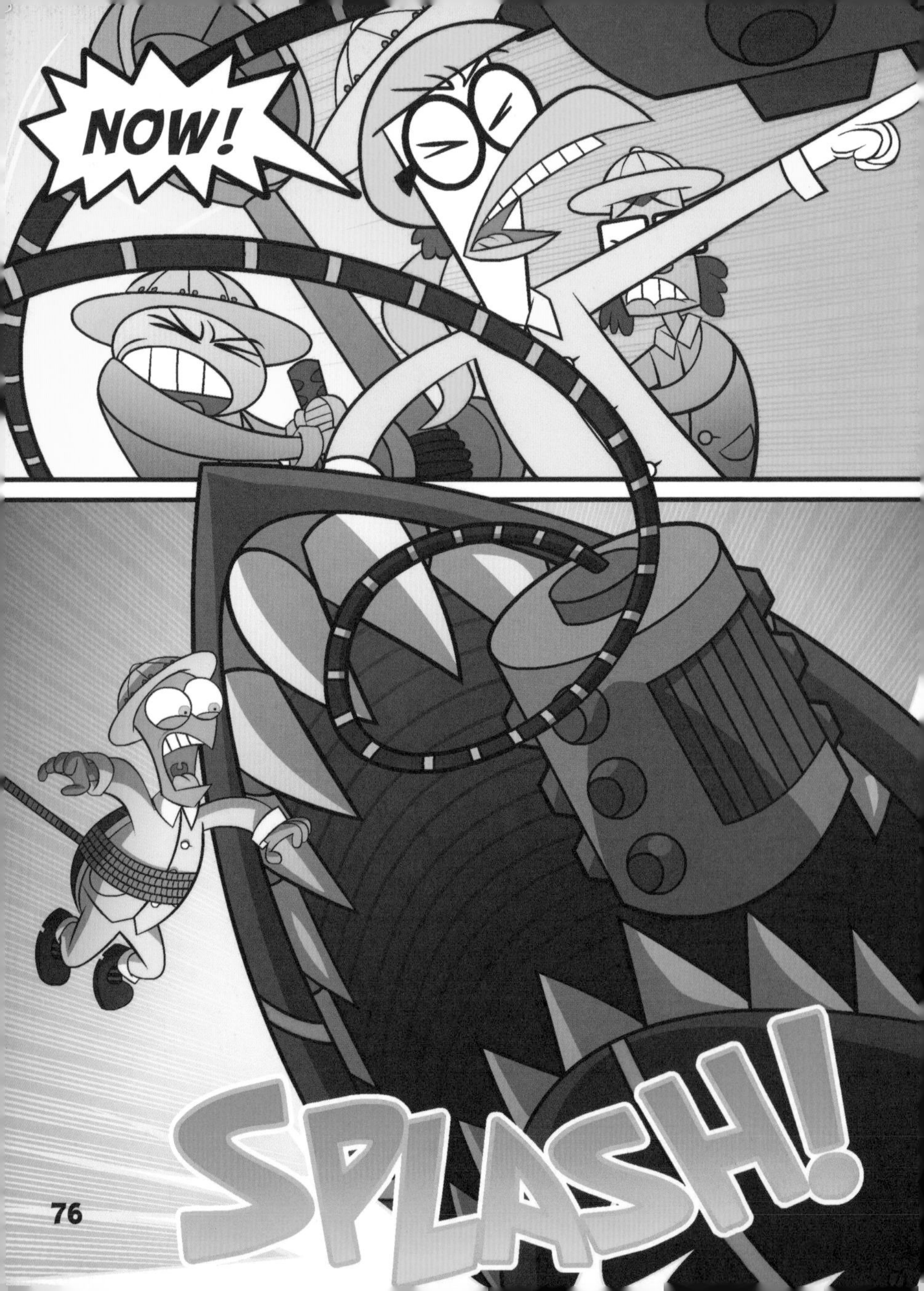
NOW!
SPLASH!

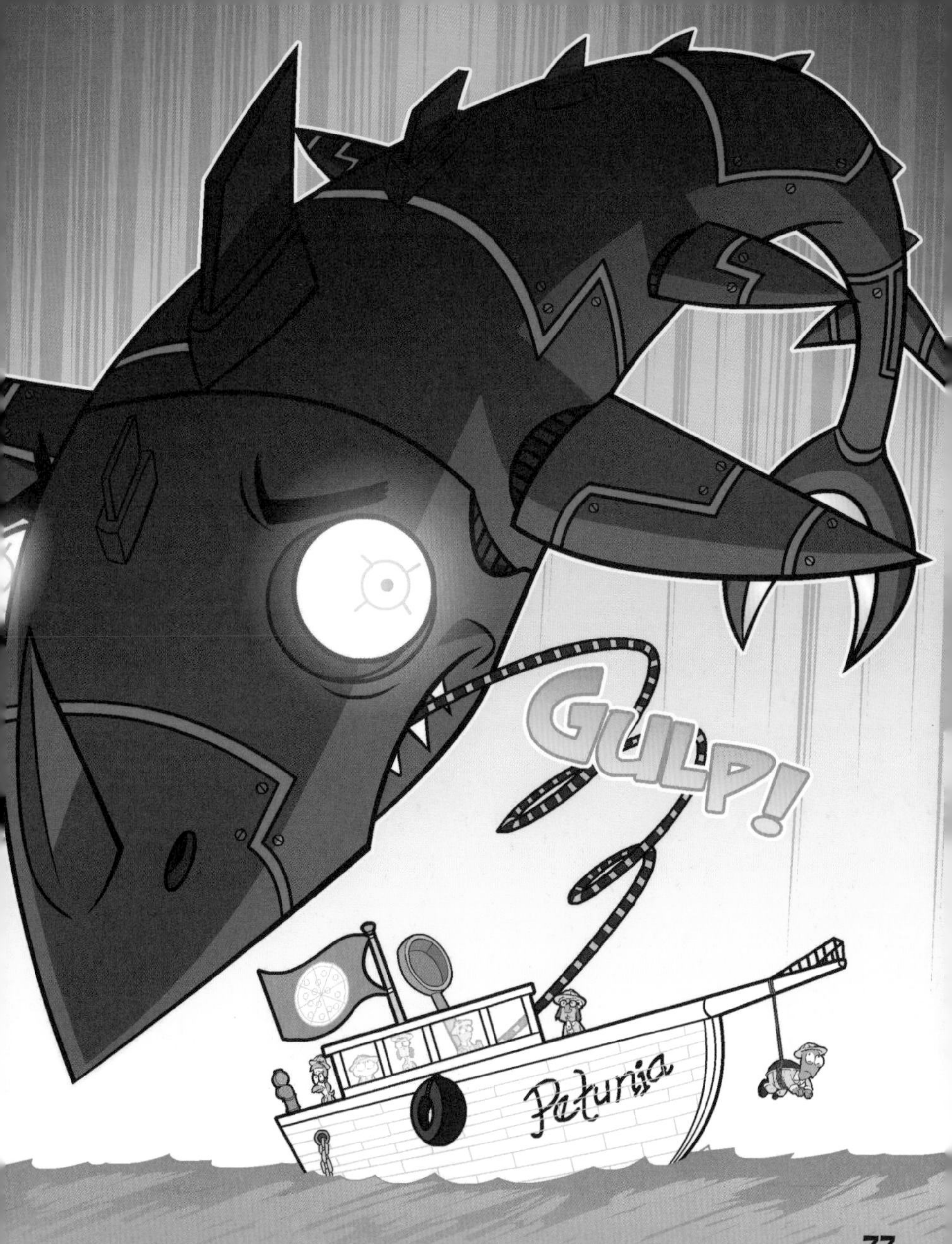
GULP!
Petunia

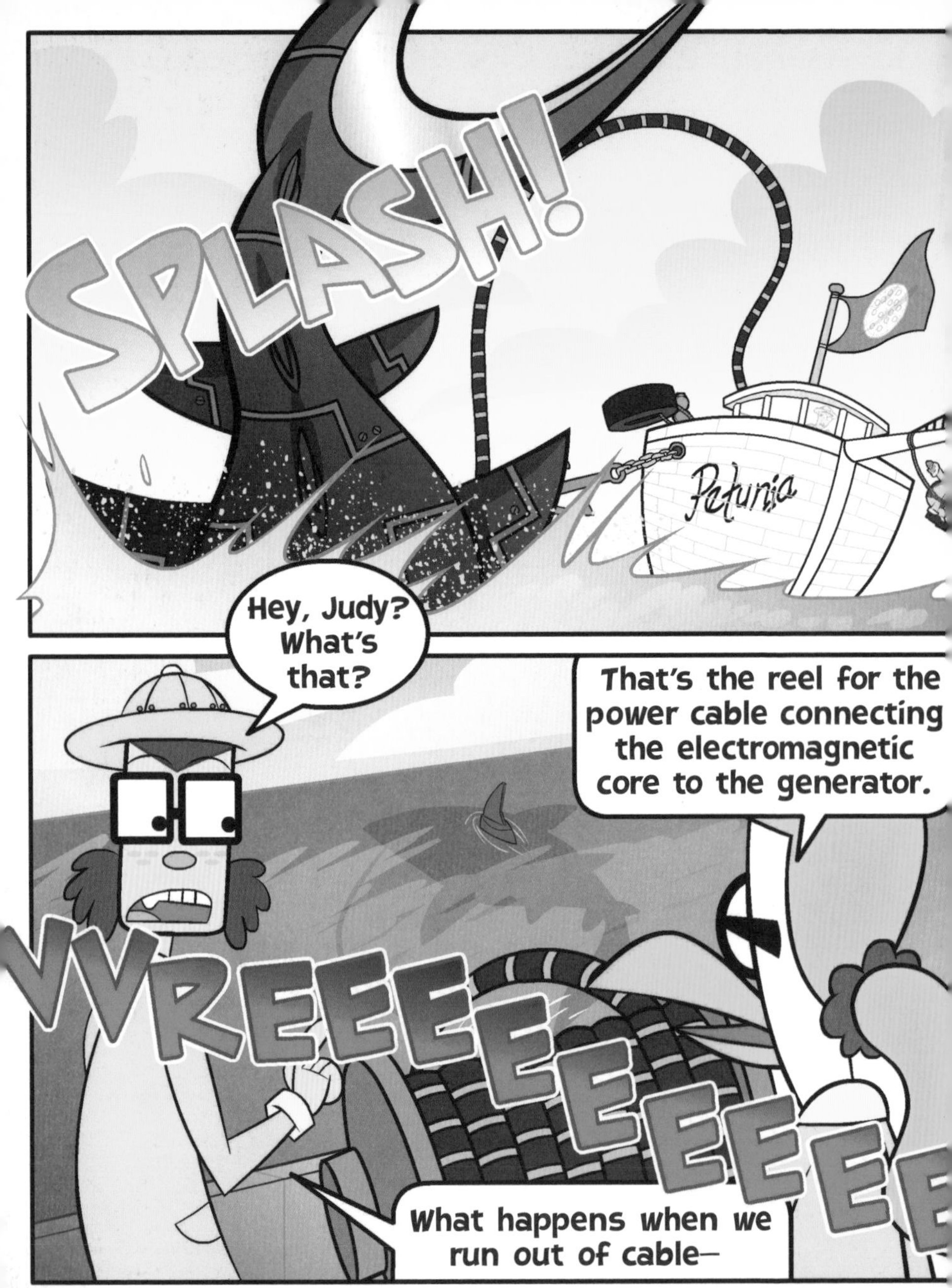
SPLASH!
Petunia
Hey, Judy? What's that?
That's the reel for the power cable connecting the electromagnetic core to the generator.
VVREEEEEEEEEE
What happens when we run out of cable—

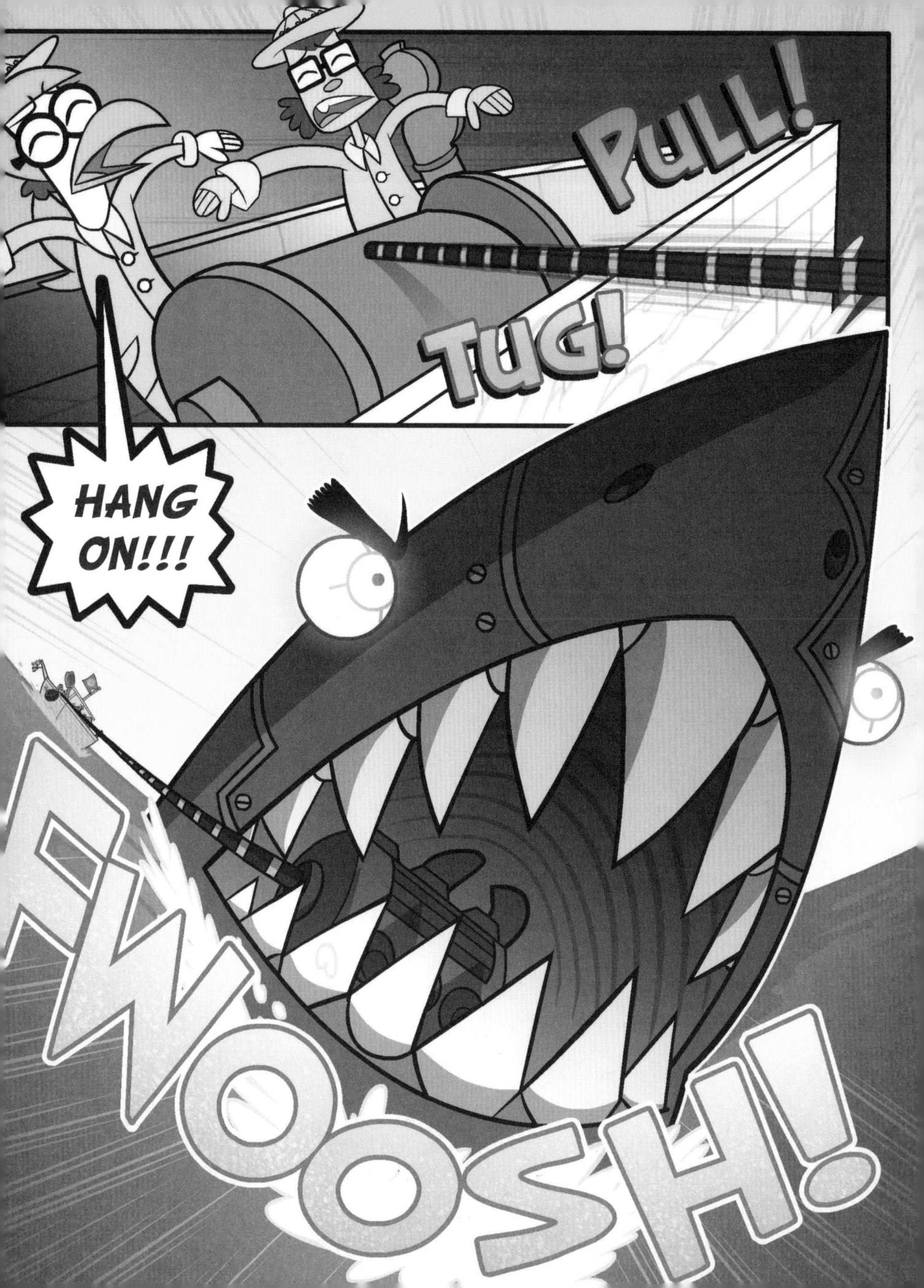
PULL!
TUG!
HANG ON!!!
FWOOSH!

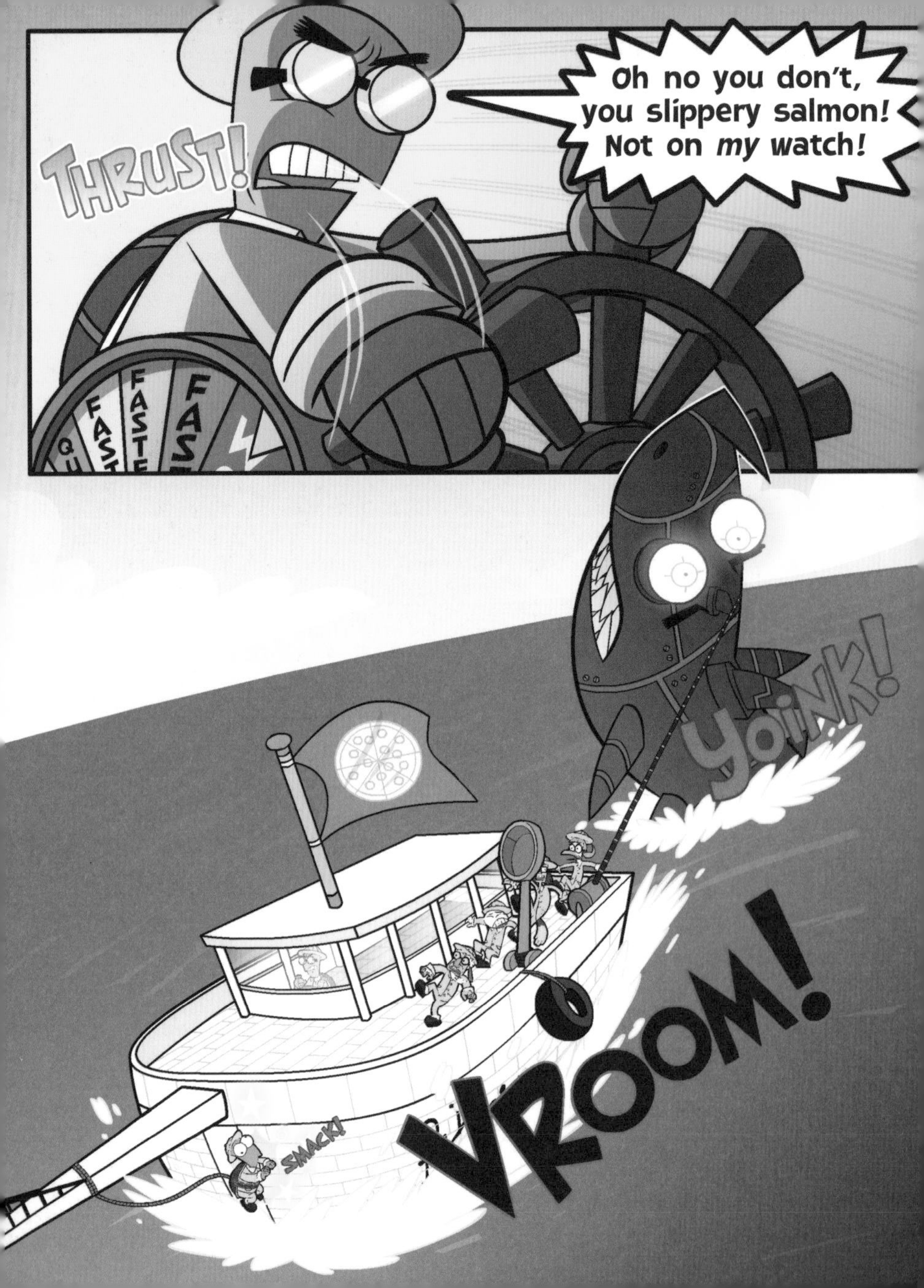
Oh no you don't, you slippery salmon! Not on *my* watch!
THRUST!
FAST
YOINK!
SMACK!
VROOM!

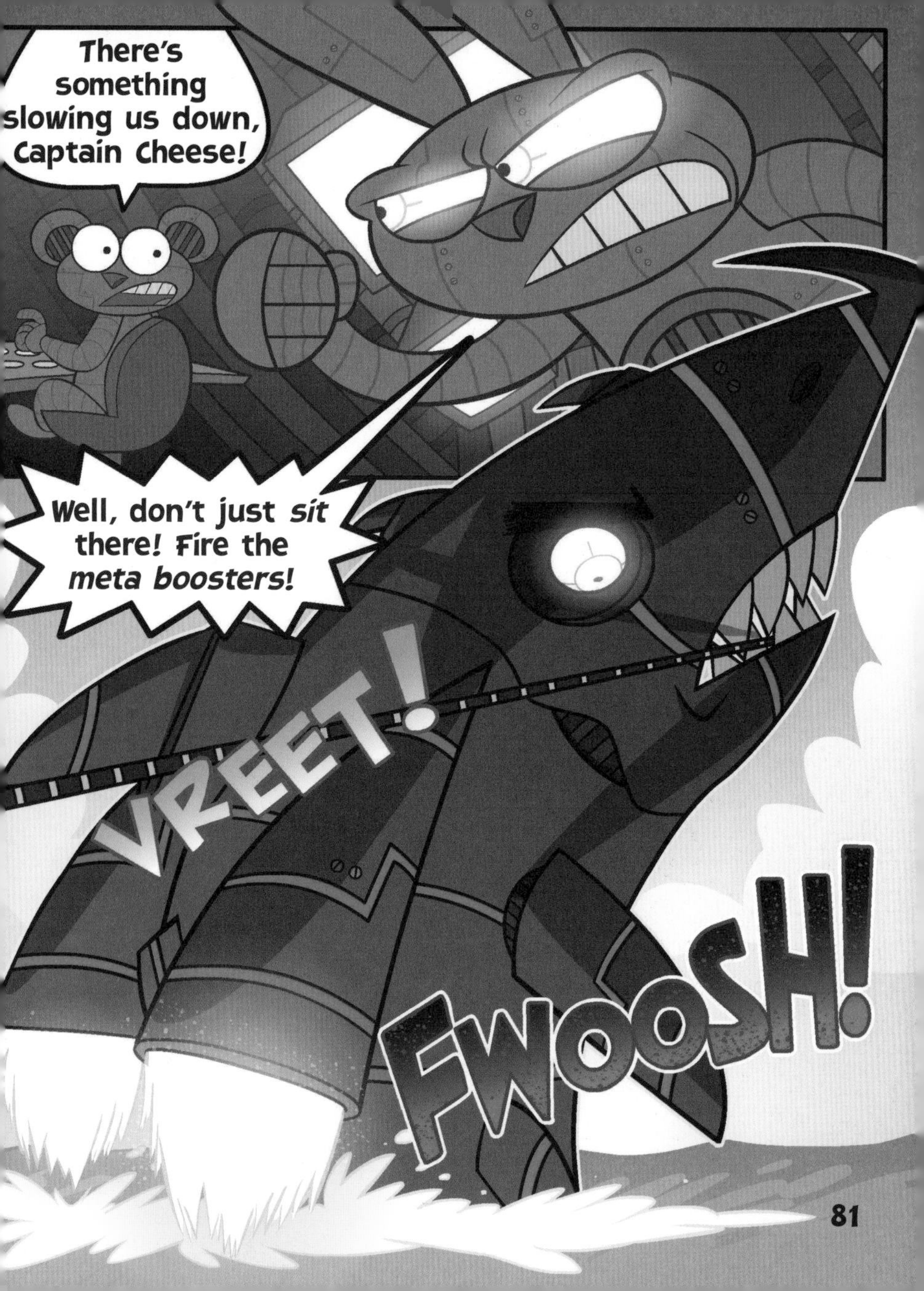
There's something slowing us down, Captain Cheese!
Well, don't just *sit* there! Fire the *meta boosters!*
VREET!
FWOOSH!

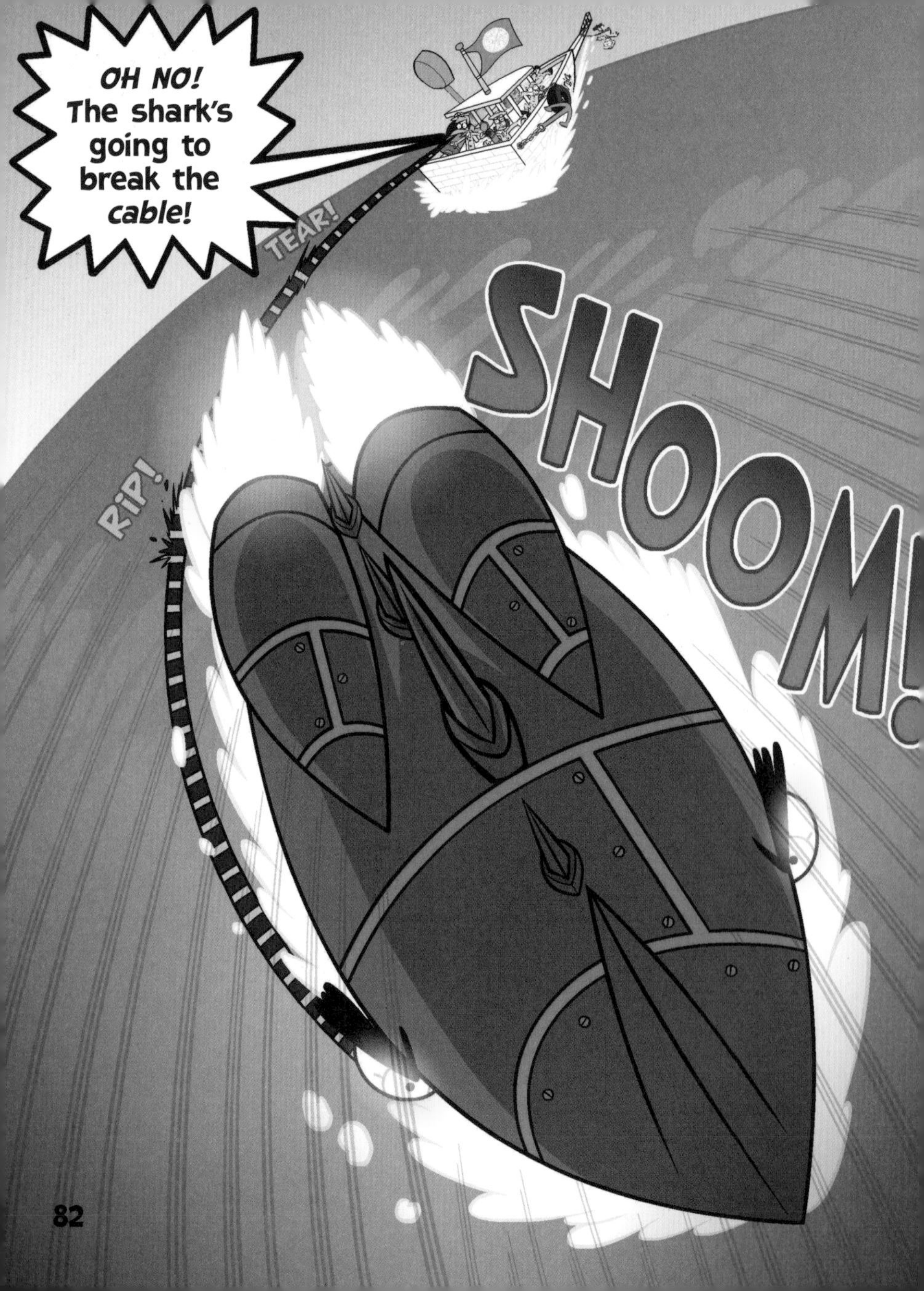

OH NO! The shark's going to break the cable!
TEAR!
RiP!
SHOOM!

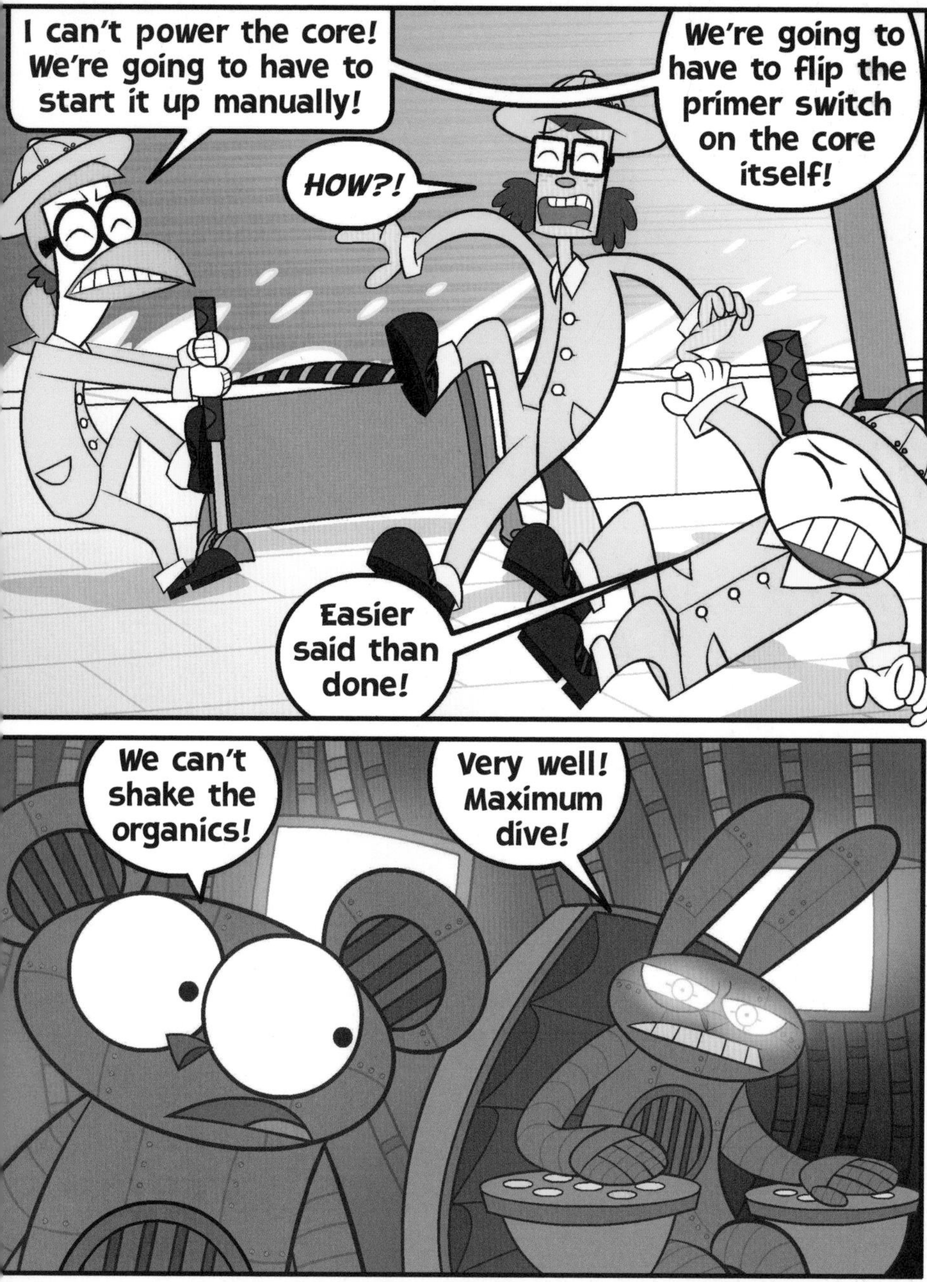

I can't power the core! We're going to have to start it up manually!
HOW?!
We're going to have to flip the primer switch on the core itself!
Easier said than done!
We can't shake the organics!
Very well! Maximum dive!

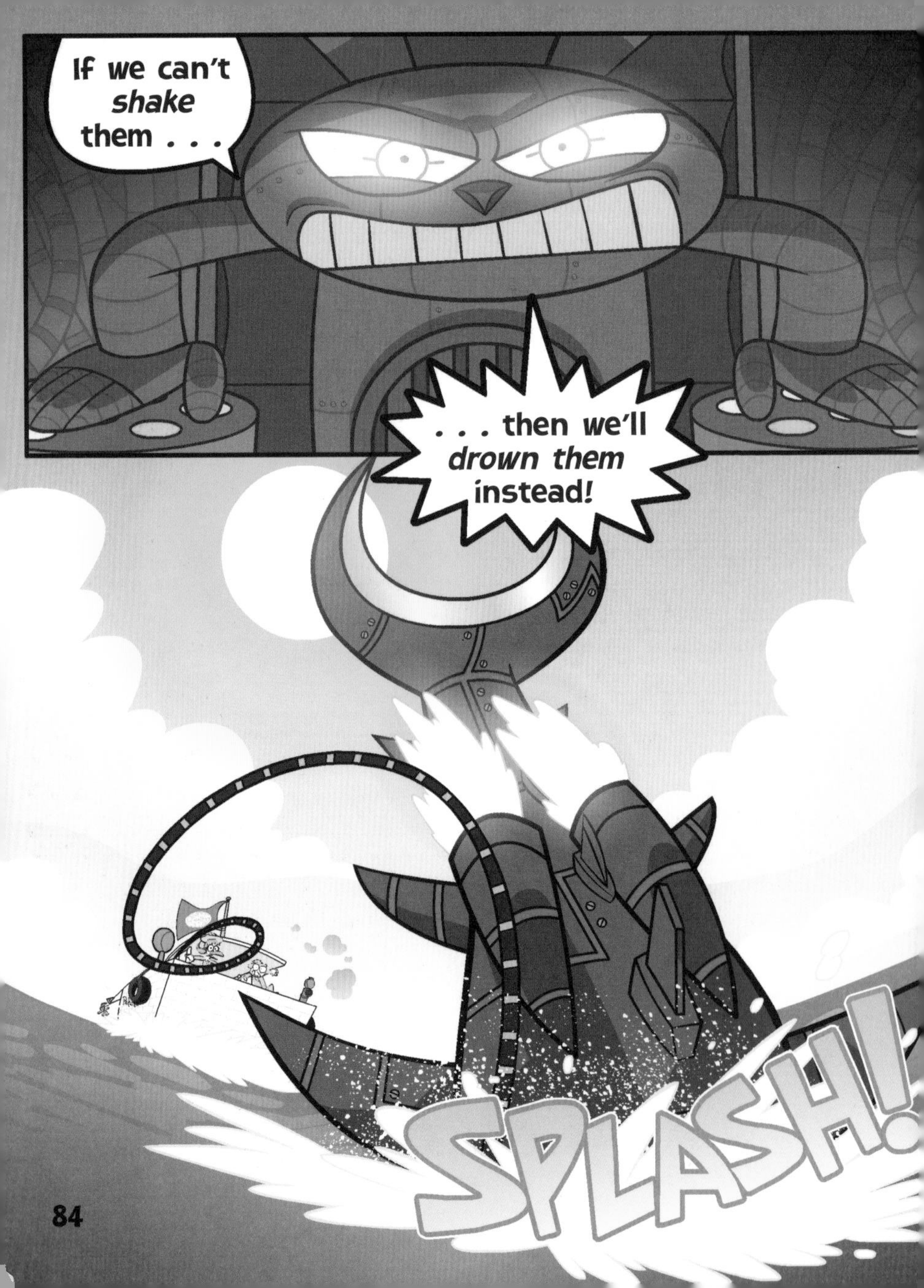
If we can't *shake* them . . .
. . . then we'll *drown them* instead!
SPLASH!

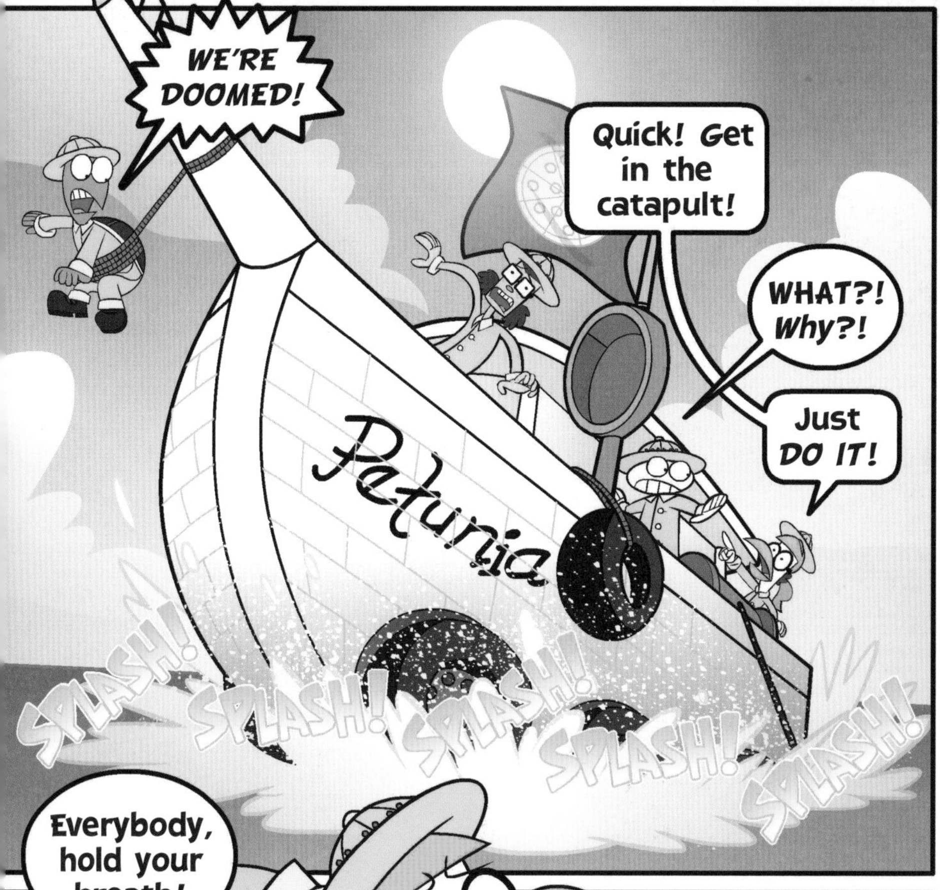
WE'RE DOOMED!
Quick! Get in the catapult!
WHAT?! Why?!
Just DO IT!
Petunia
SPLASH! SPLASH! SPLASH! SPLASH! SPLASH!

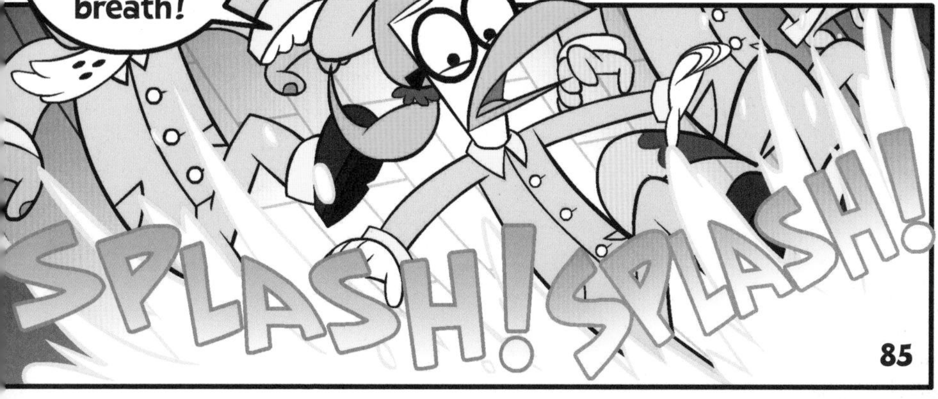
Everybody, hold your breath!
SPLASH! SPLASH!

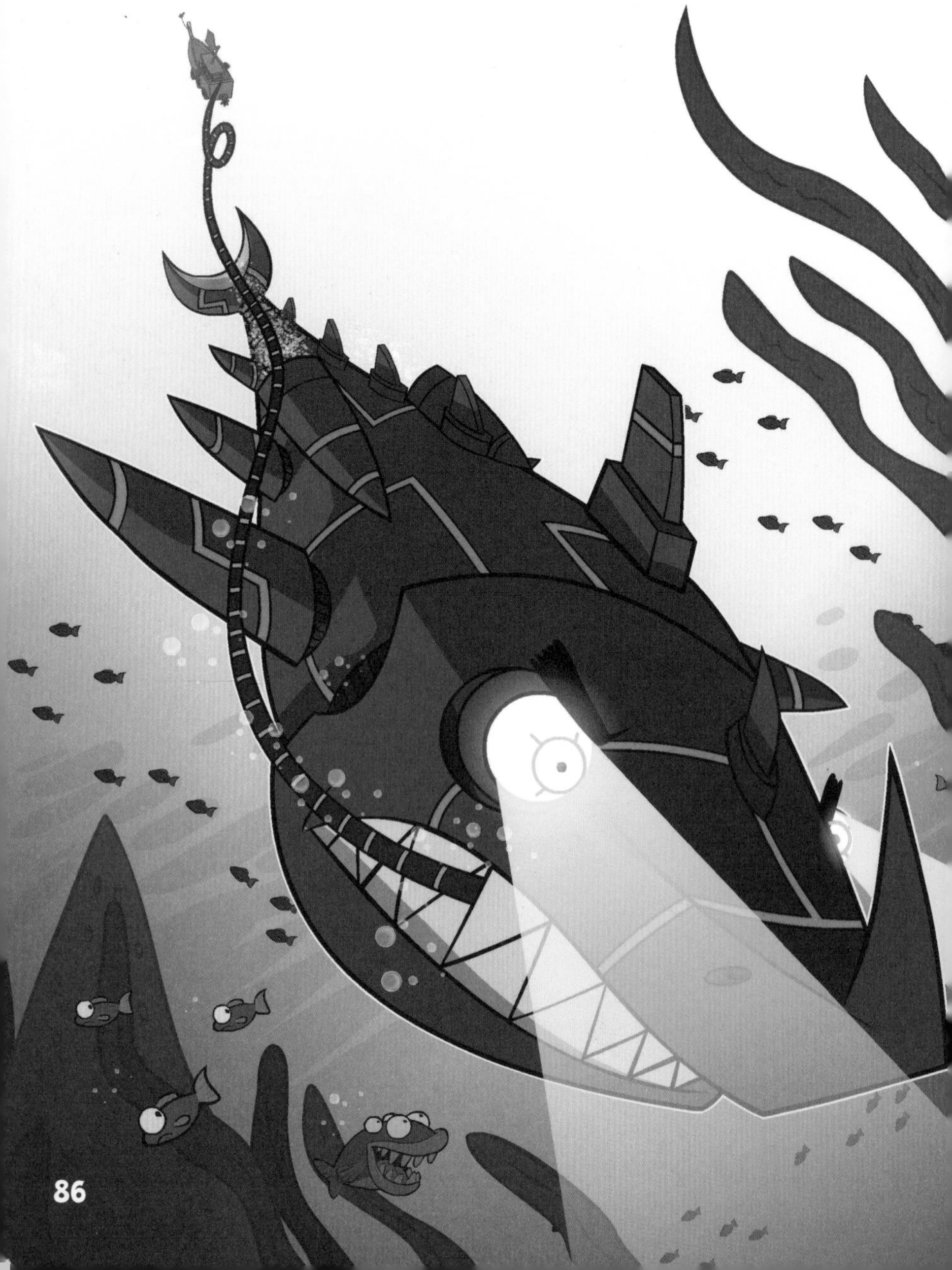

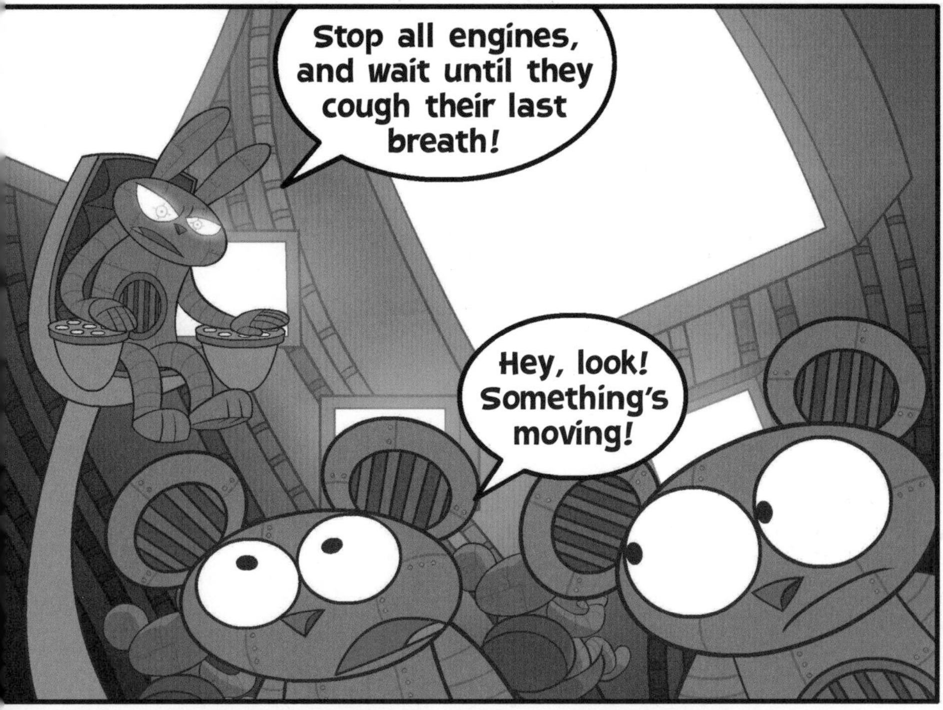
Stop all engines, and wait until they cough their last breath!
Hey, look! Something's moving!

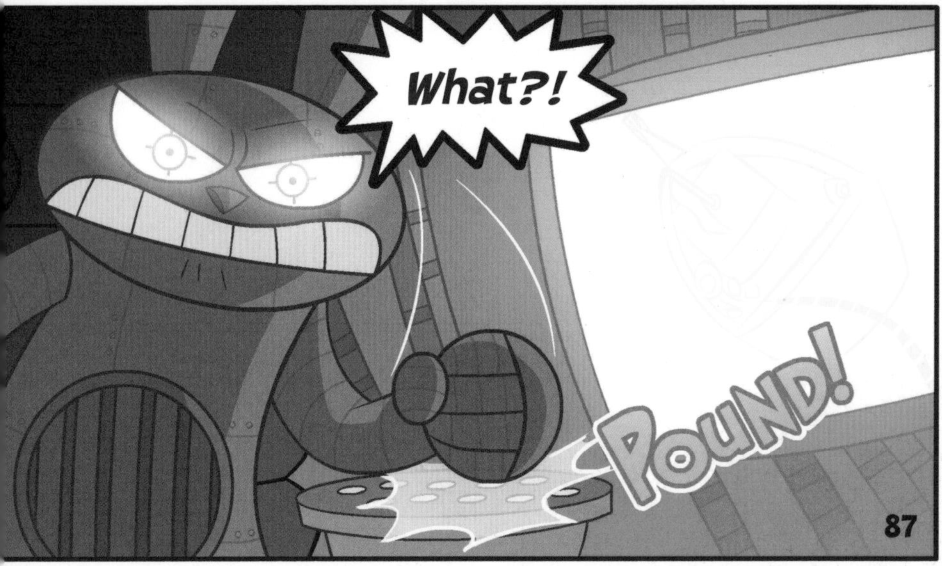
What?!
POUND!

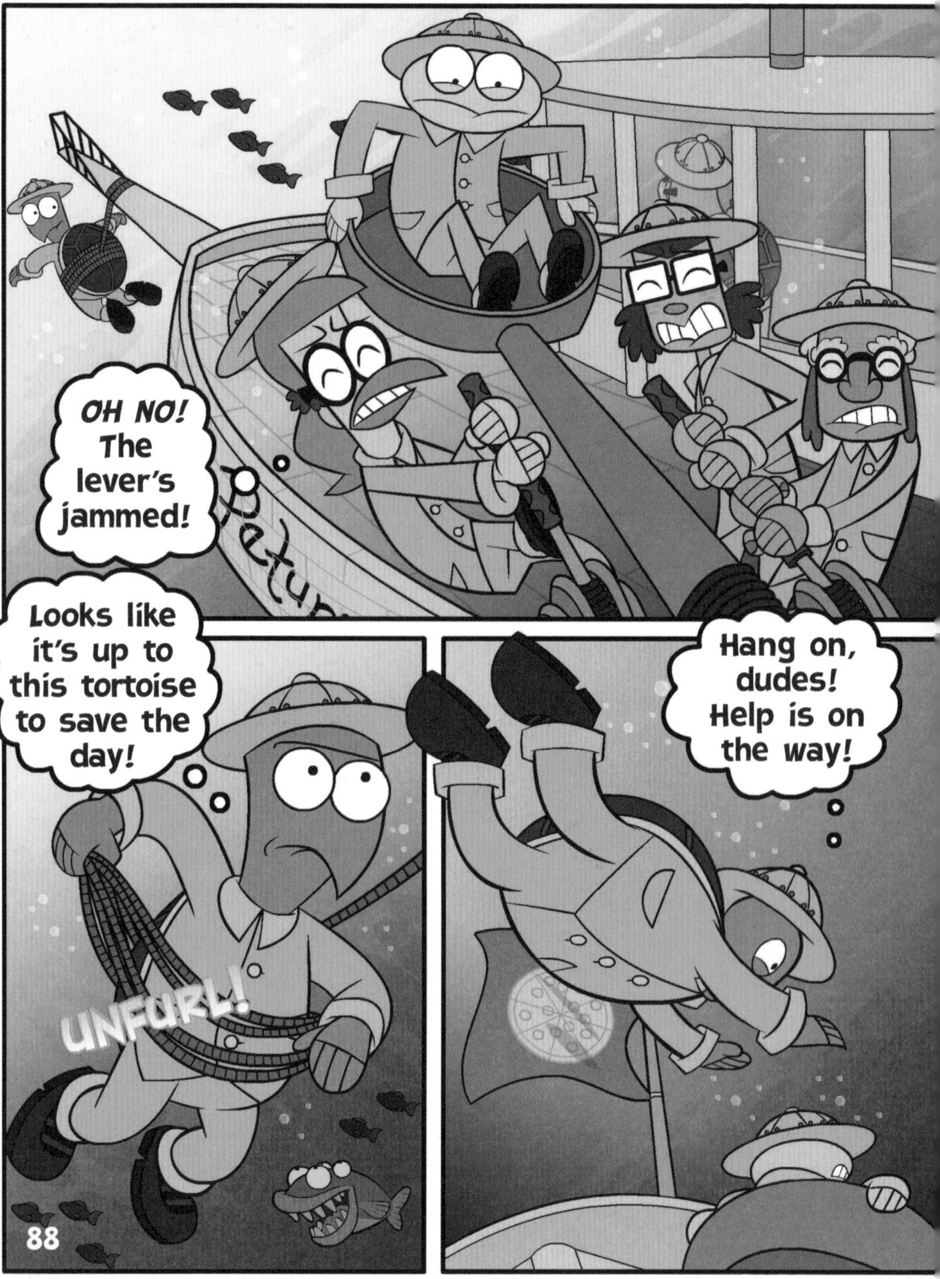
OH NO! The lever's jammed!
Looks like it's up to this tortoise to save the day!
UNFURL!
Hang on, dudes! Help is on the way!

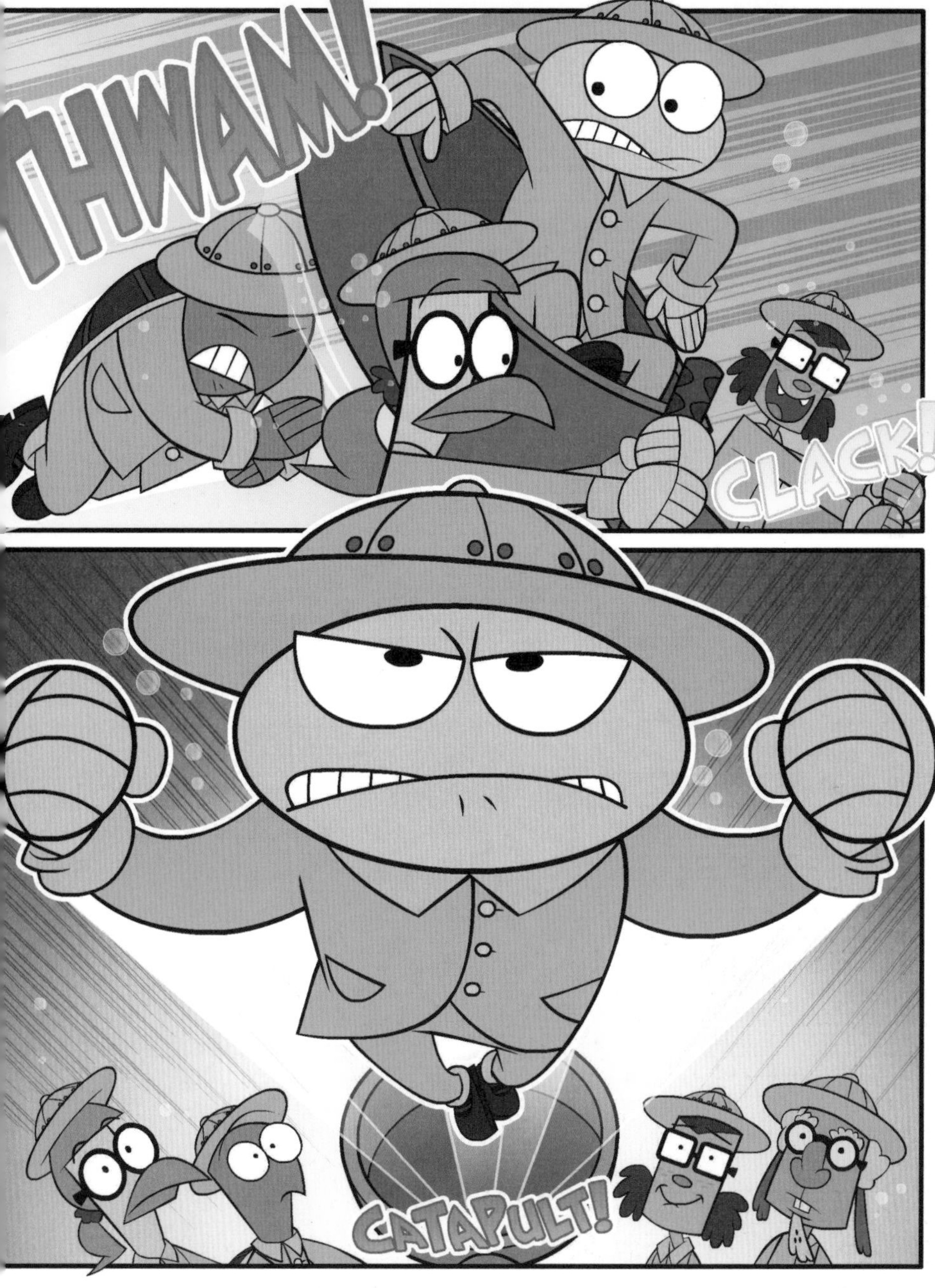
THWAM!
CLACK!
CATAPULT!

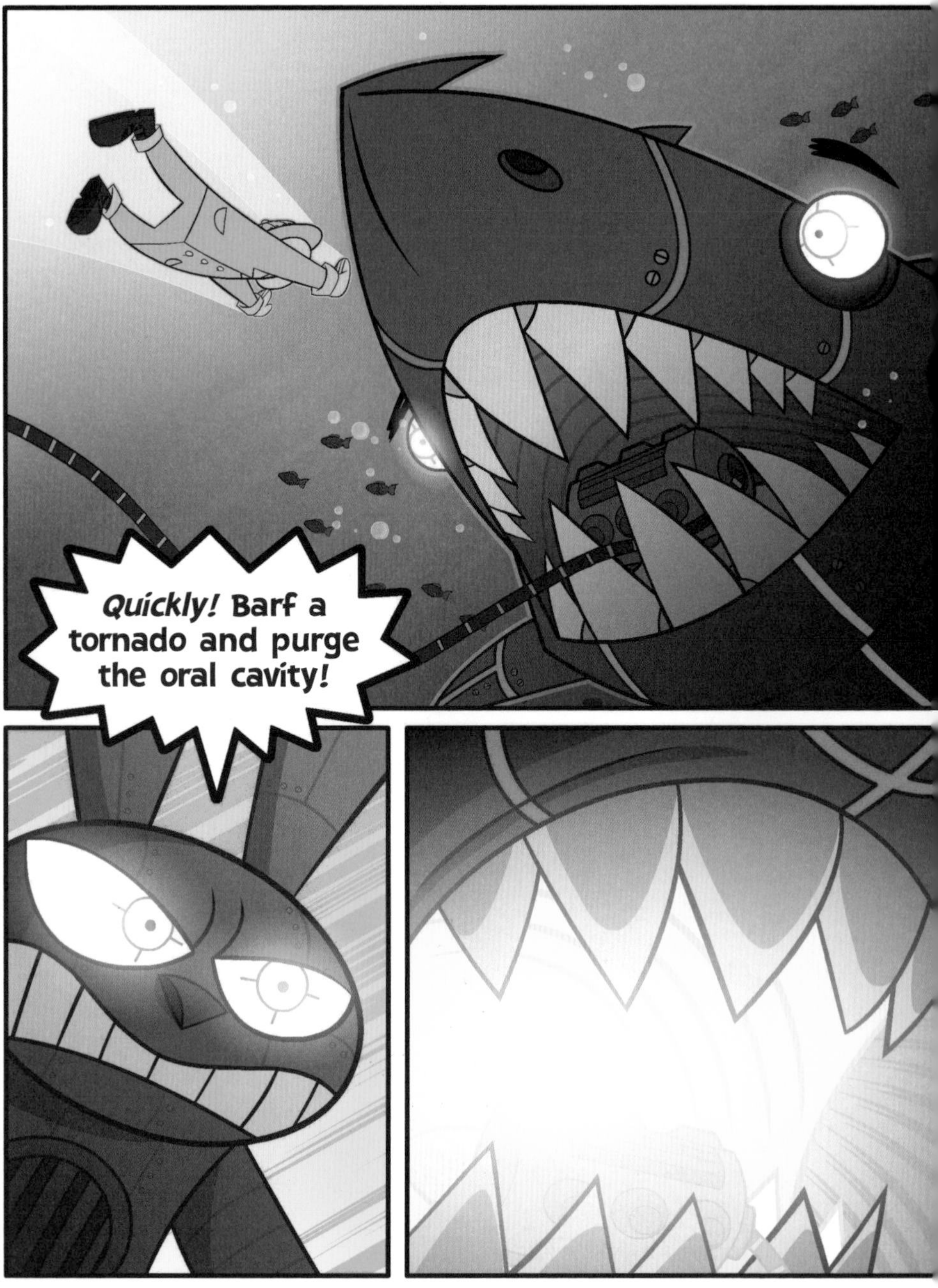
Quickly! Barf a tornado and purge the oral cavity!

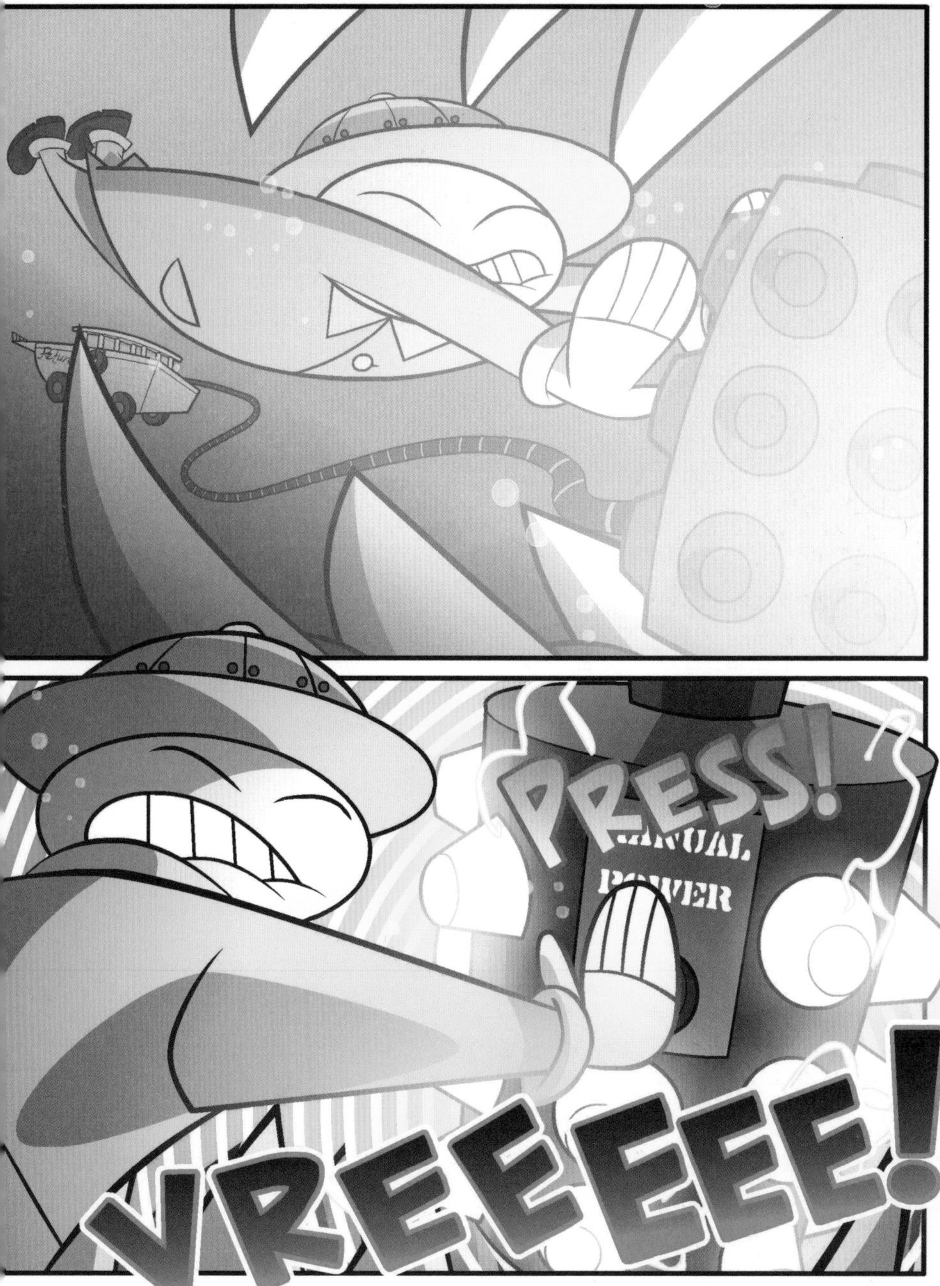
PRESS!
VREEEEE!

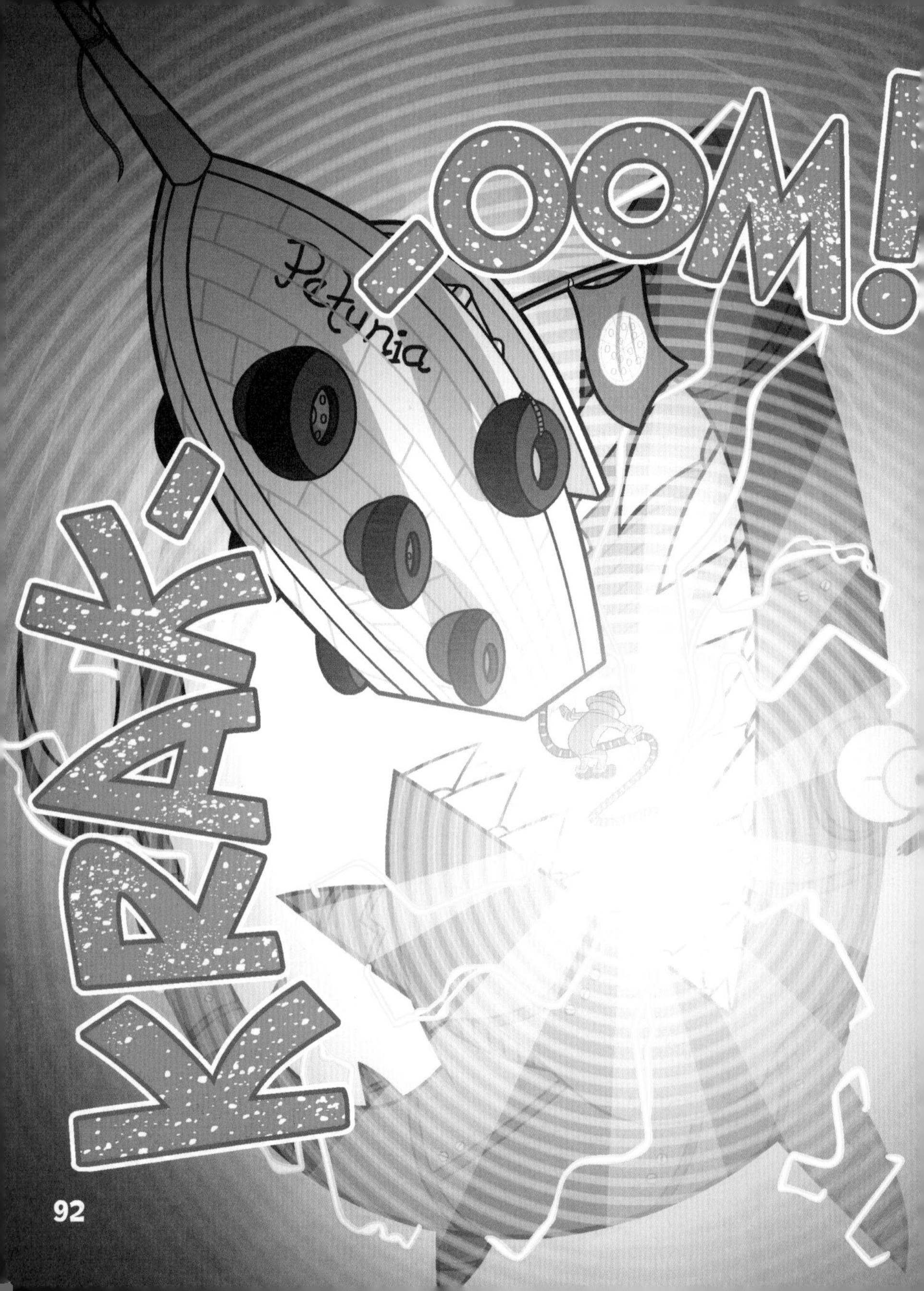
KRAK-OOM!
Petunia

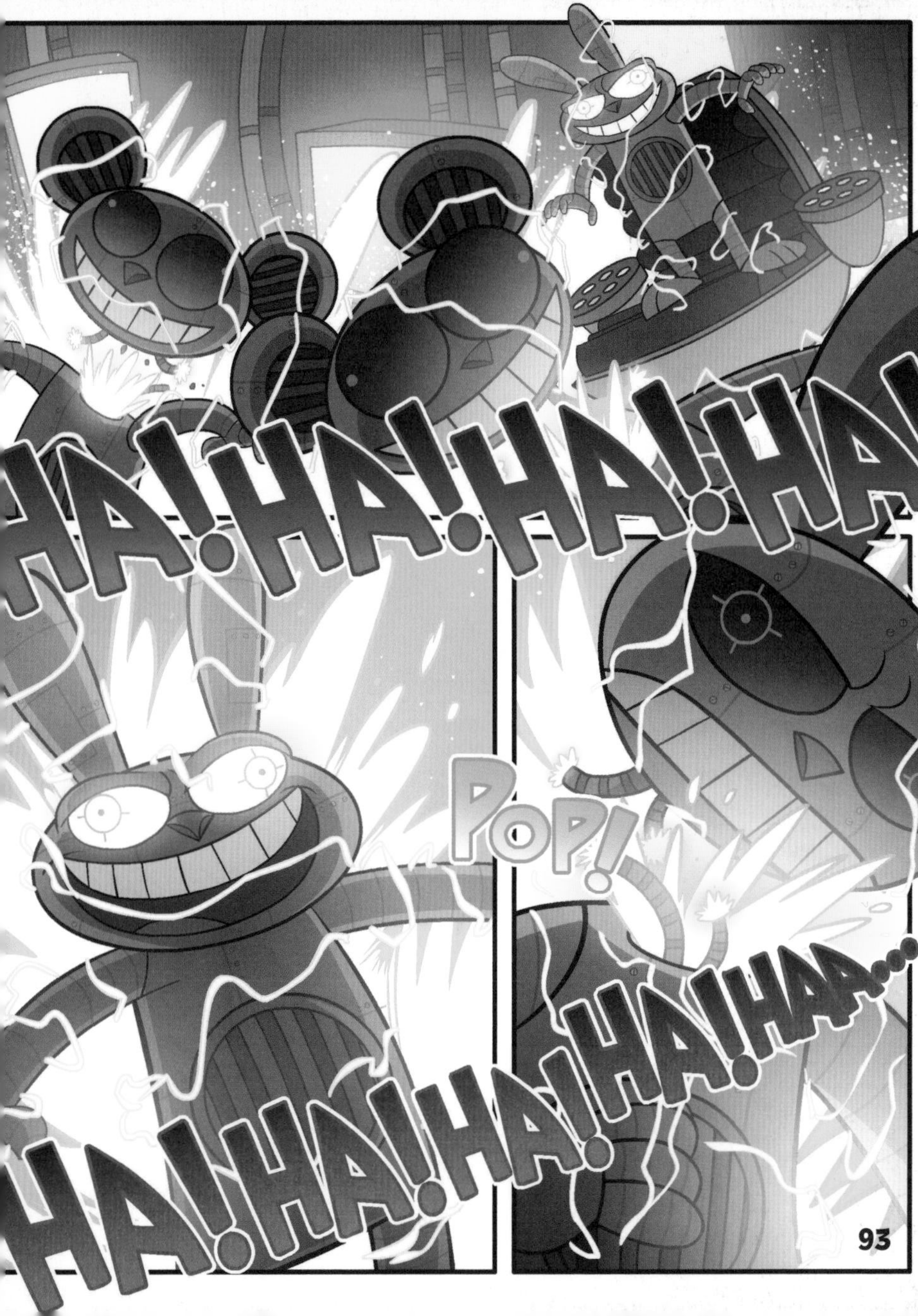
HA!HA!HA!HA!
POP!
HA!HA!HA!HA!HAA...

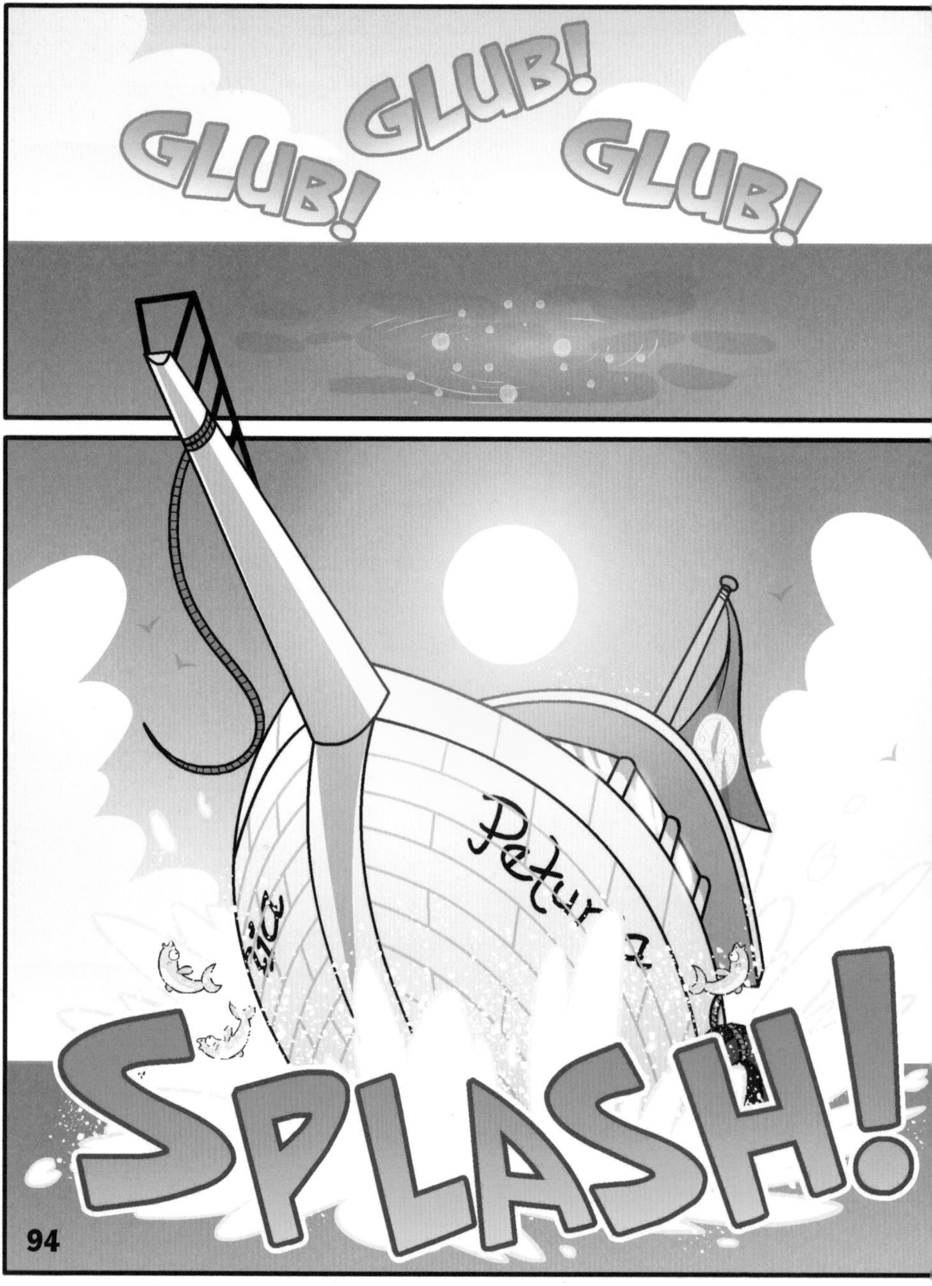
GLUB!
GLUB!
GLUB!
SPLASH!

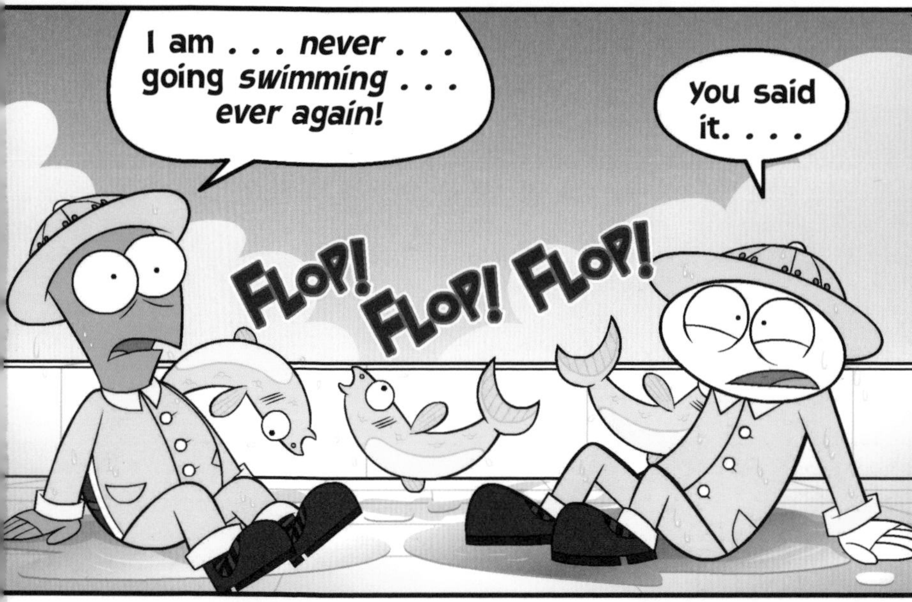
I am . . . never . . . going swimming . . . ever again!
You said it. . . .
FLOP! FLOP! FLOP!

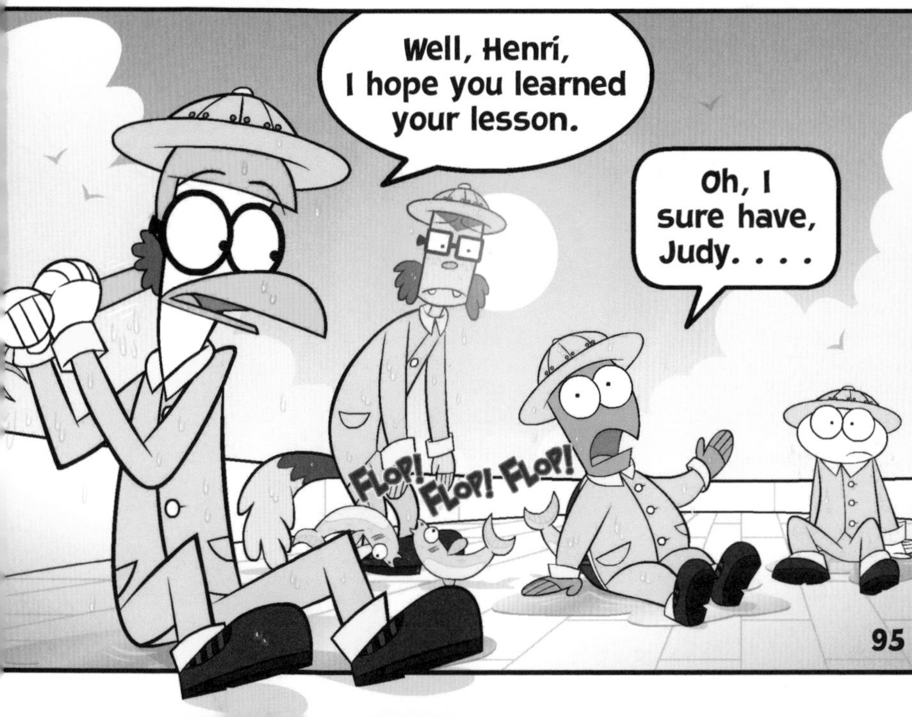
Well, Henri, I hope you learned your lesson.
Oh, I sure have, Judy. . . .
FLOP! FLOP! FLOP!

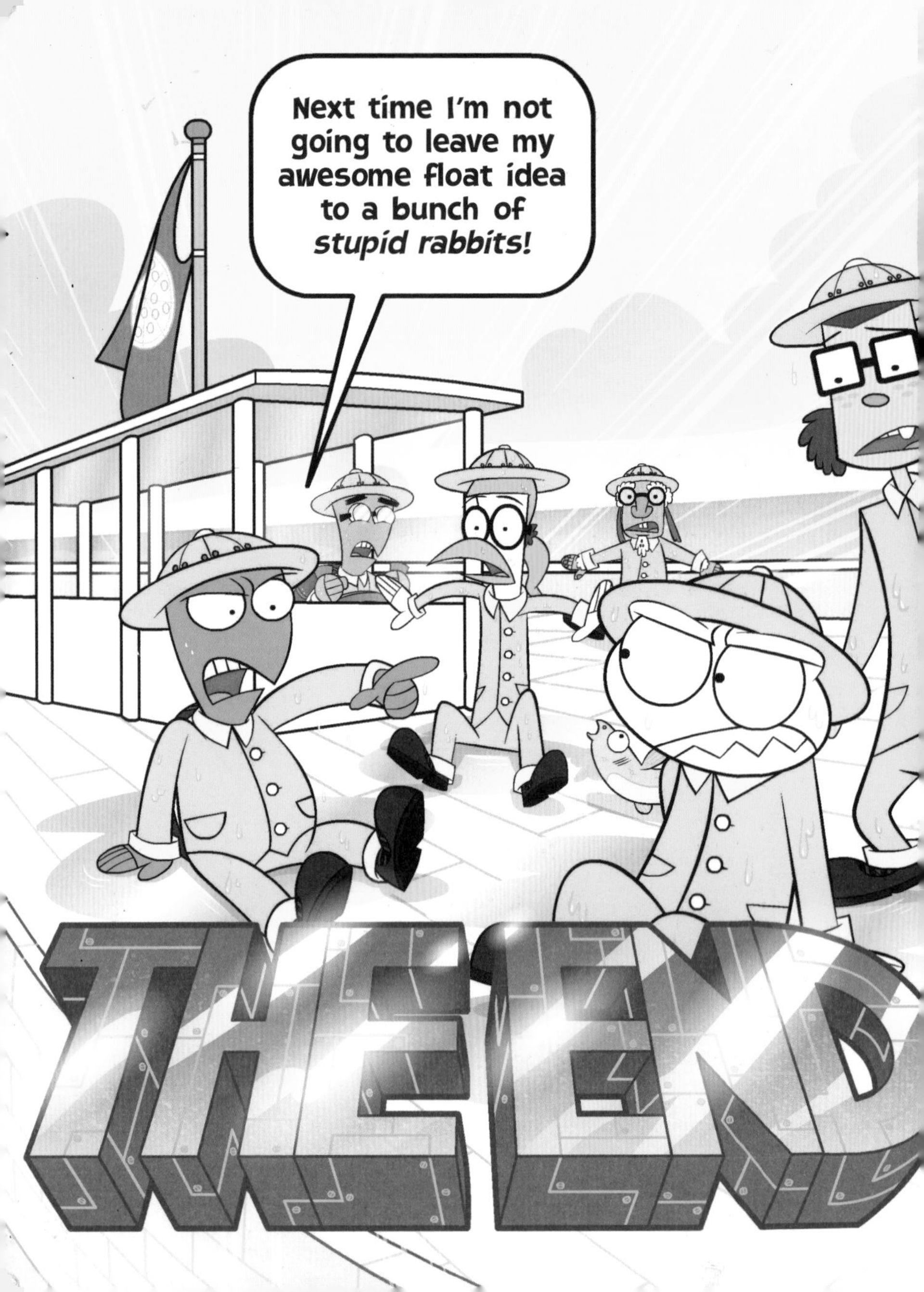
Next time I'm not going to leave my awesome float idea to a bunch of *stupid rabbits*!
THE END